Trust Issues

Katherine Nichols

Black Rose Writing | Texas

First printing

ISBN: 978-1-68513-086-2
PUBLISHED BY BLACK ROSE WRITING
www.blackrosewriting.com

Printed in the United States of America
Suggested Retail Price (SRP) $21.95

Trust Issues is printed in Baskerville

*As a planet-friendly publisher, Black Rose Writing does its best to eliminate unnecessary waste to reduce paper usage and energy costs, while never compromising the reading experience. As a result, the final word count vs. page count may not meet common expectations.

Dedicated to the memory of my grandmother Jenny Holland, the woman who believed I could do anything I set my mind to.

Trust
Issues

1

According to family legend, my mother was conceived in a van almost immediately after Janis Joplin's iconic performance of "Piece of My Heart." My grandmother Sarah Claire Davis, or Jams as she preferred because it reminded her of her "jamming" days, loved to repeat the story of Mom's less than immaculate conception at every possible and inappropriate opportunity. As enthusiastic as she was about the details of the event—concert and conception—Mom was equally unenthusiastic.

"For God's sake, Janis, loosen up" had been Jams' refrain to her for as long as I could remember, but she wasn't a loosening-up kind of woman.

Unfortunately, neither was I. This aspect of my nature never seemed like a big deal to me until my relationship with my fiancé, Rob. He said I couldn't be happy unless I was in control. My best friend Anna insisted Rob's lack of transparency threatened our upcoming nuptials. Mom suggested we try Christian counseling, and Jams volunteered to do a Tarot reading for me.

After weeks of online research, I discovered Relationship Builders. Based on the building blocks of a solid marital foundation—trust, commitment, intimacy, respect, communication, empathy, and equality—the group promised hope for couples lacking in these areas. Although Rob and I had difficulties with all seven, his biggest complaint concerned my lack of trust, not only as it related to him but also with the rest of the world.

My denial of his accusation was honest, at least the part about not distrusting all of humanity. My issue was more specific, a troubling little voice in the back—sometimes the front—of my mind expressing doubt about us.

I had no history of being victimized by unscrupulous men. Yes, my junior year in high school Randy Blumenthal dumped me for a nice Jewish girl, but I only dated him to drive my mother crazy. And it was true Greg Fisher, my on-and-off boyfriend throughout college, had been a serial cheater. But I didn't find out until after we graduated when I realized that, without the drunken frat parties and football games, he was duller than dishwater. By then, his philandering held no interest for me. My post-graduate love life was almost as dull as Greg and not at all fraught with betrayal.

Nor did I experience any deep-seated childhood issues that might have been the root of my skeptical nature. Married for thirty years, my parents never had any serious problems. Grandpa Walter adored my wild-ass grandmother, and she had been devoted to him.

Rob insisted something in my past made me resistant to accepting love, that whatever it was, caused me to be suspicious of anyone who loved me. I considered his condemnation extreme but didn't deny it because it meant he hadn't guessed the truth—I couldn't accept the concept of us. Since I had never been in a committed relationship as an adult with an adult, I didn't know what one should feel like. But this nagging fear told me ours wasn't it. Still, he was handsome in a button-down kind of way and charming at least fifty percent of the time.

After reading what Relationship Builders offered—hope for uptight, control freaks—I decided to give it a try. Their website promised to "help couples achieve greater fulfillment through transformational counseling."

Hell, fulfillment sounded good to me. The price tag was steep, but wasn't my relationship worth it? I signed up.

On the morning of the workshop, I left my apartment early to find the perfect seat. Like Wild Bill Hickok, I always chose a spot with my chair pushed against the back wall. Today, however, fate and Atlanta traffic conspired against me, and I made it just as the speaker slipped behind the podium. My face burned with embarrassment as I took one of two remaining chairs in the front of a group of forty or so other untransformed people.

A slender woman in a well-tailored black suit welcomed us. Her chin-length chestnut hair glistened with auburn highlights that were an exact match for her thin-rimmed glasses. She introduced herself as Dr. Sheila Norton.

"Welcome and congratulations for taking the first step toward building strong relationships and emotional freedom. Freedom from the shackles of suspicion and doubt that have been keeping you up at night. Prepare to toss out the debris of the past and clean your house of fear and cynicism."

Dr. Sheila's delivery combined earnest and inspiring. Like Weight Watchers meets Gamblers' Anonymous. Her references to housekeeping, however, made me squirm. An urgent need to race home and reorganize my perfectly organized closets overcame me.

While I calculated whether I should arrange my shoes by hue or frequency of use, the good doctor—doctor of what, I wondered—conducted some arranging of her own.

"That's it. Stand as close to your partner as you can get without touching."

Because I was sitting in the front and engrossed in color-coding my footwear, I didn't notice the people to each side, standing and pairing off. Seems I hadn't made the connection that "couples counseling" required both parties. I skimmed over the part explaining putting Rob's name in the space designated "Significant Other" meant he should be there. Or maybe I ignored that requirement rather than ask him to come.

My heartbeat quickened and blood rushed to my face. Hemmed in by pairs scrunched against each other, I couldn't breathe. I scanned the room for an escape route. The chairs were flush against the wall, and the aisle was blocked. Dr. Sheila stepped from behind her podium and slithered among the participants, pushing and pulling at them until they achieved optimum discomfort. One couple presented a challenge: the woman stood about a foot taller than the man, and he kept ending up with his head nestled between her enormous breasts.

If I made my move while the duo distracted her, I could slip by and—

"There's plenty of room for you and your partner." The doctor stood directly in front of me and leaned in to scrutinize my name tag. "Ms. Kincaid, I see. Or may I call you Claire? Oh dear, Claire. You aren't alone, are you?"

Although I shared my mother's compunction for being in control, I also inherited a bit of Jams' whimsy, especially in the fantasy department—a genteel way of saying I'm one hell of a liar.

"My fiancé was unexpectedly called out of town." Not my most creative effort, but a good lie stays as close to the truth as possible. And, as a forensic accountant, Rob was frequently unavailable.

"There you are." The voice, deep and smooth, tickled the hair on my neck. "Sorry I'm late. It took longer than I expected to rearrange my schedule."

Sheila's smile broadened into a toothy grin as she shifted her focus. "Welcome, Mr. Evans, is it?"

"Please, call me Rob."

"Well, Rob, I'm so pleased you made it. We're about to begin our trust exercises. First, I want you all to know that I'm here for you. That means if you fail, I fail, so there will be no failure." She tossed her hair and laughed—a hollow sound bordering on sinister. "Teasing." She drew the word out and giggled. "Everyone will gain from this experience. So, no worries."

She might not have any, but I had one—a big one. The man whose sexy baritone rescued me from the humiliation of going solo at a couples' conference wasn't my fiancé.

2

Sheila gave me no time to make sense of why this stranger was pretending to be my fiancé. Oblivious to my confusion, she barreled ahead. "You two can help demonstrate some of our moves." She took my arm and dragged me toward the podium.

"Please," I began, "I'm not good at this." *Especially when I was clueless as to what this was or the identity of my handsome partner. Had Rob found out about the conference and sent a friend to prank me? Could he be watching from a distance, to gauge my reaction?*

In the nine months of our time together, I met only one of Rob's friends, also a forensic accountant who didn't seem prone to pranks.

If Sheila heard my protest, she gave no sign. She dropped my arm and spoke to the crowd.

"Attention, everyone. Quiet, please."

I focused on a spot above Sheila's head while thirty pairs of eyes locked on my back.

"Our first exercise is simple. Make sure you're standing as close as possible to your partner." She paused as the group tested the boundaries of personal space. "Now gaze past the physical directly into the soul of the person you trust above all others."

Her tone and choice of words reminded me of a tent revival my mother dragged me to when I was thirteen. People shouting and galloping down the aisles toward salvation sent me running in the opposite direction.

I turned to the far left, then to the right, searching for the baptismal dunking booth. Relief at not seeing one faded quickly as I realized I was about to come face to face with the man who claimed to be my fiancé.

Sheila put her hand on my shoulder and said, "This is Claire and Rob. Aren't they a cute couple?" A few nervous titters from the audience rewarded her.

"Claire, you need to turn this way." I kept my head down as she scooted me until I faced the right wall. "That's good. And Rob, you should be here."

She maneuvered us until the tips of our shoes touched. Deep burgundy and shiny, his looked expensive.

She lifted my chin. "There, now lose yourself for the next two minutes."

The man standing so close I noticed the flecks of gray in his otherwise dark blue eyes bore a passing resemblance to my fiancé. At five feet four, I stood about shoulder level to both men. But the real Rob was thicker through the chest and wore his light-brown hair in a buzz cut to fit his serious demeanor. The fake love-of-my-life's was a similar shade but longer and curled above his ears. Rob's lips were thinner and his cheekbones less defined than his imposter.

And not even on the night he proposed had the real Rob examined me with the intensity of this stranger.

"Who the hell are you?" I hissed through clenched teeth.

"Claire, no talking, please. Let yourself live in the moment."

I took a breath and tried to relax my jaw. You can do anything for two minutes, I told myself. That total eclipse in Oregon lasted less than two minutes. And it takes only two minutes to cook a delicious Hot Pocket or delete Twitter from your phone with time enough to regret your decision and reinstall it.

But peering into the "soul" of another human being was different. It was intensely personal—almost painful. And when that person was a total stranger, it was frightening.

I shifted from one foot to the other, thinking as soon as our instructor moved on, I would turn away from the man. Then I noticed that besides having flecks of gray, his eyes weren't totally dark blue. The irises were outlined in a lighter shade. And they were almond shaped with a slight upturn where light etchings of laugh lines marked their territory. His nose was more prominent but not too—

"Excellent job everyone. Let's take a few minutes to share how doing nothing but basking in your partner's loving eyes made you feel."

Basking? Loving eyes? Jesus, Sheila. How corny can you get?

"We'll begin with our lovely volunteers."

I glanced around the room, then realized we were those lovely volunteers. I shot faux-Rob a desperate look and was relieved when he took the lead.

"I felt as if I were seeing myself through a different lens."

I rolled my loving eyes. Sheila oozed enthusiasm. "That's incredibly perceptive. Wouldn't you agree, group?" Murmurs of assent rose from the audience. "And you, Claire? Did you see Rob through a new lens?"

Definitely new. "I can honestly say I saw him for the first time."

"Good, Claire. Very good."

I detected a note of surprise in her voice, as if she discovered her dog could talk.

Sheila spent the next ten minutes coaxing similar revelations from participants while I stole glances at my partner beside me.

The man I planned to marry favored dark suits with white or beige shirts and striped ties. This one dressed more casually in a pale-yellow polo and black jeans. Although slimmer than my fiancé, my current partner's shoulders were just as broad, and his biceps were more defined.

Sheila's cheery voice interrupted the body scan. "Okay, everyone. Get ready for some real fun: the trust fall."

. . .

"That was interesting." My trust-fall partner grinned as we sat across from each other in a booth at the hotel restaurant.

Mildly traumatized, I let him lead me out of the room for lunch.

"That's easy for you to say. You weren't the one blindfolded, throwing herself into the abyss. Who does that? I mean there's trust and then there's full-on lunacy."

We'd spent the last fifteen minutes attempting to follow Sheila's instructions. But no matter how hard I tried, I couldn't make myself fall into his waiting arms. I would lean back, then stiffen before snatching off the blindfold and skittering away.

Sheila gave up on using us to showcase the move but promised she would return to check our progress after she assisted the others. I expected the couple who required so much help getting into the staring position to be in worse shape than we were. Turned out the woman was an idiot who flung herself backward with abandon, and the little squirt caught her with ease.

"I've got a plan," Rob—as I'd come to think of him—said. He moved sideways so that he blocked Sheila's view. "I'll hold you here." He looped his arms under my armpits. The position turned me into a life-size rag doll, but at that point, I would have hung from a ceiling harness if it meant getting that woman off my back.

"Don't panic, okay? I'm just going to let go of your right arm, so you can cross it over your chest." I forced myself not to struggle and did as he asked, keeping a death grip on his left wrist.

"Great," he whispered in my ear. "When I say *now*, do the same thing with your other arm."

"But won't that mean—"

"Now!"

He yanked his arm free, propelled mine forward, and shouted, "Look, Sheila. We got it!"

My blindfold slipped enough for me to see the doubt in her expression, but she gave us a tight-lipped smile and said, "Congratulations. I knew you could do it."

Sitting in the relative safety of a plush booth sipping iced tea and picking at a Caesar salad, I could appreciate the humor in the situation.

"I don't think for a minute she believed we had done it." I smiled at the thought of Sheila's face at the moment of our triumph.

"Me, either. But remember, if we fail, Sheila fails. *And there will be no failure.*"

I snorted, sending a spray of golden fluid out my nose. Then I remembered the seriousness of my situation.

"Like I said before, who the hell are you?"

"I'm Kevin Thomas." He plucked a name tag from his back pocket. "My girlfriend Judy and I registered for the conference. She's always late, so I didn't worry until everybody started pairing off. I wanted to sneak out the door, but then I heard Dr. Norton giving you a hard time about not having a partner. There were only two nametags left, Judy's and Rob Evans'. I said to myself, what the hell. The workshop wasn't cheap, and I took the day off work. Why not stay?"

Her betrayal must not have been too devastating unless he'd been so upset, he hadn't been able to leave. If that were the case, he disguised it well. And it didn't explain the ease with which he stepped into the role as my rescuer.

"Sheila will not be pleased if she finds out we broke the rules," I said.

"How about you?" he asked.

"What do you mean?"

"I get the impression you're a bit of a rule follower yourself."

Whether from irritation at being put in the same category as our annoying instructor or something a little closer to home, I bristled at his remark.

"I don't know where you got that idea. I'm totally not a rule follower. Finish your coffee, and I'll show you what a rule breaker I can be."

3

Anna Ramirez poured herself a second glass of wine and topped mine off. During our five years at Reynolds and Schultz, a public relations and marketing firm, we became close friends. She was the only one I could talk to about the strange day I had.

"You spent all that time building the foundation for a lasting relationship, and at the end you just walked away?"

"In case you forgot, I am engaged to be married."

"Oh, I didn't forget. But I was hoping you had."

My friend made no secret of her distaste for my fiancé. After Rob and I dated for a month, I invited Anna and her husband for dinner. The next day when I asked her what she thought, she'd been her usual direct self.

"I don't trust him. His eyes shift to the right whenever you ask him a question. And you know what that means." She was referring to our introductory session for the public relations portion of our roles at the firm.

I reminded her she skipped the follow-up workshop debunking the theory that you can tell if someone's telling the truth by the direction they look. The latest data suggested looking for telltale signs—hesitation, face-touching, throat-clearing—provided a more accurate picture. The consensus among researchers, however, was that it was almost impossible to detect a good liar, especially if he was a sociopath.

"In that case," she paused to clear her throat and smooth an eyebrow, "I'm crazy about him."

I told myself all that mattered was my impression of the man I planned to spend the rest of my life with, but it stung that she disliked him. Today, her comment about forgetting I was engaged struck a nerve. I hadn't exactly forgotten my engagement, but I had experienced one or two memory glitches during the day.

"Did you find out where this Kevin Thomas works?" she asked, picking up her phone and scrolling down the screen.

"I told you it's not like that. Hold on a minute. Tell me you are not searching for him on Facebook."

"Of course not. Google. But there were too many. Speaking of that, how many Judys can you think of within twenty years of our ages? My abuela works with someone named Judith, but that woman's closing in on seventy."

"She could be British," I offered.

"Or maybe she's not real."

"Seriously, why would a man come to a couple's conference with a made-up girlfriend? He'd be stuck without a partner."

"Only Kevin wasn't stuck without a partner. He was stuck with you. And from some of the trust *activities*," she put air quotes around the word, "it sounds as if he enjoyed himself."

"There was absolutely no inappropriate touching. He was a perfect gentleman."

"Too bad." She sighed. "So where is Rob, and why wasn't he with you?"

"He's out of town and won't be back until next Thursday."

"That man's away more than he's here."

"Forensic accountants travel a lot. All over the world even."

"Right. But enough about him. You might not have gotten details about where this Kevin Thomas worked or other boring stuff, but there must have been some exchange of personal information."

"It wasn't like that, not really. The questions were a little weird, but I wouldn't call them personal. As for our goodbyes, I thanked him for stepping in, we shook hands, and went our separate ways."

I didn't tell her how I glanced over my shoulder and experienced a stab of disappointment when he disappeared into the crowd.

Anna finished her wine. "I'd love to hear more, but it sounds like you've told me all the good stuff, and I have a hot date with my husband."

I walked her to the door, wishing I had a date, hot or otherwise, with Rob—only I wasn't sure which one.

After putting away our glasses and the empty bottle, I surveyed the kitchen of my small apartment. The landlord let me paint it a soft shade of yellow. I loved the way the color reflected the sunlight as it filtered through the window. As I passed through the living room, I straightened a floral pillow on the sofa I stumbled across in an antique store. Once a deep red, the piece looked as if it belonged in a bordello until I recovered it in a cheery navy and white striped fabric.

Rob commented that my choice of colors and furniture was "cute, but old-fashioned," unlike the ultra-modern theme in his Buckhead condo, where we planned to live after we got married. Sleek metal, spotless glass, and gleaming leather—the place exuded minimalist elegance, but I could never get warm enough there. Wrapped in one of his cashmere blankets, I would stand in front of the never-ending windows, taking in the night with its dazzling skyline. Despite the beauty of lights flickering through gauzy clouds, I couldn't shake the feeling some rooftop pervert was staring back at me through a high-powered telescopic lens.

As I brushed my teeth, I tried to imagine what Kevin Thomas had seen when he stared into my eyes. Greenish gold, they weren't as beautiful as his, but they were one of my more interesting features. Had he noticed the scar above my right brow, from where I tumbled off the tricycle Jams let me ride when Mom had been shopping? He'd been close enough to take in the freckles that spilled across my cheeks and notice how full my lips were. Had he found my face appealing or at least pleasant?

After I climbed into bed, I considered the last time I'd taken such a detailed inventory of myself and came up with nothing. If I asked Rob what he liked about my appearance, what would he say? It was obvious he approved of my fairly generous breasts, but I doubted he had a clue about the color of my eyes or the heart-shaped mole on the inside of my left thigh.

We never discussed specifics like that—not even in our most intimate moments.

I adjusted my pillow and tried to conjure an image of me lying there with Rob. When I couldn't, I attributed it to my lack of character and my encounter with Kevin. Still, there had been nothing guilt worthy about our meeting. As I explained to Anna, our exchanges had been limited to innocent responses to our instructor's commands.

But that wasn't entirely true.

•   •   •

Most of the questions Sheila posed demanded more than a surface response, and many made me downright uncomfortable. Like the one where we told each other what frightened us. A woman in the back asked if snakes counted. The good doctor had been adamant they did not. Nor did claustrophobia nor fear of heights. She insisted we go deeper and warned she would be moving among the group, making sure we were baring our souls to our partners.

My hands began to sweat as I tried to come up with something that would satisfy Sheila without revealing too much. Once again, Kevin rescued me by getting emotionally naked first.

"This is an easy one for me. After years of therapy, I guess it should be. My greatest fear is abandonment. My dad disappeared when I was five and never came back into my life. And my mother, let's just say she didn't take it well. I suppose being stood up at a couples' conference is par for the course for me. But if I'm being honest, as Sheila insists we must, I don't feel as sorry as I should that Judy flaked out. If she hadn't, I wouldn't have learned how much fun a trust fall can be."

I turned away, hoping to hide the blush traveling from my chest to my throat.

"Your turn," he prodded.

"It's not so much a fear, but I hate losing control." From the corner of my eye, I saw our leader approaching, so I elaborated. "It makes me a little crazy when I can't predict what's coming or what's expected of me."

Sheila paused long enough to take in the last part of my confession. My back stiffened as I waited for her judgment. She nodded and moved on to make another couple wish they'd stayed home.

"If you don't mind my asking, why do you think that is? It's pretty obvious what screwed me up. Your situation seems more complicated."

"You wouldn't say that if you met my mother. Compared to her, I'm Miss Spontaneity. If it's Sunday, it's pot roast and potatoes. Every other Tuesday, she gets her nails done, always cherry red. Her calendar is precisely highlighted according to domestic, social, and medical. I suspect she schedules sex with my dad under either domestic or social, and don't want to know."

He laughed, and I realized my palms had stopped sweating.

"I can't believe I said that." But I was surprisingly unembarrassed.

"Coming from a house where chaos was the norm, I envy you a little."

"You shouldn't," I responded without thinking. "Of course, I love my mother. But sometimes when I look at my own multi-colored calendar, I wonder what it would be like to have a rainbow day. You know? A day where you couldn't tell what category you were supposed to fit into."

"What about him?" He pointed at his name tag. "What's Rob's designated color?"

"Well, he, uh, I never thought of it that way."

Thankfully, Sheila called time and directed us into our next adventure: couples' charades.

. . . .

My phone buzzed from my bedside table. It was a text from Rob.

Sorry I didn't call, but this place is unbelievable. Some of the worst record-keeping I've ever seen. Not sure if I'll be able to get everything wrapped up by Thursday. Love you.

I searched my mind, trying to pull up the location of *this place* and was certain he hadn't told me. But if I asked where he was, I knew he would be annoyed. He would insist he'd given me a detailed account of his schedule, and his tone would imply I had failed to give him my full attention—a serious infraction of the girlfriend code.

So instead of pressing him about his travel agenda, I searched for the kiss emoji, although I was pretty sure Rob hated emojis, then hit send.

I replayed my conversation with Kevin and wondered what calendar category Rob fit in. I decided it didn't matter because he'd somehow bled into every day, whether he was with me or not. Seconds before I drifted off, it occurred to me I should be less afraid of losing control and more afraid of losing myself.

4

Sunday was wet and gray, a perfect morning for lounging in bed. A quick look at the clock told me it was only 6:30. Burrowing deeper under the covers, I tried to fall back to sleep. But the sound of raindrops on the roof went from soothing to annoying—reminiscent of my mother's voice urging me to return to church with her and to bring Rob. Because everybody knows a Godly marriage is a goodly marriage.

As a child, it never occurred to me to rebel against joining my fellow Methodists every damn Sunday. Mom would outfit me in full, lacy-skirted dresses with itchy material. In the hard-backed pew, I would lean against Dad's scratchy wool jacket, breathing in the smell of cigars and Old Spice, until my mother tugged on my arm and hissed at me to "sit up straight and keep my legs together."

The closest I ever came to rebellion was to ask why I couldn't stay home with Jams.

Mom replied, "We're going to let Jesus deal with your grandmother. I'm dealing with you."

I begged Jams to use her influence in the matter.

"All that moaning and groaning and begging God to step in to fix things we'll just screw up again has never been my thing, but it's important to your mother. She's afraid if you don't go, you'll turn into a heathen like me and be headed straight to hell."

"If you're going to hell, I want to go, too."

Jams laughed but refused to intervene.

When I came home from college, I got the nerve to tell Mom I would no longer be going to church.

"I can't say I'm not disappointed, but I understand. You need to find a place to worship with people your own age."

That was over six years ago, and I remained one of the unchurched.

Thoughts of eternal damnation made it impossible for me to go back to sleep. I kicked off the blankets and squirmed under the sheets. Most days, my bedroom is my happy space. The airy lace curtains framing white shades allowed a soft glimmer of sun to shine through. Beams bounced off the mirror over my antique dresser and created colorful prisms of light against the pale blue wall. But there was no sunshine today. The room was drab and filled with shadows. It offered no comfort. Instead, its compact nature tightened my chest, and I was back in the second grade when the class bully locked me in the supply closet.

I picked up my phone to see if Rob had tried to get in touch since last night. He hadn't.

Neither coffee nor my cheery surroundings improved my mood. For the first time, I saw my favorite room through Rob's eyes. Maybe it was too old-fashioned, too cute. But when I attempted to picture myself standing at the counter in his house, I quivered and the hair on my arms stood on end.

I ate a toasted Cherry Tart and finished my second cup of coffee a little after eight, leaving me with four hours before I was due for lunch at my parents'. That gave me enough time to catch up on some work from the firm. At first, whenever Rob was home, I left everything at the office, even though he was usually on the phone with business associates or shut away with his laptop, creating spreadsheets or proposals or whatever forensic accountants did. With the increasing frequency of his absences, however, I got into the habit of checking in on some of Reynolds and Schultz's more demanding clients.

I started as an assistant after majoring in marketing because a professor asserted there were seldom life or death emergencies in the field, and that, although somewhat tedious, it could be very rewarding. And he'd been right—about the tedious part. After six months of analyzing data, I still waited for the reward. Then my boss came down with a stomach virus the night before a big presentation on the viability of a campaign strategy for a state congressional hopeful. Since I was the only one who knew how to run the projector, the vice-president drafted me to fill in for him.

The head of PR attended the meeting and arranged my transfer to his team. I suspected my gender played a role in what was a slight promotion. It turned out I was better suited for the work than expected and four years later, they put me in charge of handling damage control for some of our biggest clients.

When people asked me what I did for a living, I replied I was a fixer. The joke lost its appeal because I'd become exactly that: the person called to prevent or clean up messes. I didn't break kneecaps with a baseball bat or pay off mistresses. I did, however, try to anticipate problems that might necessitate those actions and spin things when I failed at averting disaster.

My most challenging case was the one I was currently working on: a state judge up for re-election. Wade Harrison, affectionately known as Hanging Harrison, had come under scrutiny for sentencing discrepancies hinting at racial bias. But that wasn't why he came to us for help.

In Georgia, a little racism wouldn't hurt him at the ballot box. Rumors of affairs and illegitimate children might, since he portrayed himself as a righteous man, one who was not only a faithful worshiper but also received his orders directly from the Big

Guy. When pressed on the method of delivery of those commands—were they presented in tablet form or issued from the flames of a burning azalea bush—he'd been vague. But his assertion that he was following God's will never wavered.

The polls favored him by double digits, but his opponent Paul Margolin was gaining on him. Less of a bible thumper than the Judge, he was also a man of God when he wasn't frequenting illegal gambling clubs. While there's no specific biblical edict condemning wagering, many associated the practice with the love of money and lumped it under avarice. The way Margolin did it ruled out any affection he might have for personal riches, since he won little and lost big. We had researchers in the field trying to connect his financial losses with some of his courtroom decisions.

The campaign was turning into a race to the bottom with hints of salacious videos on both candidates, and Harrison wanted to make sure Margolin sank first. He hired us to do counter-research, to uncover what his opponent's team had uncovered on him and preemptively squelch it. I expected a few breadcrumbs as guideposts on our journey to dig up dirt on our own client, but the judge refused to provide any.

"There's nothing there, but I wouldn't put it past the sonofabitch to make a mountain out of a molehill. That's why I need you to find that molehill first," he said.

The reference to moles was unfortunate. With his elongated nose, flaring nostrils, and beady eyes lost in folds of droopy lids, he bore a striking resemblance to the annoying little rodents. I choked on unreleased laughter and gulped down half a bottle of water.

We decided, in addition to overseeing the excavation of molehills, I would oversee setting up focus groups to test-run political ads. The goal was to see how far we could go before the public disgust factor kicked in. It had already kicked in for me.

I brought up my emails and saw one from Sarge Alfonsi. His given name was Alberto, but during his years in the Marines, Alberto became Sarge. Well over six feet with a thick neck and torso, he had the build of a professional wrestler. He wore jeans stretched tight across his thighs with short-sleeved shirts that allowed a partial view of a skull with Semper Fi inscribed on his right arm and the talons of an eagle holding an American flag on his left.

A man of few words, he maintained a solemn demeanor, making it difficult to tell whether he was pleased or displeased. This lack of emotion made him the perfect investigator. Most of the time, I appreciated his pithy communication style. Today's email, however, fell short. I needed more.

Got a guy working on M's gambling debts. But H may have bigger problems than we thought. Sit tight on campaign strategies.

With Harrison breathing down our necks urging us to get a jump on his opponent by rolling out defamatory material first, sitting tight wasn't an easy option. I set up a focus group for tomorrow and had plans to hold at least two more. Other than that, I doubted how much longer I could postpone the roll-out, and Sarge's information stinginess offered no guidance in the stalling department.

I shot him a quick response, asking for detailed updates as soon as possible. Then I speculated on what the judge's bigger problems might be. Everybody knew his great-grandfather had been active in the KKK. But in the South, what well-to-do Caucasian politician didn't have a distant relative who had donned a white robe from time to time?

Harrison distanced himself from that branch of his family tree, but had he been able to slice off those limbs? I dove into the internet, searching for dirt on his tribe: arrests, lawsuits, divorces. I found a few drunk driving and disorderly conduct charges, but they had either been dropped or punished with a fine and a slap on the wrist. Not a big surprise, since Harrison's clan had enough influence to buy a judge or two before they produced one.

Damn it, Sarge. What had Harrison done? Or was it who had Harrison done? His second wife divorced him over five years ago, which made the probability our client might have had a juicy affair with a colleague's spouse a strong possibility. Even better—or worse, I supposed—had he had a fling with someone from the other side of the political aisle? If so, his constituents could decide he picked up a dose of liberalism, for which there was no excuse or cure.

5

After three hours staring at my computer, I came up with nothing but a stiff neck. I spent the forty-minute drive to Mom's preparing myself for my weekly interrogation.

"Rob wanted to come, but his flight was delayed." Had I used that excuse the previous Sunday? No, last week I concocted an emergency call from his boss.

"Working too hard? No, these dark circles must be hereditary on your dad's side of the family." A low blow since Mom had never met her biological father, didn't even know who he was.

"We're very close to setting a date for the wedding." We had no idea when or where we'd marry.

"I am well aware that I'm not getting any younger." And *"No, I will not consider freezing my eggs."*

I parked behind my grandmother's shiny black Mustang and headed to the three-bedroom ranch house where my mother grew up. After Grandpa Walter died, Mom tried to talk Jams into moving in with her and Dad. She refused. As usual, Mom dragged me into the discussion during one of our Sunday dinners.

"Momma, what if you fall and break a hip or God knows what else. Claire, don't you agree your grandmother would be safer living with us?"

I held my hand over my mouth, pretending to chew on a piece of chicken I'd long since swallowed.

"At my age, dear, the last thing I'm interested in is being safe. And I have no intention of being taken down by a slip-and-fall. I plan on something more interesting, like pulling a muscle raking in my winnings at the blackjack table or swing dancing over the side of a cruise ship or having a heatstroke in bed with a—"

Dad changed the subject.

Still, my mother continued her campaign to ensnare Jams. She clipped horror stories from the paper of injured elderly women lying undiscovered for days, of widows tied up by home invaders, and of confused senior citizens disappearing in the woods, never to be seen again. My grandmother tossed them unread into the trash, and Mom seemed to be running out of steam.

As I walked through the door, I selfishly hoped she hadn't given up because if she stayed focused on Jams, she would have less time to interrogate me.

"There she is." Dad must have been standing by the window waiting for me. He whispered, "It's not pretty in there, baby." Then he flung an arm around my shoulders and steered me toward the family room. "Ladies, Claire's here."

"Who else would it be, Martin?" Mom snapped from inside the kitchen.

Jams rose from the chintz-covered rocker by the fireplace. I wrapped her in my arms and breathed in the clean floral fragrance she'd worn for as long as I could remember.

"How about I get everybody a nice, cool drink? Let's make that a naughty stiff drink, the stiffer, the better." Without waiting for a response, she strode through the salon-style doors separating the two rooms. I heard bottles rattling.

"Really, Momma. Don't you think it's a little early for wine?" Mom asked as she attacked a pan of gravy with a wooden spoon.

"That's why we're going with Bloody Marys."

Dad and I retreated to the sofa, the farthest point from the kitchen, and discussed the weather: unusually warm for this time of year. My job: all good, thanks. His latest woodworking project: harder than he expected to carve bird wings.

Jams delivered our drinks complete with olives and celery sticks. We sipped in silence, except for the sound of silverware slamming onto the table. I was two-thirds of the way finished with my Bloody Mary when Mom announced lunch was ready.

"This looks great. How in the world do you do it?" I piled my plate with ham and green beans.

"It's not magic, dear. Learn to cook and voila: Mystery solved." She slapped a spoonful of potatoes on my dish.

What the hell did I do?

"Now, Janis. There's no use taking it out on Claire when I'm the one you're pissed at," Jams said.

"I'm not angry. I'm frustrated because you won't even talk about it." There was a catch in her voice.

"I thought we agreed not to bring it up again, that's all."

"You agreed. I didn't get a say in the matter. Not once in my whole life have I ever had a say in it." Mom pushed her chair back, snatched her plate, and fled from the room.

Dad and I stared at the door for a few seconds before he asked, "Think I should go talk to her?"

Jams shook her head and kept buttering a roll.

When I was growing up, I sensed the hard place between my mother and my grandmother. They tried to keep it from me, but I'd walked in on too many abruptly ended conversations not to get an idea of what repulsed Jams with the same intensity it lured her daughter. I knew they were fighting over the topic of Mom's father.

Jams sighed and said, "I hoped she would let it rest."

Mom burst through the door, sending a shock wave over the table. "How can I let it rest when you never tell me the truth?"

"I have told you everything I can. I thought we made peace with it."

"You made your peace with it. But you know damn good and well I never did."

"I hate fighting with you about this."

"Don't worry, Momma. The fight's over. Or it will be soon."

She whisked a piece of paper from behind her back and thrust it in my grandmother's face. As Jams read it, she grew paler and paler. She relaxed her grip, and the colorful sheet slipped from her hand and landed beside her plate.

"Oh, Janis," she whispered.

I saw the bright orange letters of the logo:

Close Connections

Let your DNA unlock the mystery of your past, present, and future.

•   •   •

Jams drained the rest of her Bloody Mary and left without saying a word. Dad stuck a slice of ham inside his roll and ate it in two bites while I rearranged green beans on my plate. Mom returned to the table, carrying a glass of wine. She initiated the required cross-examination, but I could tell her heart wasn't in it.

"Have you and Rob talked more about having your ceremony in the church?"

"It's still a possibility," I lied.

Instead of a hard-hitting line of follow-up questions, she mumbled, "That's good," and began clearing the table.

The printout from Connections remained on Jams' place mat.

While Mom was banging dishes around in the kitchen, I pointed at the offending paper and asked Dad, "Did you know about that?"

He shook his head, stood with his plate, and left me alone with the report. I slid it closer but didn't pick it up.

As a child, I never questioned why he was Grandpa Walter and not plain old Grandpa. I just loved him—his great booming laugh and pockets filled with caramels, the way he threw me into the air and knowing he'd always catch me. He was one of the constants in my life and that was enough.

Spring of my freshman year in high school, my history teacher introduced the decades project. She assigned my group the sixties, and I became obsessed. The music and flower children and social unrest convinced me I'd been born in the wrong time period. I watched videos of Woodstock, hoping to spot my grandmother in the crowd, and listened to The Who day and night. As part of the assignment, I interviewed Jams for hours.

During our third session, I sat across from her at the kitchen table. She explained how she became the victim of gradual enlightenment. Stuck in a small Southern town, she awoke to the hateful discrimination she never noticed before. She identified with the oppressed, but a good girl from the South wasn't supposed to question leaders—mostly men, of course. She was dismissed or ignored. Her one act of wild rebellion had been her trip to Woodstock, a journey that changed her life forever.

I was furiously scribbling notes when Grandpa Walter came into the kitchen.

"What are my two lovely ladies up to?" he asked.

"Talking about old times, honey." She smiled up at him, and he patted her shoulder before pouring himself a cup of coffee.

"Jams was telling me about going to Woodstock. That must have been totally amazing. What was your favorite band, Grandpa?"

He stopped stirring and stood straighter. Except for the sound of Jams tapping her fingernails on the table, the room was silent.

"Your grandpa didn't make it to the festival," she said. "But I told him all about it."

It wasn't until later when I was typing up my notes from the interview, that I caught the discrepancy. If my grandfather hadn't been present in that rocking van, he couldn't have been Mom's father. I considered asking Jams for clarification and don't remember why I decided against it. I guess I liked the mystery of it all. Or maybe I was too self-absorbed to dwell on ancient history. And it was around the time I started kissing boys on a regular basis.

Even now my curiosity about my real grandfather wasn't based on what he might have contributed to my biology or destiny. My interest sprang from what there was about the man that caused such a rift between Jams and Mom.

Beneath the logo was the personalized heading *Possible DNA Matches for Janis Brady Kincaid.*

My parents were whispering in the corner of the kitchen, but their conversation could end at any minute. If I was going to check out those secrets, I needed to do it now. But did I have the right to read it? Wasn't it the ultimate invasion of privacy, like reading someone's diary only about a hundred times worse?

Spared from this ethical dilemma by the sound of my mother's sobbing, I barely had time to slide the paper back to its original spot before Mom burst through the swinging door and ran through the room. I hopped up to follow her, but Dad caught me by the shoulder.

"Let her go," he said.

A wave of guilty relief washed over me. I had no idea how to comfort my mother. Like Mom, offering consolation wasn't my strong point.

6

At home, I logged onto Connections. Images of grandmotherly types embracing smiling men and women filled the screen before being replaced with laughing people gathered around picnic tables. None of them wore the look of grim-faced terror I'd seen on Jams' face.

I scrolled through a menu of options on "connecting the dots." Choices ranged from assistance with building family trees "branch by branch" to thorough DNA testing guaranteed to "answer all your pressing questions about where you come from to help you get where you want to go."

I wondered how that might work. For every person who discovered a relationship to George Washington's footman, there had to be dozens more who found out their great-great-great whatevers had been hanged for stealing horses. Or that a distant cousin had been married to Mussolini's nephew. Regardless of the uncovered material, there was no way finding out what a long dead ancestor had been or done had the power to shape the future.

Taking a stroll through my family history held no interest for me. Unlike Mom, I didn't care who her real father was. The only grandfather I'd known was Walter, and he'd been excellent at the job. Piggy-back rides when I was little, letting me steer the riding lawn mower, a new car when I turned sixteen. And even a kid like me could tell he made Jams happy.

I could, however, see how having a substitute dad might be different. And Jams' refusal to provide a single clue as to her biological father's identity seemed to increase my mother's need to find him. I assumed my grandmother's reluctance to discuss the man who'd rocked her world so many years ago had more to do with a painful break-up or a one-night stand. Now I wondered if she had a darker reason for erasing him from her life, something that provided more motivation to keep the truth from Mom.

Before I had a chance to explore what terrible secret Jams might be hiding, my cell phone rang. Rob's name popped up on caller ID, startling me because he usually texted. It was more efficient. I didn't know if I should be excited or frightened.

"Is everything okay?" I blurted.

"Why wouldn't everything be okay?" His voice was one of his most interesting qualities. He never raised it in anger. It never cracked with emotion. Anna said it reminded her of watching golf on TV.

"No reason, just surprised you called. In a good way, though. When will you be back?"

"That's why I'm calling, babe. I finally cleaned up that mess I told you about when I got another call from the home office."

This time, I knew he hadn't told me much of anything about that mess, not even where it was.

"Home office," I echoed, wondering if my voice had become as flat as his.

"I hate it, but I won't be able to make it back until early next week."

I separated a strand of hair, examined it for split ends, and made a mental note to schedule a haircut.

"Claire, are you listening?"

"You're not coming home until next week. Got it."

"You sound upset. I'd come sooner if I could."

"I'm not upset. It's just stress from lunch with the family. Mom and Jams got into it again about—"

"That's a shame. You should get some rest. I've got to run, but I'll check in tomorrow. Love you."

"Love you t—" I stared at my phone, asking myself if it made sense for me to expect more from the relationship. More what, though? Interest in my day? Concern over my family conflicts? But that wasn't fair. Things were crazy for him at work. When they settled down, he'd be back to—I searched for what we would return to—and came up with the way we were at the beginning.

The night Rob and I met, my boss had insisted I go with him to a Harrison fundraiser. He wanted me to get a feel for the judge before meeting him. After listening to his donors drone on and on about how the state was desperate for a man like him, someone tough enough to stand up to the people who were out to destroy time-honored traditions—traditions including singing "Dixie" while rallying around statues of Jefferson Davis and Robert E. Lee—I needed a drink. Others must have shared my sentiment. Instead of an orderly line, the crowd swarmed the bartender, pushing past one another while shouting their demands.

Wishing I'd taken Anna's advice to carry a flask in my purse, I almost gave up when the man behind me tapped my shoulder.

"A beautiful woman like you shouldn't have to get her own drink. What are you having?"

I couldn't decide if he was being patronizing or polite and decided if he could speed up the alcohol-procurement process, I didn't care.

"Bourbon, please. On the rocks."

"A girl after my own heart."

Once he had the drinks, he introduced himself and insisted on escorting me back to my table. I don't know if I invited him to join me or if he simply took my boss's vacant seat, but he stayed. Handsome in an understated fashion, Rob wasn't like other men I dated. As early as middle school, I'd been a sucker for the class clown, but not the bra-flipping, fake-farting types. I liked the quick comeback kind who understood comedic timing.

Not a funny man, he had excellent timing when it came to delivering the type of compliments I needed to hear.

"I hope I'm not coming on too strong," he said. "It's just that you're so perfect."

Perfect. No one had ever called me that.

His mouth dropped open when I told him I wasn't seeing anyone.

"You're kidding right? How can it be that someone as irresistible as you isn't taken?"

Warmed more by his compliments than the bourbon, I assured him it was true. Then he went on and on about this being his lucky night. When the speeches concluded, I agreed to go to dinner with him. That date led to a series of others and before I knew it, we were a couple.

Unlike less mature relationships, we didn't tear each other's clothes off every time we were together, but that didn't worry me. I read in numerous surveys that people who made love as seldom as once a month claimed to be satisfied and happy. Rob and I were far ahead of that curve. Not that I kept count.

My boyfriend approached sex in what I imagined as the same manner he did forensic accounting. He meticulously collected evidence that might be valuable in some future venture. While this meant he became better at ferreting out my preferences and producing the desired effect, there was something mechanical about his performance.

He more than made up for his lack of passionate abandonment in the bedroom with his keen interest in every aspect of my life. At first, this intensity intoxicated me. Soon, I started to believe I was as fascinating as he thought I was. He asked questions about my family and friends, where I went to school, places I'd traveled. He seemed most intrigued by my job. I remember how disappointed he'd been when I explained that much of my work was confidential.

A few months into our relationship, his enthusiasm for the details of my daily life waned, and I realized how little I knew about him. Born in a small town near Philadelphia, because of his father's job, he moved around a lot. He told me both his parents had died in an automobile accident soon after he left home.

"My God," I said, moving close to him on the sofa where he sat reading the paper. "That must have been terrible."

"It was," he responded and turned to the sports page.

Later, when I pressed for more information, he provided the basics. He'd gone to a private college in Illinois and had been too focused on his studies to make friends or date that much. Forensic accounting was his passion, almost a calling. Other than that, he refused to discuss the past because it was more productive to think about our future.

He did, however, love for me to talk about my work.

"Must be fascinating dealing with all those powerful people," he repeated for at least the twentieth time.

"No, it's really dull."

I had spent the day examining photos of Margolin and his cronies sweating and yucking it up at a boxing match.

"Come on. Admit it. Looking into someone's life in search of dirty deeds can't be that boring."

I promised him it could be and ended the conversation. But no matter how many times I cut off any work discussion, he always returned to the subject.

My buzz from Jams' Bloody Mary—my grandmother was well-known for over-serving—had worn off after Rob's call. I expected to be too overwhelmed by disappointment to get anything done but wasn't. So, I turned my attention to the impending focus group.

But my creative juices weren't flowing. Thinking more alcohol might stimulate them, I took a cold beer from the fridge before returning to my laptop.

The Connections site greeted me, and I toyed with the idea of ordering a kit for myself. I decided it made more sense to see how Mom's genetic adventure ended before I initiated my own. I pulled up my files on the most recent polling data on Harrison but didn't open them.

Instead, I would check for a different connection—one that provided more in-depth information on my fiancé. Without a DNA sample, though, I would have to wing it. I started with Haderman and Associates, the forensic accounting firm Rob worked for. Their website described the services they performed, which included quantifying data for legal resolutions, preventing fraud, and working with whistleblowers. The site didn't include a list of employees. I assumed that meant it wasn't like a dating app where you swiped right on the most appealing accountant. Nor did it have client endorsements. No bells and whistles at all.

Other than a generic bio with no picture on Linkedin, Rob had no online presence. And he was incredibly camera shy.

When I wanted to take a selfie of us for my Facebook profile, he insisted he was too unphotogenic.

My persistence paid off, and he gave in. But in every photo, his face was blurred by a last-second sudden movement. I ended up creating avatars to go along with my *in a relationship status*.

About a month after we started dating, Anna voiced suspicions.

"What thirty-eight-year-old man isn't on Facebook? It's like he's a freaking ghost. Are you even sure his name is Rob Evans?"

Forgetting I told her I trusted him too much to run a background check, I blurted out my confession. "Yes, it's his real name, and he graduated from Deluca University with a major in accounting. I have proof."

Then I showed her the picture of Rob's graduating class. "See, there, third from the right on the back row. Robert A. Evans."

Anna squinted. "Kind of looks like him, but it could also be my cousin Tony and the bartender at the Ritz."

I stood firm on my belief in Rob, and we agreed to disagree. But like a song you can't stop humming, that melody of uncertainty echoed through my brain. Tonight, the faint cry took on a more strident tone.

What if my friend was right? What if he wasn't who or what he claimed to be? What if he was after ... after what?

I had a decent stock portfolio and a sufficient amount in the money market. But not enough for him to be after my fortune. Neither my family nor friends were influential people. And everything from his tailor-made suits to his Jaguar XJ and his Rolex, the one he had engraved—in an uncharacteristically romantic gesture—with the date we met, demonstrated he wasn't hurting for cash.

His persistent interest in my job troubled me some. But I never brought home sensitive information and kept a separate account for business emails. Besides, some of our clients might be big shots on the local scene, but no one stood out on the national stage.

Thoughts of work reminded me of the focus group. I set aside my personal investigation and read through bios on our recruits: twelve mostly retired, white suburban women. We planned to determine how Harrison might woo them into voting in an election with a dismal turn-out. We were paying them on the low-end of the scale but were providing coffee, soda, snacks, and lunch. I expected a fairly convivial group. However, things often turned ugly when the discussion centered on politics, so I needed to be prepared.

After reviewing information on our participants, I practiced my introduction. It had to be warm and welcoming while establishing the basis for absolute, yet unobtrusive, control. Unlike Dr. Sheila, I would mold my little group, without bullying them, into a congenial and cohesive unit. I would gently manipulate them into revealing motivations that would provide a road map to victory for our client.

I would tease out biases and unveil deep-seated prejudices. Biases and prejudices they were unaware they possessed.

Dear God. I may be worse than Sheila.

The idea she and I might be in the same line of business created an urgent need to shower. I was on my way when my phone began buzzing in my pants pocket. It was a number I didn't recognize.

I never answer anonymous intrusions, but something stopped me from dismissing it. This could be someone calling to let me know Rob had been in an accident.

I answered with a shaky hello.

"Hey, it's Kevin, Kevin Thomas, your trusting partner. Hope it's not too late."

"Not at all. I was going over some material for tomorrow's... never mind. It's boring."

"I doubt that, but I won't keep you long. I realized I've got your binder from the workshop. I must have picked it up with mine. Your number was in it, and I thought you might want it if, for nothing else, to remember our outstanding trust fall."

My stomach fluttered at the memory.

"If you're free for lunch tomorrow, I can bring it to you."

I had absolutely no interest in Dr. Sheila's packet of fluff, the one that promised relationship bliss.

"I've been looking all over for that binder," I said and agreed to meet him at a spot far enough from my office to ensure I wouldn't run into any co-workers.

Seconds after hanging up, I began regretting both my choice of restaurant and whatever impulse had made me accept his offer. I should call him back, make up some appointment I'd forgotten about. I held my finger over the callback icon, but instead of pressing it, sent a guilt text to Rob.

It's lonely here without you. I miss you so much.

Rather than end with my usual *I love you*, I selected a heart emoji and a trail of smiley faces with hearts for eyes and hit Send.

7

Twelve pairs of eyes, eight of them magnified through thick lenses, were fixed on me. My assistant Lisa set up her laptop to record the session. Seated around a giant circular table, we hoped to portray a Consumers-of-the-Round Table motif.

According to our unwritten script, I should have been beaming at the group while Lisa introduced me as their moderator. I would wrap each individual member in a cocoon created by the warmth I radiated. Then they would all emerge as beautiful butterflies eager to flitter around Judge Harrison. Complete nonsense, of course. We'd be lucky if we got a few moths drawn to false flame.

But I was off my game. I plastered a simian grimace on my face like heavy foundation but couldn't read the expressions of the women receiving it. I traced the outline of the phone in my pants pocket, wondering if I had time to call off my lunch with Kevin. I had an unofficial policy never to cancel on the day of a scheduled event. I also had a rule about not going out on my fiancé. But that wasn't this. Not at all. I would only be picking up a binder I neither wanted nor needed.

"Claire Kincaid." Lisa's voice penetrated my inner monologue, cuing me to take center stage. The protocol was simple: Welcome, overview, ground rules, first question. I could perform the tasks in my sleep. The challenge was not to look as if I were sleepwalking through the entire event.

"I want to thank everyone for taking time out of your busy schedules to sit down with us so that we can get a better understanding of what people need in a leader. Because that's what this election is all about: selecting the right person to carry the banner for our legal community. Someone worthy of your trust who will administer justice in a fair and impartial manner."

I let the weight of my words sink in. Other than a slight flinch from Lisa, the expressions of the group members remained neutral. I ignored their passivity and continued as if I'd received a standing ovation.

"Your voting record shows you're the type of people who care deeply about this issue. That's why Reynolds and Schultz asked each of you to join us today to share your thoughts."

We didn't have access to their records, voting or otherwise, and were relying on random surveys we passed out in their neighborhoods. That meant we were clueless as to whether they'd voted in previous elections. All we got from their survey answers was that they preferred law-and-order candidates and were available to meet during the day.

"Please feel free to share your opinions, even if they differ from others in the group. We're not just looking for positive feedback. We want to hear from all sides. Speaking of feedback, I'm sure you've noticed the microphone in front of me."

Lisa rewarded my lame joke with an obligatory chuckle. No one else cracked a smile, but that wasn't a surprise. I became more determined to melt the iceberg between me and my new best friends.

"Lisa is an excellent note taker, but these discussions can get pretty lively, and we don't want to miss anything. The cards in front of you have only your first names because we respect your privacy. We won't identify anyone in our final report. This session is absolutely confidential."

We rarely had a need for confidentiality, but it made people feel special, maybe even a little naughty, to imagine they were part of something worthy of keeping secret.

"Before we start, let's take a few minutes to go around the table and get better acquainted. You can share where you're from, your favorite movie or book, or any other interesting tidbit. Remember, we won't tell anyone."

Because it will be duller than dog shit, as Jams liked to say.

Icebreakers like my moment of sharing were designed to create a more relaxed atmosphere that would make it easier for the members to share their honest opinions because in most focus groups the participants often shy away from expressing dissenting viewpoints. Lisa says I have a way of coercing my people into disagreeing in a civilized, if not necessarily dignified, manner. She considers it one of my strong points, but I'm not so sure.

"Why don't I begin?" I always began but tried to inject just the right amount of spontaneity into my voice. Falling back on agency training that emphasized sprinkling in as many absolute and partial truths as possible in a narrative, I started with the obvious.

"You all know my name is Claire. I've lived in Marietta, Georgia all of my life." Verifiable fact.

"I love the classics like *Casablanca* and *To Kill a Mockingbird*." Partially true: I loved sitting beside Jams on her sofa watching her choices of black and white movies. Left on my own, I'm more a *Pulp Fiction* or *Kill Bill* kind of girl.

"My favorite book is *Jane Eyre*. Not married yet, but I hope to find the right man and have a house full of kids someday." Mostly true. I enjoy the high jinks of the plucky orphan, but there are other characters I like as much or more. However, Jane is the safest choice. It's the story of an unfashionably independent woman who, despite her independent spirit, can still snag a husband—he's burned and blind, but a husband, nonetheless.

The house full of kids fell into the total fabrication category. Maybe one or two someday, but filling my home with a bunch of unpredictable little hooligans held no charm for me.

Most of my group were or had been married and had children. Whether they would see my responses as affirmation of their choices or future membership in their misery, I couldn't be sure. Research suggested they were more likely to identify with my misdirection than with the truth. The smiles and nods they exchanged confirmed the theory.

Lisa followed with her own well-rehearsed introduction—also part fact, part fiction. Yes, she had moved to Atlanta from New York City to be closer to family, but no, she had not fallen in love with Southern gentility. Although she developed a tolerance for piddlers and drawlers, she detested what she referred to as all that "bless your heart bullshit."

She didn't share those feelings with the group. Instead, she pretended to adore good ole Dixie. She gushed about the proud history of antebellum days. No matter how many times she delivered her spiel, when she got to the part where she assured them that both her favorite book and movie were *Gone with the Wind,* she winced. And I suppressed a giggle.

She turned the program over to the group members. For the next few minutes, I smiled and nodded at each woman as she mentioned her love of baking or taking care of her grandchildren or playing mahjong.

"Wow, Lisa! This might be in the top ten of our most interesting groups."

As orchestrated, my assistant clapped her hands and gave everyone the thumbs-up sign.

Then I explained the ground rules.

"Because everyone's opinion is too valuable to miss a single word of it, only one person should talk at a time. This includes crosstalk. Whenever you want to add to the conversation, raise the index card with your name on it. And, even though I can tell this group doesn't need to hear it, most important of all, be courteous and respectful."

After pausing for questions they wouldn't pose—no one wants to ask why she should be polite—I walked to the whiteboard and wrote the open-ended topic designed to launch the rest of the discussion.

"When you think of a leader, what qualities come to mind?" I read aloud what I had written.

The answers were predictable, but I responded with gusto to each one as if she had solved the mystery of dark matter. As usual, I had trouble distinguishing between group members, except for one.

Younger and more stylish than her counterparts, Mary Saunders caught my attention, and not only because of the blonde and highlighted hair unlike the grays and whites surrounding her. And not just her choice of trendy jeans instead of polyester pull-ons. The directness of her gaze set her apart.

During our first break, I thumbed through the applications. Mary's file had been added less than a week ago, much later than the others. Not unusual; we often needed replacements at the last minute. Unlike most, she hadn't marked retired on the form. We didn't require anyone to provide place of employment because we rarely had volunteers who were employed. Who would or could miss work to take part in something as nebulous as a focus group? And there were no marks beside married or children. Could she be a kept woman or very private or both? I made a note to have our research people run a background check to uncover who Mary worked for in the unlikely event she might be an opposition plant.

The rest of the morning went according to plan. After we established the qualities every leader should have, I followed with questions digging into what these values would look like in action and rounded third base—all baseball analogies were part of the firm's training program—by providing specific examples from Harrison's term in office that met their criteria. I didn't mention the judge himself until everyone—with the exception of Edith, a white hair who fell asleep, and Mary, who refrained from comment despite my encouragement—agreed the instances I cited did, indeed, qualify a person as a good leader.

I slid across home base by revealing the identity of the unnamed judge. As expected, a few women smiled and nodded as if they'd already guessed my mystery hero. Some registered what I took for genuine surprise, and several maintained blank looks as if they had tuned out long before my announcement. I couldn't read Mary's face.

I ended with effusive thank-yous as Lisa passed out handouts that asked questions like those we posed during the discussion. We would compare their responses to transcripts from the sessions to determine how effective we'd been or how unreliable they were. They exchanged their surveys for vouchers to be mailed in for cash and a special bonus of a Chicken Delight gift card.

When our guinea pigs left the room, Lisa began packing up the equipment. "Some of the gang are going to Catfish King for lunch. Join us?"

"Thanks, but I brought my mine," I lied as I noticed the first survey listed honesty as the most important quality in a leader. "And I want to go over the responses while everything's fresh in my mind."

"You work too hard," she said and closed the door behind her.

I wondered what it revealed about my character that I would choose lying to a trusted co-worker and friend rather than mentioning an innocent lunch with a recent acquaintance. Of course, that statement qualified as a lie, too. A folder exchange wasn't a business deal, and Kevin wasn't only an acquaintance. He was the man whose impersonation of my fiancé might have been better than the original.

8

As soon as I got to the hostess stand, I saw Kevin waving from the back of the room.

"It's great to see you without Dr. Sheila around as a chaperone." He stood as I sat across from him.

I felt a blush coming on and picked up the menu.

"I definitely don't miss her enthusiastic approach to relationship coaching," I spoke from behind the daily specials.

"How about a drink before we order, unless you're short on time and want to go straight to the main course?"

The correct response would have been to pretend I had a tight schedule. Instead, I put my menu down and said, "A cold beer would be good."

"Pictured you as a wine girl."

When he grinned, I noticed the way the fine lines at the corners of his eyes tilted upward.

"I'm flexible." His smile widened, and I added, "When it comes to alcohol, that is."

Oh, my God. Was I flirting? No, engaged women don't flirt.

The waitress appeared before I could continue with my non-flirting. I selected a pale ale from a local brewery and Kevin ordered a Pilsner.

"I have a confession to make," he began.

My grip on the menu loosened, and it slipped from my hands to the table. "Confession?" I echoed.

"Nothing monumental. Only that I did some research on you."

Our server arrived with water. She told us the drinks would be up soon, then asked if we were ready to order.

Kevin said, "I think we need more time." He gave her a smile similar to, but certainly not as bright as, the one he'd given me.

"Facebook."

"I'm sorry?" Still lost in comparing smile intensities, I had forgotten my question about what he found out about me.

"There aren't too many Claire Kincaids in Marietta."

"Interesting." I didn't mention how overloaded the internet was with Kevin Thomases.

"See anything you like?"

"Anything I like?"

"For lunch. No hurry, but I don't want the marketing department of Reynolds and Schultz mad at me."

"How did you—oh, right. Facebook." I retreated behind the menu again.

We spent the next few minutes discussing the merits of the turkey Reuben versus the traditional.

"How 'bout we get one of each and share?" he asked.

I agreed before I had time to consider what signal such an intimate food arrangement might send.

When I returned to work, the front office was empty. I dashed by the reception area and into the bathroom. My urgency had less to do with my second beer and more to do with not wanting to be seen. Not that Lisa or anyone else would have questioned where I'd been for the past two hours. It was doubtful they would have even noticed, and they wouldn't have cared. Still, I couldn't avoid having mixed feelings about how easy it had been to talk to this man I barely knew.

"That's absurd," I said facing myself in the mirror. "All you did was have a lunch."

From a dark corner of my mind, my mother's voice asked, "If it was so innocent, why do you look so guilty?"

I squeezed my eyes shut and refused to answer, but I couldn't unhear it. For as long as I could remember Mom found a way to ruin whatever good time I came across. From my first make-out session with Johnny Fowler to lying about being at a friend's sweet sixteen party when we were partying at the lake with college boys, my enjoyment was laced with guilt.

I asked Jams once what had made Mom such a spoilsport. "Just because she hates having a good time, why does she want to destroy my entire life? Why can't she be more like you?"

"Honey, your momma's not programmed that way. For me, there's nothing better than to load up the car and head out on a road trip to Who Cares or We'll Figure It Out When We Get There. Your mama? She's more into a good guilt trip. Not that a little guilt's a bad thing. That's pretty much all that stands between us and that fiery pit your mama's sour-faced preacher is always harping about. Janis's problem is she insists on the guilt without any of the fun."

"Well, I'm going to be like you," I'd sworn. But I wasn't at all like Jams.

"Never too late," I said to my reflection, then freshened my lipstick. Fluffing my curls, I remembered how Kevin reached across the table to brush a breadcrumb from my cheek. Although his fingertips only grazed me, I jerked away from the touch. Irrationally certain Rob was hiding in the crowd watching me, I revolved in my seat to survey the area.

A distinguished older gentleman wearing gold-framed glasses glanced in my direction. His hair was the salt-and-pepper color you see on Just for Men dye, and his gray pin-striped suit was a perfect match. As soon as I saw him, he waved at the waitress standing at the table behind us.

"Are you okay?" Kevin asked.

I assured him I was fine and ordered my second beer. We spent the next hour laughing over our time with Sheila, speculating what it would be like to live with a woman who insisted on constant eye contact. Before I had a chance to feel uncomfortable about being so comfortable, I shifted the subject and discovered that after a stint in the Marines, Kevin had opened his own small home security company. I wanted to ask if he was still with Judy after the shameful way she stood him up but didn't want to reciprocate if he questioned me about my missing partner.

He followed my lead and asked about my work. Kevin expressed interest in what I did. Unlike my fiancé, he asked if I enjoyed it, found it fulfilling. I told him it wasn't what I planned to do when I graduated, but I had a flair for it. Then I shocked myself by admitting what I had always wanted to do was write, something I'd never said out loud.

Immediately regretting my candor, I prepared for comments about the impracticality of writing for a living or a condescending smile of faux encouragement. I hadn't been ready for inquiries regarding my genre or sources of inspiration.

"I wrote a few short stories for my college literary magazine."

"Are you working on anything now?"

"Not much since then unless you count campaign ads. Most of that is fiction, but not even a tiny bit inspiring."

Although he seemed unaware of it, his interest in my writing changed the atmosphere. We shifted from a pleasant exchange of not-so-personal information to a whole other level of intimacy. Now we were venturing into dangerous territory. Afraid of revealing too much of myself talking about my desire to be a writer,

I switched topic and asked how he liked working for himself. He shrugged and said it was okay, but his boss could be a real jerk.

I noticed the restaurant had emptied and checked my watch. Shocked at how late it was, I thanked him for lunch and for returning my folder, then gathered my things and scurried away.

Checking for mascara smudges in the company restroom, I had to admit my time with Kevin had turned into another example of how I was nothing like my free-spirited Jams.

The door swung open, ending my depressing self-evaluation. Two chattering girls from the accounting department lowered their voices when they saw me.

Back at my desk, the surveys from Judge Harrison's focus group were where they'd been when I left. They were a reminder of my duplicitous nature. To quiet my overactive conscience, I reached for the stack, planning to read through them and make notations in the margin.

Before I began, I remembered Rob and looked at my phone to see if he had responded to my sappy emoji. I had two texts: one from Anna asking if I wanted to grab a drink after work; the other, a message from the apartment manager telling me the exterminator had sprayed my unit, per my request. Still nothing from Rob.

I told Anna I was taking some files home to catch up but would schedule something with her later in the week. Then I reread my landlord's text. I hadn't asked for an extra treatment, so I decided he must have me mixed up with another tenant. Since that person would contact him as soon as a roach skittered across the kitchen counter, there was no need for me to reply.

Rob's lack of communication gave me an uneasy feeling. The man might be romance-impaired, but he had never taken this long to respond to a text. Possibly because he knew I would follow up with a phone call, which is what I did. I was sent straight to voicemail and was informed the mailbox was full. My unease threatened to become distress.

I turned to my computer and searched for Haderman & Associates. After clicking on the contact number, I counted the rings as I waited for an answer. I was on twelve when Lisa tapped on my open door. She placed some papers on the corner of my desk and hesitated.

Ring fifteen and still nothing.

"It's okay. Nobody's home." I tried to keep my tone light, hoping I was overreacting to what was most likely a problem with Rob's cell service and his firm's work overload.

Lisa pointed to the stapled packet on top. "I know you like to have a hard copy, so I printed the transcript of the first hour. You were so eager to get started I didn't want to make you wait for the whole thing."

She scooted the file to the side to reveal a nine by twelve mailing envelope underneath it. "Someone left that for you."

Puzzled, I picked it up. Other than my name printed in bold block letters, there were no other identifying marks.

"Did they leave it at reception?"

"No, I found it lying on my desk this afternoon. I asked the front office if they'd seen anyone drop it off, and no one had. Do you want me to run it by security?"

"Thanks, but I'm guessing it's from a group member: a complaint about the quality of the snacks or the gift card or the sound of my voice. I'll check it out before I leave. Speaking of leaving, you must have gotten here before seven; go home."

"I think I will. And you should practice what you preach since you only came in a few minutes after I did."

"I promise I won't be far behind you."

As soon as she left, I retried both Rob and his firm and got the same results. I had no number for the friend of his I had met; hell, I didn't even know his last name. Once again, I realized how little I knew about the man I planned to marry.

I stared at the phone, trying to convince myself I imagined a problem where none existed. Most likely, he had gotten tied up with a demanding client and would call me as soon as he could. Or maybe he had lost his cell or wanted to surprise me by coming home early.

Then I spent an additional minute or two shooting down each of those possibilities. Hadn't he said things were a real mess wherever it was he was going? He had mentioned on multiple occasions how hard he tried to spend as little time as possible with difficult clients. Checking in with me would have given him an excuse to extricate himself from whatever irritating circumstance he was dealing with. With his compulsion for keeping his phone with him at all times, it was unlikely he wouldn't have noticed it was missing. As for surprising me, that was pure fantasy.

Frustrated, I logged off my computer and began clearing my desk. I stuck the transcripts and the surveys into my purse, then turned to the mystery envelope. Remembering my plan to check it out before I left, I reached for the Egyptian letter opener Anna had given me.

"It's Hathor, the goddess of just about everything," she explained when she placed the ten-inch figurine in the center of my desk. The long-haired deity held an orb with cattle horns above her head.

"Sun, sex, beauty, fertility, dirty dancing—you name it, she's your girl. There's a rumor she was involved in high-level mass destruction, but her specialty is protecting women. And, honey, in this testosterone-infested business, you're going to need as much protection as you can get."

I popped off the deity's head and slid out the attached eight-inch dagger-shaped opener. Her cold, dead eyes conjured images of the goddess dancing around an open flame one minute and cutting down armies the next. The blade complemented those scenes. It was perfect for slicing through everything from stubborn wrapping tape to the thick necks of any man who offended her. I drew it through the paper, put Hathor back together, then turned the envelope upside down and shook it.

A four-by-six, black-and-white photo fell out. Clipped to the front of the picture was a neatly folded note. I removed it and stared at Judge Harrison, standing beside an overweight man with a thick mop of silvery hair. The judge had tilted his head back, and his mouth hung open. He seemed to be laughing. With his overbite and non-existent chin, I couldn't be sure. The background was blurred but could have been a bar or restaurant. On the other side, someone had neatly printed *Meeting with Delmar October*.

Like his face, his name rang a distant bell, but I had no time to answer it.

I read the note.

I'm afraid to trust anyone, but I can't keep quiet. You seem like a decent person who would want to know the truth, who wouldn't do anything to put another person in danger. I need your help. Meet me tonight, 7:30 at the Iron Horse Tavern.

M. Saunders.

A quick check for directions explained why I was unfamiliar with the place. It was over twenty miles north of my office. Since it was almost 6:30, I would have to hustle and pray there would be no serious issues on the road. I grabbed my purse, the note, and Mary Saunders's personal info form, then raced to my car and out of the parking deck.

Despite Atlanta's usual slow and slower traffic pattern, I arrived at historic downtown Norcross only a few minutes after 7:30. I parked about a block from the tavern near the train station. Brick sidewalks led to shops and restaurants with facades reminiscent of an earlier time, one devoid of shopping malls and golden arches. On a normal day, I would have enjoyed strolling through the area, would have found its quaintness soothing. But I didn't want to keep Mary waiting. If she was as paranoid as her note sounded, I worried she wouldn't stick around if I was late.

When I reached the Iron Horse Tavern, a red brick building with colonial-style trim work, I rushed through the shiny black door. The thick smell of spicy cheese wafted over me as I passed the gleaming wooden counter of a well-stocked bar. To my side, onlookers laughed and cheered as serious dart-throwers landed their shots.

"You can sit anywhere," a hostess in a white ruffled shirt and dark pants greeted me.

I thanked her and looked for Mary, but she wasn't there. I chose a small booth facing the door, ordered a draft beer, and waited.

Mary Saunders never showed.

9

Watching TV with a bowl of cereal and a glass of wine, I was still fuming when the 11:00 news came on.

At least five vehicles with flashing lights gathered in front of the apartment building. A dark-haired woman with a microphone stood off to the side. Behind her, a group of teenage boys jockeyed for camera time. Passersby stopped to gawk at uniformed officers.

"Victoria Nunally here at the Scenic Manor Apartments in Roswell." The slender brunette spoke in a solemn tone that matched the serious expression on her precisely made-up face. "Police discovered the body of a woman behind a building here. We don't have all the information, but her death does not appear to be from natural causes."

I jumped from the sofa and dashed to my office, where Mary's file lay on my desk. I slid my finger down to her address: *Mary Saunders, 1559 Scenic Manor Drive.*

.   .   .

After a restless night filled with dreams of bodies buried in pine straw, I eased into morning traffic, made even more challenging than usual by the light drizzle. The early edition of the news said authorities were waiting until next-of-kin notification to announce the identity of the woman found behind the Scenic Manor apartment building. But I knew it was Mary Saunders.

Unlike my mother, who insisted coincidences were God's way of remaining anonymous, I didn't believe in those quirky little twists of fate. Mary could have been in the wrong place at the wrong time, but I was certain her death had something to do with what she planned to share with me, information about Judge Harrison.

Traffic ground to a stop as the rain came down in torrents. Trapped between a semi on one side and an SUV on the other, I would be stuck long enough to contact Sarge. He picked up on the second ring.

"Hey, Miss Kincaid." Although I'd urged him to call me Claire, he hadn't been able to do it. "I've got a lead on Margolin's gambling debts. Should know more by the end of the week. I'm worried if I push too hard, my source will get spooked. But I can try to speed things up if you're in a hurry."

"Margolin? Oh, right, Margolin. Later is fine. In the meantime, I need you to check on something else, please."

I told him I needed clarification about some follow-up responses from a focus group member, and she wasn't answering her phone. Then I gave him Mary's name and address.

"And try to find out her employment history for the past two years." I kept the details to myself but not because I didn't trust him. It was because I was reluctant to tell anyone about the meeting I was supposed to have had with a murdered woman.

Traffic slowed to a crawl when I saw the exit to Rob's apartment, only a mile away. There had been no message from him when I checked after the morning news. I imagined that while Kevin and I were enjoying lunch, Rob had been fighting for his life.

Someone had whacked him on the head and sent him to the hospital with amnesia. An angry client could be holding him against his will to keep him from reporting cooked books.

Or maybe he was on a flight out of the country.

Nothing he had ever said or done indicated he wanted out of the relationship. He pushed for me to move in with him and stayed focused on the details of my job: who I'd met with, how my latest campaign was going. And me? I had shown no interest in his occupation, didn't even know what a forensic accountant did. Nor did I have any idea what *my* forensic accountant did. But the time had come to find out.

From the front, Rob's building looked like a thin slice of a multi-layered cake made of steel and glass. From the side, it was less cake and more pie with its wedged shape, designed to ensure maximum views of Atlanta's skyline.

I drove around to the underground garage and used the pass card Rob slipped into my box of Valentine's Day chocolates. My application for an assigned space was pending, but during a weekday, it was easy to snag a visitor spot not too far from the entrance. A white sedan with darkened windows ignored the rows of available spots and backed into the one next to me.

Not wanting to get stuck in an awkward elevator conversation, I grabbed my purse and leaped out of my car. I needn't have worried. The driver stayed put, and I began my ascent alone.

Unlike the rickety structure outside my apartment that wheezed and shuddered its way from floor to floor, this one was as sleek and smooth as the building itself. If not for the bright neon green lights that signaled our progress, I'm not sure I would have known I was moving. At the nineteenth floor, the doors opened onto a pale gray and blue carpet, creating the illusion of gliding across a smoky sky.

I concentrated on steadying my breathing as I made my way down the wide hallway to Rob's apartment. This wasn't the only time I stopped by unannounced, but I never enjoyed being alone and on display in the expensive and tasteful but cold fishbowl Rob called home.

I rang the bell three times and followed up with a series of increasingly loud knocks before inserting my key. My first thought after opening the door was that I had the wrong apartment or the cleaning lady had been overzealous. As usual, I could see my reflection in the gleaming black marble floor of the foyer. Morning sunlight from the window-wall pooled in buttery golden splotches on the otherwise snowy carpet. Unlike my home, there were no straw baskets brimming with unopened utility bills, no books scattered by the sofa, or papers strewn across tabletops.

My tennis shoe screeched against the smooth surface, and I almost lost my balance.

"Shit," I whispered and crouched to erase a sneaker smudge from the spotless floor. Then I noticed no one had tidied the place. Instead, someone had emptied it.

The sunken living room—once a frosty arrangement of glass, metal, and leather—had been stripped of its chic. Skirting the barren space, I forced myself to walk toward the kitchen. I shrank from the stark silvery gray walls, once lined with paintings splashed with discordant shapes and startling colors. As disorienting as the artwork had been, the naked walls were worse.

Polished granite counter tops cast an eerie glow from beneath recessed lighting. I opened one immaculate stainless-steel cabinet, then another and another. No dishes, glasses, not even those stupid little ramekins Rob thought were so classy. When I reached for the handle of the Sub-Zero refrigerator, images of doomed horror movie heroines superimposed themselves over my own reflection. I hesitated, fearful of what or who I might find inside, then made myself fling it open. It, too, was empty.

I rushed from the kitchen to the master bedroom and bath, then the guest room, the office. All empty, as if Rob never existed. But he had been...no, he *was* real. And he wanted us to start a life together. So why would he disappear?

Despite the size of the apartment, those pale and paler gray walls narrowed and trapped me in a metal and glass box. My chest constricted and my pulse pounded in my temples. I dashed for the exit and didn't slow my pace until the elevator doors closed behind me.

Inside my car, I gripped the steering wheel tight enough to whiten my knuckles. I turned the key, then opened all the windows and took deep breaths of stale air laden with the smell of gasoline and general garage funk. I wanted to be above ground as soon as possible and had to make myself slow down and look both ways twice before I backed out.

The roar of a nearby engine startled me. I must have been so deep in thought I missed seeing my parking neighbor enter his car. I tapped the brakes, planning to let him go first, but he didn't move. Although I couldn't see the driver's face, I acknowledged his patience with a half-wave and eased out of the space.

After exiting the garage, I realized I was too rattled to return to the expressway, so I stayed on side streets. Morning traffic forced me to maintain the speed limit, but my mind raced. I needed someone who could be objective. Jams might qualify. While she never said anything negative about Rob, she wasn't her exuberant, irreverent self around him. But with Mom's sudden desire to explore her heritage, my grandmother's plate was overloaded. Anna's distrust of him made it impossible for her to give me an unbiased opinion, but for now, she was my best bet for clarity.

In my eagerness to get to my friend, I almost missed the white car behind me. If it hadn't sped up to pass me when I turned into my building, I doubt I would have noticed it. I ignored the sound of the tiny bell ringing in the back of my brain and dismissed it as coincidence.

10

From the hallway, I saw her staring at the computer screen. Normally, I wouldn't have disturbed her. I would have come back at a better time, but there was nothing normal about a fiancé vanishing without a trace.

"Got a minute?" I walked in and shut the door.

Anna rolled her chair away from her desk and faced me.

"You don't look so good. Sit down and tell mami everything."

I sat, uncertain where to begin. "It's about Rob."

I expected a monumental eye roll, but she only nodded. "Okay. What's going on?"

I hesitated and her expression hardened. "Did that bastardo hurt you? Because there are people who will—"

"Nothing like that, but it is something terrible." My throat tightened and I tried to hold back tears. "He's gone, Anna." And for the first time during my awful morning, I broke down.

She came from behind the desk and held me until I was cried out. "It's going to be okay. But I cannot help you until you tell me what happened."

I told her about the unanswered calls and messages and no one picking up at his office, finishing with an account of the empty apartment.

"Please, don't say it. That he probably dumped me, that he never loved me at all. That's not it. Something horrible has happened to him." I plucked a tissue from the box on her desk and blew my nose.

"Honey, there are at least fifty ways to leave your lover, and none of them require the services of a moving company. And I never thought he didn't love you. It's more that he's a little shady. Okay, a lot shady. But that doesn't matter. What matters is, whatever the reason, he is missing."

"Someone must have kidnapped him."

"Possibly, but I've never heard of a kidnapper who emptied out the victim's apartment. And where's the ransom note?"

"Maybe Rob's employers got one."

"If they did, it doesn't look like they paid it."

I closed my eyes and pictured Rob handcuffed to exposed pipes in some dark basement or stuffed in the moldy trunk of a car.

"What if he's with some secret government agency that snatched him to work on infiltrating a terrorist organization and uncovering tax fraud or some other accounting blunder that would land the bad guys in prison?" I offered.

"Or maybe aliens abducted him. And because they wanted to help him relax while they picked and probed at him, they beamed up his overpriced furniture and flashy artwork."

This time I was the one who rolled my eyes.

"Too soon?" She stuck out her lower lip. "Sorry. This really is some serious shit. We should get the cops involved."

"And tell them what? That my boyfriend ran off before we even set the date for the wedding?"

She tapped her bright pink nails on the desktop. "You're probably right," she conceded. "What about Sarge?"

"I hate to involve him in a personal issue. Anyway, I've got him working overtime on the Harrison campaign." I didn't add that I had him looking into Mary Saunders's death.

"I'll ask Luis to see what he can find out," she said.

Anna's husband, Luis Ramirez, was a rising star in the district attorney's office. His contacts extended to law enforcement, politics, business, and—sometimes—the less than legal world. He would be the perfect choice, but if he found out Rob had done something illegal, he would have to report it.

She seemed to sense my discomfort. "I can ask him to be very discreet and not dig too deep until you give him the okay."

"Thanks, Anna. Having you in my corner means a lot to me, especially since you're not Rob's number one fan."

"But I am crazy about you. If he left you before you got to the altar, I have people who can make him disappear for good.

I snorted out a nervous chuckle, then noticed the grim expression on her face. Like her husband, Anna had a wide array of friends, many of whom operated by their own moral code. I thanked her again and hustled away.

There were no mysterious envelopes waiting for me at my desk, nor were there any disturbing voicemails on my business or personal lines. Too soon to expect information from Sarge, and Rob never communicated through email, so I skimmed through my inbox looking for messages requiring immediate attention.

The first was my apartment manager asking if everything had been good with the exterminator treatment. I decided equivocation would suffice and responded that I hadn't seen a single crawling or flying insect.

The sight of the second one shot my guilt index off the charts. It was from Kevin.

"Don't even read it," I told myself as I opened the text.

Had a great time at lunch. I'd love to do it again sometime soon. How about next week?

"Okay, you can read it, but don't answer it," I warned as I typed: *Me, too.* The image of Rob unconscious and helpless in a dark alley came to me and I added: *Work is crazy right now and won't ease up until the election.*

I suspected by that time he would have forgotten all about me. The thought should have been a relief, not the let-down it was.

After answering a few emails from clients and forwarding a request for help with another ad campaign to Lisa, I came across one with a puzzling subject line: *Reconstruction.*

Suspecting it was an advertisement for penile enhancement that slipped through my spam filter, I checked the sender's address: *happyharrison69*— yep, penis related. I was ready to delete, then looked closer at the source: harrison. The word *happy* never crossed my mind when I thought about my cranky client. As for the topic of reconstruction, I was at a loss as to what it had to do with our work on the campaign. And I really, really hoped there was no connection between the judge and penile enhancement. But I needed to make certain Happy wasn't my Harrison.

Braced for dancing phallic images in various states of good humor, I double-clicked on the subject. Instead of frightening before and after pictures of willies and weenies, there was a cryptic one-line message.

The meeting of RDR rescheduled. Time and place TBD.

There was no signature. Not a surprise. Who would go to the trouble of making up a silly moniker like happyharrison and then use his personalized signature: *The Honorable Judge Wade Harrison*? The question was why he included me.

Including an outsider to a private group email wasn't the same as carelessly hitting *reply all*. That often resulted in serious hard feelings; it might even get a person fired or at least banned from the break room. But adding the wrong name to what appeared to be an extremely private group could have more severe and far-reaching consequences. Lucky for the sender, I was in the dark about what it meant.

I searched my contact list; no Happy Harrison. As for the rescheduled event, RDR remained a mystery. I considered the possibility it had come up during our conversation about getting dirt on Margolin and I had forgotten it. I opened the shared folder where Lisa and I posted our individual notes and read through them, hoping something would jog my memory. But there was no reference to anything with those letters. And we hadn't set a date for our next meeting, much less postponed it.

The quickest way to learn both the identity of the sender and the meaning of the message would be to respond to Happy. But our IT people drilled it into us the many ways we might unleash a deadly virus by venturing into the unknown. I could also use the judge's business address, but if he sent the strange communication by mistake, I risked embarrassing my client. Despite my growing curiosity, I decided the best course of action would be to do nothing. If Judge Harrison intentionally included me in the mystery group and I ignored it, he would be certain to follow up, so I closed both the file and the email.

Patience had never been one of my strong points. Now it seemed as if I had no other choice in so many areas of my life. Even before the man I planned to marry went missing, I spent most of our relationship on hold. Along the way, I'd scattered pieces of my independence like birdseed. I let Rob make all the decisions, from where we would live to what I should wear. Who would I be if he never came back?

"You got a minute?" I recognized the gravelly voice. Sarge. He strode into the room, closed the door behind him, dropped a thin packet on my desk, and squeezed into a chair.

He tapped the folder. "The good news is I found out your girl's been working for some fancy pants joint called Temp of the Town the last couple years. They advertise themselves as a boutique agency with efficient and discrete personnel. Smells fishy to me. Not sure how much it matters though since it doesn't look like you'll be getting answers from Mary Saunders." He shifted in his seat, causing the chair to squeak in protest, then ran his hand over his close-cropped hair.

His solemn face revealed his discomfort at delivering bad news. A pang of guilt over not sharing I learned about her death on television shot through me. But I didn't want his assessment clouded by knowledge of my involvement with her.

He squared his muscular shoulders and looked me in the eye. "I'm sorry, but Saunders is dead. Happened last night. The cops haven't released anything yet, so this is on the down low. Looks like she was murdered outside her apartment. My guy swears he can't talk about the cause of death, so I canvased the neighbors. One old lady says she thought she heard a car backfire, and a kid said fireworks were popping."

My stomach lurched and my throat constricted against a rush of bitter fluid.

Sarge leaned forward. "Shit. I shouldn't of blurted it out like that. Need some water or something?"

"No, no. I'm okay." I was about as far from okay as imaginable. The possibility I played a part in the violent death of a woman, even one I barely knew, made me queasy and disoriented. I didn't want Sarge to know how terrible I felt, so I sat up straight and gripped the arms of my chair.

"Have they mentioned anything about why someone would, would uh," I searched for a gentler synonym for murder and came up empty. "What possible reason anyone would do that to her?"

"No idea why or who yet, but it doesn't look like a robbery, since the only thing missing was her phone. I did find something else on Margolin. It's nothing that can't wait if you're not up for it."

I assured him I was fine and tried to concentrate as he recounted what he'd learned about Margolin's gambling problems. Not only had our opponent racked up some hefty debts with his Vegas connections, but there were also rumors of his involvement with the convenience store video ring in Georgia, an enterprise that had resulted in fines, imprisonments, and deportations.

I should have been thrilled at this exciting news for my obnoxious client. But the thought of Mary Saunders with her open, straight-forward gaze distracted me. Despite my canned speech, practiced responses, and choice of profession, she trusted me. And now she was dead.

I realized Sarge had stopped talking. "Sorry. I'm a little overwhelmed with the other issue. I don't think I've ever known anyone who was, uh, well." I still couldn't bring myself to say the words. "Someone who died under suspicious circumstances. As for Margolin, I trust your judgment."

"Got it." He stood and took a few steps toward the door. "There's something else about the Saunders case. But I can come back later."

Part of me wanted to agree to picking up our discussion at another time, but Mary thought I was a good person, one who cared about the truth. She trusted me, and dammit, I owed it to her to set things right, or at least try.

"No, I'm fine. What else did you find out?"

"Her contact sheet has her living alone. The neighbors say different, that there's a kid, a teenage girl. The lady next door says she hadn't seen her since the night of the shooting."

"A child?" I fumbled through the folders on my desk until I came across hers, opened it, and flipped through the pages. "Nothing in here about Mary having a daughter."

Sarge shrugged. "Could be a relative staying with her. Sounded like she and the girl kept to themselves. Want me to keep poking around?"

His expression offered no clue to what he might be thinking. We both knew any further investigation would have nothing to do with me getting follow-up information for our survey. Still, I couldn't let it go.

"Would you, please?" I gave him what I hoped was an innocent-looking smile. "I've never lost a focus-group member before, and it makes me feel weird. Like I should help the family."

What you should do is contact the police. But what if her death had nothing to do with what she had to tell me?

"Sure. Not a problem." Sarge put an end to my debate about talking to the cops. He strode to the door, then turned to face me. "I don't give a shit which scumbag politician sticks it to some other crook. It's all part of a day's work to me. But if you ever need something not job-related, something or somebody making trouble for you, I'm your guy."

He paused and looked at me for a second, then walked through the door and shut it behind him.

Tears clouded my vision, possibly a reaction to Sarge's generosity or to my growing concern I had facilitated a murder. It was most likely a combination of the two. While I hadn't lied about wanting to do something for the family, I was more concerned about the identity of the teenage girl the neighbors reported seeing. Whether she was Mary's daughter or niece or even a distant cousin, she could be in danger. And I might be the one who had put her there.

Writing insipid copy for Harrison's roll-out campaign ads or getting anything else accomplished was out of the question. So, I emailed Lisa to let her know I'd be working from home, logged out and closed my laptop. Along the way, I grabbed the Saunders file.

By the time I reached my car, I remembered the temp agency Mary worked for. I intended to see if Sarge had found out the name of the business. If he had, it would be part of the material in the folder. If not, I could ask him to—but no. The company included a training session on the art of gentle persuasion: coercing people to spill their guts about sensitive information without realizing they'd said too much. I would visit the place myself.

I was preparing the script in my head of what I might say to the agency supervisor when a call from my father interrupted my flow.

"Hi, Dad. How are—"

"Claire, you need to go over to Jams' as fast as you can."

"Oh, God, Daddy. Is—"

"She's fine. Well, not exactly fine. Jesus Christ, honey, the woman is losing her mind, and I don't have time to deal with her."

"I'm on my way." I veered into the exit lane without signaling and was rewarded with an angry honk from the driver behind me. "But, please, what's going on? Is Jams sick?"

"It's nothing like that. It's about your Mom. She's gone."

11

After Dad's mic drop about Mom, he gave me enough information to keep me from having to pull over and breathe into a paper bag. Before I reached my grandmother's, he told me he got up at his regular time to find a note on the refrigerator door. He read it to me.

I'm following a lead in Jacksonville. Can't say how long I'll be gone but will call when I get there. Don't worry. Love, Janis.

P.S. Your breakfast is on the table.

I almost asked what the hell she meant about following a lead, then remembered the DNA report. Instead, I checked to see about when she left.

He couldn't say for sure, but his egg-white omelet with Canadian bacon and spinach had gotten cold. Like me, he suspected her disappearance had something to do with finding out the identity of her father but didn't understand the Jacksonville part. He got in touch with Jams to see if she had any idea why his wife chose Florida. After a silence long enough for him to become concerned about the older woman, she told him she had no clue why her daughter took off on a crazy-ass, wild goose chase. Then she hung up without saying goodbye and hadn't answered when he called back. That's why he wanted me to check on her.

"I don't like to accuse your grandmother of flat-out lying," Dad said as I reached Jams' street. "But there may be more to the old girl than any of us imagined."

Surprised he was just catching on that there was a whole lot more to his mother-in-law than any of us knew, I pulled into her driveway.

"I'm here now. The garage is open, and the Mustang's in it."

"That's good. You see what's going on with your grandmother. I'll be heading to Jacksonville."

"But Dad, Jacksonville's a big city. You'll never find her."

"Remember when your mom flipped out about that guy who had a heart attack and croaked before anybody figured out his location? Well, she didn't want something like that to happen to us. The woman couldn't get it off her mind. You know how she is. So, I agreed to install tracking apps on our phones. Been over a year ago, and she only used it once when I had my ringer off in Home Depot. I gotta go."

"Okay, but be care—"

He hung up. I shook my head, then walked into the garage and tapped on the door before turning the knob. As usual, it was unlocked. I stepped inside and called out, "Jams, it's me." No one answered. "Jams," I continued calling as I moved through her kitchen with its pale peach walls. A breeze from an open window ruffled through the lace curtains behind the sink.

She wasn't in the small family room or the attached sunroom where the his-and-her rocking chairs sat. Walter's had been sitting empty for years. On the way to her bedroom, I caught movement from the backyard—a Braves cap bobbing up and down as my grandmother yanked at unfortunate weeds cropping up in the wrong garden.

Watching her from the window, I thought of the times I spent tagging along behind her as she worried over knobby yellowish tomatoes and cursed clusters of aphids intent on destroying them before they were table ready. I'd listened when she'd explained the art of when to pick green beans.

"If you get them too early, you'll lose a lot of the little suckers. But too late is worse. That's when they're all tough and stringy." She would frown and shake her head. "Nobody wants to floss their teeth with their dinner."

No matter how many times she said it, I always laughed at the thought of Dad tugging at a ropy bean thread stuck between his molars. Even now it made me smile. But today, the closer I got to Jams, the less I felt like smiling. Because my grandmother wasn't pulling weeds, she was attacking them. And not just physically but verbally.

"That gall-darn son of a biscuit eater," she said loud enough to start the neighbors' dog barking.

She crouched with her behind resting on her heels, ripping out dandelions and thistle. Continuing with language only her Southern Baptist upbringing would classify as vulgar, she added,

"That mother-loving piece of poop. If I get my hands on him, I'll tear off his head and shove it up his—"

"Hey, Jams," I half-shouted to avoid hearing the exact location said head would be shoved. "Need some help?" I wondered who was in danger of decapitation.

She jerked upward and turned toward me, a distant look on her face. For one awful second, I feared she didn't recognize me. But the expression passed, and Jams returned.

"What's my favorite granddaughter doing here in the middle of the day?" I smiled at the joke we'd shared for years, that I was both her favorite and only granddaughter. She wiped her hands on her jean-clad thighs before wrapping her arms around me and pulling me close. A combination of sweet onions and Jams' lavender perfume filled the air.

"Whew, it's getting hot out here. Let's go get some iced tea," she said.

Neither of us commented on her unanswered question. We both knew why I had come.

We sat at the kitchen table with its wooden surface, scarred from my early years of banging with my spoon until my food arrived and indelible marker hearts I drew as a Valentine tribute at age eight or nine. I waited for the familiar sense of comfort to wash over me.

Instead of lifting my spirits, the bright, cheery kitchen presented a stark contrast to my mood. And Jams' face as she filled my glass with the sugary liquid brought me even lower. Although she avoided looking directly at me, I noticed her puffy, red eyes.

When she finished her tea, she asked, "How about a chocolate and pecan chip cookie?" She made it halfway to the fat-cat jar before I responded.

"Thanks, but I'm not hungry. Please, Jams, sit down with me so we can talk."

Her shoulders sagged as she sat, and I reached across the table to clasp her hand. I traced my fingers over the topographical map of veins.

"I guess it's no secret why you're here. And I wish I had more to tell you, but like I told your daddy, I can't think of a single reason your momma would take off for Jacksonville."

Whether it was the slight tremor in the hand I still held or the rapid blinking or the special bond between child and grandparent, for the first time ever, I knew for certain Jams was lying to me. And it frightened me.

I released her and tried to steady myself as I took a sip of tea. This was going to be more difficult than I had imagined.

"I can believe you're confused about where she's headed, but you have to know why. The only reason she would take off like that would be to find her biological father. Please, Jams, Mom might be in trouble."

Now I wasn't being honest. Yes, the idea of my mother alone on the highway concerned me. But my increasing sense of urgency about Mom's obsession with her father's identity had become more powerful.

This secret created a rift between the two most important women in my life. That and Rob's disappearance had thrown my entire world out of orbit. For now, at least, I could do nothing to solve the Rob problem. But I might help to ease the tension between Mom and Jams.

She pressed her lips together as if hoping to contain her secret, then sighed. "I never have been able to tell you no, even though this time it might be better if I did."

She stood and walked to the cabinet where she kept stronger spirits.

"We're going to need more than tea for this conversation," she said as she removed a bottle and set it on the table. Maker's Mark, the good stuff, usually reserved for special occasions or funerals.

I watched as she filled two glasses with ice. Her brown bob— Color Me Happy Cinnamon Pecan—was plastered to her face in front and uncombed in back. Her signature smile lines turned to deep, grim parentheses marks. It occurred to me I might be better off not hearing what she had to say.

"Lots of people think the sixties and seventies were the *Peace, Love, and Rock 'n' Roll* generation," Jams began. "But in South Macon where I grew up, peace was for sissies, love was okay if you were married and didn't enjoy it all that much, and the only rock we rolled was *Rock of Ages* from the Baptist hymnal.

"By the time I was sixteen, I had enough hell, fire, and brimstone to last a lifetime. If you had fun doing something— dancing or kissing boys or sneaking out to the movies—you better look out because the fiery pit awaited you. And if Momma or Daddy caught you, God help you, only He wouldn't because you'd thrown in your lot with Satan. The way things were going, it's a good bet I would have ended up marrying the first boy who asked me and becoming just like my mother."

She swirled her drink before taking a sip.

"Then Nichole Anderson moved to town. Her parents had divorced, forcing Nichole and her mother, Carol, to move in with her parents. Even worse than having to live with her Baptist grandparents, who attended the same church we did, her mom dragged her from the magical land of Los Angeles."

Jams stopped to refill her glass; I covered mine with my hand when she reached to top it off. I needed to stay clear headed. She stood and walked to the refrigerator.

"I better fix us a little something to nibble on. You might be young enough to handle it, but if I keep drinking on an empty stomach, I'll be drunker than Cooter Brown." She took out a bunch of plastic containers. "And I've got homemade bread and butter pickles and potato salad." She began putting together chicken sandwiches and laying out an assortment of leftovers.

While she worked on the meal, I remembered the first time poor old Cooter's name came up. It was Jams who mentioned him right here in this kitchen. I asked her who he was and what had driven him to drink. When she admitted she didn't know, had never even thought about it. I checked it out and found out he'd been a Civil War double draft dodger. He lived on the Mason-Dixon line, which made him vulnerable to service on both sides. He declined to serve either and came up with a plan. Since neither army wanted heavy drinkers in their ranks, he vowed to stay drunk every day until the fighting was over. My research didn't say if he ever sobered up.

Trying to create neutral territory between Mom and Jams gave me newfound empathy for Mr. Brown.

We took a break from her narrative and Mom's disappearance to eat and talk about the weather, who was cheating in her bridge club, and how the neighbors weren't taking care of their pitiful little dog.

"Come over here and look." She stood and motioned for me to follow her to the window. "See. There she is." She pointed to a pitiful looking creature huddled in the corner of a chicken-wire pen. "Not much more than a pup, I bet. They leave her outside all day and into the night. I have half a mind to call the humane society, but I'm afraid they'll take her to the pound. As matted and dirty as she is, I doubt anyone would adopt her." She sighed and we sat back down.

She turned to the subject I hoped to avoid.

"What's up with you and that boyfriend of yours?" Jams rarely used Rob's name and never referred to him as my fiancé.

"We're fine."

She raised an eyebrow. "Hmm. Finer than frog hair, I bet," she said as she began clearing our plates.

I insisted on helping. Once we loaded the dishwasher and put the food away, Jams resumed her story.

"I'll never forget the first time I saw Nichole. Her grandparents sat in the same pew right in front of us, and everybody was belting out the second stanza of 'Amazing Grace' when a gust of air signaled somebody was trying to sneak in. Mostly, tardy sinners slid into the back row, hoping they could make a dash for the door before folks identified them. I kept on singing like I always did, loud and off key enough to keep from getting recruited for the choir."

Jams' eyes clouded and a half-smile played across her lips, as if she had retreated into happy recollections. She cleared her throat, then continued.

"I noticed the preacher had dropped his hymnal and was standing there with his mouth open. The congregation was blasting into saving wretches when voices started dropping out. The music director had his back to the rest of us and kept pounding away on the piano until he realized he was going solo. He and I turned to see what the fuss was about.

"A lady with long wavy curls floated down the aisle in one of those kaftan things with all different shades of blue and gold. I thought she might be the most beautiful real-life woman I'd ever seen. However, as usual, I seemed to be out of tune with the rest of the congregation.

"People started throwing out judgment stones. *Shameful, disgusting, sinful.* I couldn't figure out why everybody was getting their panties in a wad. What if she looked like a peacock? She had everything interesting covered up."

Now, my grandmother's smile was broad and uncomplicated.

"Turned out, she hadn't gotten the congregation all stirred up. It was the girl walking behind her. She wore this itty-bitty plaid miniskirt, a tight red t-shirt, and white boots that went way up to her thighs.

"My momma let out a little yelp and started fanning herself with the program. I swear, that woman passed out at the drop of a hat. Anyway. She pulled herself together and said loud enough for the back-row slackers to hear, *I swanee! That skirt's so short I could see her religion if she had any.*"

Jams explained Nichole and her mother ignored the uproar. They picked up hymnals, thumbed to the right page, and stared at the preacher. He nodded to the choir director and instructed everyone to start from the beginning.

She stopped to take a slug of bourbon. I resisted the urge to ask what any of that had to do with my grandfather. My grandmother hated to be rushed. When she showed no signs of resuming, I felt the need to prod her with a few gentle questions.

"So, how did you and Nichole become friends?"

"That's a funny story," she began. The shrill ring of the landline startled me. Jams jumped up. "I better answer that."

The phone was mounted on the kitchen wall. We finally persuaded her to go cordless, but she had yet to get the hang of being untethered and still walked within the boundaries of her old model. Today, however, as soon as she answered, she made a beeline to the next room.

I recalled the poor woman from down the street who couldn't get her hearing aide to adjust to phone calls, and Jams had to shout to be heard. I assumed she relocated to shield me from the volume. Only she didn't raise her voice at all. After a few minutes of quiet, I went to the den to check on her. She wasn't there.

I stood in the hallway and noticed her closed bedroom door. Her sudden need for privacy was uncharacteristic for a woman who had no problem asking for help checking out a mole on her backside.

Like some character in an old sit-com, I pressed my ear against that door at the same time she yelled, "No."

I kept listening and didn't realize she had terminated the conversation until she started shouting a string of curse words. At first, I thought she had taken up where she left off in the garden, replacing more colorful expletives with genteel swearing. As she moved closer, I realized she'd abandoned any attempt at self-censorship. She let loose with the real deal. And from what I made out, it was impressive.

After listening to my grandmother dish out enough X-rated language to make a hooker blush, I sprang to action at the sound of her footsteps on the hard wood floor in her room. I skidded into the bathroom off the hallway seconds before she came out.

When I joined her in the kitchen, I could tell by the look on her face our interview was over. She gave me an excuse about feeling a migraine coming on—Mom insisted Jams didn't get migraines; she got tired of fooling with you—and made it clear it was time for me to leave. I talked her into promising me we would meet again the next evening.

I sat for a minute in the driveway and checked my messages, hoping to find one from Rob. There were none. Only a text from Anna.

Two men came by looking for you. Badges said FBI but could have been fake. Told them you were out of town. Be careful.

12

Despite the warmth of the sunshine flooding the car, a crop of goosebumps popped up on both of my arms. I answered Anna's text with a confidence I didn't feel. I told her I had nothing to hide from the feds and wasn't worried, which I totally was.

Why in the name of God would the FBI be interested in me? In my line of work, I dealt with some obnoxious people, several of which were into some crooked shit. None of whom were important enough for a federal investigation. Judge Harrison came to mind. His petty corruption was worthy of the government's contempt but not their time.

I had always done my best to remain ignorant about criminal involvement among my clients. The less I knew, the easier it was to make up pretty stories about them. Because of Mary, I had been more involved in that area but had discovered nothing that would be of interest to the feds.

Unless the men who visited Anna had something to do with Rob's disappearance. But I had nothing to offer there either.

By the time I got to the parking deck, I almost convinced myself the whole thing was a mistake. Although I saw no suspicious-looking cars following me, I passed my regular spot and parked another flight up in the area reserved for visitors.

Before I stepped from the car, I gathered my purse and work stuff, then darted to the stairwell. Inside, I held onto the handrail, taking the metal steps two at a time until I reached my floor. Winded, I paused and listened for the sound of footsteps. The silence should have reassured me, but it only served to make me more anxious. I pushed the heavy door open, then eased it shut.

I peered into the hallway, where no men in suits waited for me and dashed from the stairwell with my key in hand. My hands shook so badly I had trouble unlocking the door. After three tries, it worked. I stumbled inside, and immediately re-locked it.

Pausing to catch my breath, I debated turning on the lights or keeping it dark and pretending no one was home. A rustle from behind the sofa made me forget about light altogether.

With my back still against the wall, I waited. Other than the pounding of my heart, the room was quiet. I dropped to my hands and knees and crawled to the door, planning to retrieve my purse and the pepper spray in it. Halfway there, I remembered it wouldn't be there because I stuck the canister in the drawer of my bedside table when I switched to a smaller bag.

I grabbed it anyway and rummaged around in search of something to use as a weapon. All I found was a combo lipstick and blush that might pass for self-defense spray in the darkened room. After a second look, I decided trying to convince my intruder Pink Posy Pick Up had the power to incapacitate was too much of a risk. So, I took out my cell instead, then scrambled backward, dialed 911, and kept my finger over the call button. Pressed against the wall, I slid into a standing position and waited for what seemed like hours but was most likely less than a minute.

This time the rustle morphed into a swish seconds before a silhouette, back lit from behind the gauzy curtains, confirmed my suspicion someone lay in wait for me.

"Stay right where you are and don't move," I shouted, hoping to mask the tremor in my voice with volume. "I have pepper spray, and I will use it."

"You mean the one by your bed? Unless you have two, which would be smart. Sorry, I got bored waiting for you, but I didn't take anything. Snooping's a bad habit of mine. Mom says it will get me in trouble someday. Anyway, the pepper spray's expired. You should try hairspray. She says it's just as good and way cheaper." She paused, then added, "I guess I should say Mom said."

The proverbial light flickered on the second I flipped on the real ones. This girl had to be the one Sarge had mentioned. Despite the information on her contact sheet, Mary Saunders had a daughter, a daughter who was at this very moment emerging from behind my sofa.

She was tall, almost model thin. Unlike Mary's fashionable highlights, her hair was dark brown. It fell across her shoulders like a shawl. I had no clear memory of what color eyes or other distinguishing features the older woman had, making it impossible to confirm my hasty conclusion about her relationship to the girl who was now standing much closer to me.

"Stop right there, or I'll call the police."

"Please, you don't need to do that. Besides, it takes like forever for them to come."

While I wasn't particularly reassured by the thought of what could happen in that nebulous "forever," the youthful female voice of my uninvited guest made me feel less threatened.

"Okay, but who are you and how the hell did you get in my house?"

Instead of answering, she stared at me with the same intensity that Mary had. Her wide-eyed scrutiny transformed her into a younger version of the woman whose association with me might have gotten her killed.

"Sorry about that whole breaking in thing. But you shouldn't hide your key on top of the door frame. It's the first place burglars look. You should keep one under the mat in your car. YouTube has a bunch of good ideas." She stepped back and settled on the sofa, one long leg tucked under her, the other dangling.

"Thanks," I said in a sarcastic tone, which seemed to be lost on her. "But you didn't answer my question. Who are you and why are you here?" I asked, hoping I was wrong, and that she was some random teen who had stumbled into my apartment. Not the girl whose life I'd helped ruin.

"Oh, right. I'm Emily Saunders and I came here because your number is the last call on Mom's phone." She swiped the back of her hand across one eye, smearing black eyeliner along the way, then sat up straighter.

"I'm so sorry about your mother." She looked away. Despite having just met her, I wanted to go to her and put my arm around those frail shoulders. But I sensed how fragile she was and suspected the touch of another person might cause her to break. And although Emily's revelation that she had picked up her mother's phone explained what had happened to it, there was still the disturbing question of how Emily had gotten my address.

I resisted the urge to show too much compassion and made myself respond with a forced coolness. "How did you know where I live?"

"I don't want to cause problems for anyone," she began.

"You're the one in trouble if you've been stalking me."

"That's not true. I'm not a stalker. It's just your receptionist seems like a nice person, and I wouldn't want to get her fired or anything."

"Nobody's going to get fired. Now tell me how you found out where I lived."

She rolled her eyes. "Fine. I have a friend who used to work for a delivery service. Pierce quit when his boss accused him of tossing packages on porches. He swears he would never do anything like that, and I believe him because—"

"Emily, please."

"Okay, okay. He kept his company shirt. I borrowed it, went to your office, and waited for you to leave. I told your secretary I had a super important delivery that you had to have right away, and my boss would kill me if you didn't get it on time. I guess she felt sorry for me because she gave me your home address."

Although annoyed with our receptionist, I didn't blame her for falling for Emily's ruse. During her recitation of the story, she slipped into the perfect rendition of a waif-like creature desperate to keep her job. She was good, so good I would have given her pretty much anything she asked for.

I kept my admiration to myself. Maintaining my righteous indignation, I asked, "How did you know who I was?"

"Your website picture."

"Well, you should have called."

In response, Emily separated a strand of hair and stared at it as she twirled it around her finger. Instead of a dangerous intruder, she became little girl lost, and I was a total ass. Interrogating her. Treating her like a criminal.

"Let's forget about that for the moment. We should talk about how we can help each other. But first I'm starving. How about you?" I wasn't the least bit hungry after stuffing myself with Jams' leftovers, but I doubted Emily had eaten much since her mother's death.

She shrugged and followed me to the kitchen where I fixed grilled cheese sandwiches and tomato soup with milk, never water—my go-to meal when life sucked. She scarfed down the first of the gooey concoctions and most of the soup while I asked questions.

I discovered she knew her mother worked regularly for a temp agency while completing her paralegal certification, but she didn't know which one.

"Mom was always on some assignment or studying, so we hadn't been spending much time together. She promised we'd catch up this weekend." She dipped the remaining corner of her sandwich into her soup and watched as the thick red liquid saturated it.

I needed her to tell me if her mother had mentioned our meeting. More important was whether she had any idea who stopped Mary from coming to the tavern. However, I sensed that, like Jams, the girl couldn't be rushed.

Emily used her spoon to push the soggy bread around on her plate. She leaned into the task of obliterating the last of her sandwich. Her hair curtained her face, transforming her into a forlorn little girl instead of a self-possessed teenager. Maybe she was both.

Regardless, she didn't belong in the kitchen of a stranger. She needed to be with a loving family.

"I'm so sorry about what happened to your mother. Were the police able to get in touch with any relatives? An aunt or grandmother?"

When she shook her head and smoothed her hair away from her face, she morphed back into the confident ice princess who sauntered from behind my sofa to lecture me about my poor key-hiding skills.

"It was just me and Mom." Her tone landed somewhere between defiance and defeat.

"What about your dad?"

"Just me and Mom," she repeated, definitely defiant.

"Got it." Her empty glass gave me an excuse to step away from the table.

I took my time rearranging bottles and cartons in the refrigerator, trying to determine how to ease information from the vulnerable young girl without seeming like a heartless hag. I came up with nothing. Then it hit me that there was no way the police would have let Emily wander off by herself. They would have stuck her in emergency foster care.

I refilled her glass with soda and went to the cupboard where I stored my Double Stuff Oreos.

"So," I began, after removing a cookie from its cellophane wrapper. "Are you a scraper or a stuffer?" She gave me a blank stare, and I explained. "Do you go for the icing first or do you cram the whole thing in?"

"When I was little, I only ate the icing. Mom would finish the cookie part. We'd laugh and..." I never found out what the giggling duo would do after cracking each other up over Oreos because Emily jumped to her feet and darted from the room, leaving the sound of gut-wrenching sobs in her wake.

I stood, prepared to run after her, to offer whatever comfort I could. Halfway to the doorway, I stopped. Both as a teenager and an adult, whenever I dissolved into a serious crying jag, I hated having an audience. But I wasn't an adolescent girl who might decide to take off into the night, leaving us both without information to help catch a killer, so I followed her.

I experienced a jolt of panic when I saw the den was empty. The sight of Emily's backpack on the floor beside the sofa eased my fears, and I sat in my floral recliner, trying to strike a nonchalant pose while I waited for her to reappear. If I moved the chair in an upright position, I became a mean-spirited inquisitor. If I leaned back too far, I came across as too nonchalant, as if I didn't give a damn. I maneuvered myself into an uncomfortable spot somewhere in the middle.

"Jeez, Claire," I whispered. "You're not setting up a focus group."

"Did you say something?" Emily's appearance interrupted my personal diatribe. Without her makeup, I could see a sprinkle of tiny pimples on her chin. The blemishes made her look even more vulnerable.

"Sorry. I was talking to myself. That's what happens when you live alone." I started to add I didn't live alone, not technically, since I spent most of my time at my boyfriend's place. That wouldn't be accurate either as he no longer resided there. But losing a mother trumped boyfriend trouble, so I let my half-lie stand and asked if she was okay. Stupid question. She might never be okay again, at least not for a very long time.

Instead of acknowledging my absurd inquiry, she ignored it and dropped onto the sofa, a wilted version of her earlier self.

I learned from my company training that silence can be an effective tool for drawing out information from reluctant focus groups. But the quiet that lay between Emily and me was not an effort on my part to weaponize silence. It was more of an exhausted truce. What possible question could I ask that wouldn't propel her back into a darkness she might not return from?

Then I remembered the phone. Although I had no direct expertise in being a single mother, Mary Saunders didn't strike me as the kind of parent who would forget something as important as that when her daughter was alone at home. Also, her note made it seem as if she was desperate to meet with me. I couldn't image she wouldn't have made certain she had a way to communicate with me in case there was an emergency. Like getting shot.

If I was right, Mary had her phone with her when she was killed, and it had been gone when the police found her body, which meant the person who'd discovered her was draped across my sofa.

13

The idea of pressing her on the issue, of asking her if she discovered her mother lying in the alleyway, brought about a dizzying nausea, and I feared I would be the one rushing from the room. But if her daughter found her, had she seen the killer? And wouldn't that be dangerous for her? And my self-centered desire to survive highlighted another troubling aspect. If the murder was connected to the information Mary had planned to share, that meant I was also in danger.

"Emily, I have to ask you something, and it's important, very important. And I need you to tell me everything, please."

She elbowed herself into a sitting position, grabbed a throw pillow, and hugged it to her chest. "Most people don't mean it when they say that. They believe they want the whole truth and nothing but the truth. But that's crap. Because when they get it, they wish they hadn't."

"I understand what you're saying, but lots of the time there's no choice. We have to face reality—no matter how ugly or scary."

She tossed the pillow aside, squared her shoulders, and focused her Mary-stare on me. Then she shrugged and said, "So ask."

"It's about your mother's cell phone." I paused, unsure of the best way to proceed.

"Mom's phone?"

I don't know if my question surprised her or if she was stalling.

"Yes. The police think the person who, uh, who hurt your mother took it. But you've got it, don't you?"

"So what? It's not like I stole it."

"Of course, not. Where did you find it?" I coaxed.

Instead of responding, she began peeling black polish off her thumbnail.

"Was it on the ground beside her?"

She scraped so furiously at the nail I worried she might draw blood.

"I'm so sorry, Emily. I can't imagine how awful seeing your mom like that was. You were smart to call 911 right away. Most people would panic."

"As soon as I saw her, I knew. Even before I got close." Her words became clipped, automated. "She was so still and quiet, but when I turned her over, her eyes were open, and her skin was warm. I felt so relieved and kept telling her everything would be okay. Like the time I fell off my bike and broke my arm. Only now I was the mom." She twisted her lips into a half smile before giving up the effort.

Her voice cracked, and I wanted nothing more than to perpetuate the same lie she'd whispered over her mother's body. *Everything will be okay.* But we would both know it wasn't true.

"I am so sorry, and I wish I didn't have to keep going on with this, but I have another question."

She wiped her eyes with the back of her hand and nodded.

"What made you follow your mom to the alley?"

I hadn't doubted the veracity of the girl in front of me. Not that I had any special intuition about her inherent honesty. But her composure had begun to crack along with her voice. The ferocity of her attack on her poor cuticles, the instability of her tone—tormented one moment, automaton-like the next—her lack of focus. She had been too raw to dissemble, too destroyed to pretend. Until now.

She shifted her eyes slightly to her right. I recalled my discussion with Anna, trying to remember which direction people looked when they were about to lie. Then I remembered that theory had been debunked. Since Emily was staring at a spot directly over my head, it didn't make much difference. Once again, I hoped the silence would work in my favor. I concentrated on the sound of the refrigerator humming in the background, intent on not speaking first.

I was close to breaking when she continued, "We had a fight. I wanted to go to Pierce's house. She wouldn't let me. Said I had to stay home and fold my clothes, straighten my room, do my homework. I tried to explain how I had plenty of time to get everything done, but she walked out and slammed the door behind her. If I ever did that, I'd be in big trouble. Anyway, I kept getting madder and madder. So, I ran after her." A high-pitched hiccup startled both of us. "Sorry." Another, then another one, erupted.

Fearful she might lose her train of thought and retreat into what appeared to be a state of shock, I rushed to the kitchen to get her a glass of water. She took a few gulps, then held her breath.

"That's better, thanks." She paused, either testing to see if the cure had worked or trying to decide whether to tell me the rest of her story.

"You followed her?"

"She hated going through that dark alley. But somebody had parked in her spot, and there was a full moon. Mom loved full moons."

"That's right. It was beautiful." I remembered the silver sheen it cast when I returned home from my aborted meeting with Mary.

"I saw her go round the corner after I came outside. She was talking on the phone, I thought. But there was another voice. A man's. He spoke too low for me to get what he said, but he didn't sound mad or excited even. He spoke like my trig teacher talks when he's going over one of his boring problems, like a robot. I shut off the light and stepped through the door. That was when things got weird." She drank more water, then tapped ice cubes and watched them bob.

"What do you mean, weird?"

"Oh." My question seemed to startle her, as if for a moment she was no longer sitting in my kitchen but standing on her porch, trying to make sense of her mother's last moments. "Mom got louder and sounded real strange. I took off running, missed the first step, and went down hard. That's when she screamed. Funny, because I thought she was screaming because she saw me fall. But that wasn't it at all."

I pictured the scene in my mind. Emily rounding the corner into the alley, her mother lying there bleeding. Had the killer still been there? Leaning over the body, making sure he'd finished the job? If so, she might have gotten a good look at him. Did that mean he saw her?

Before I got the chance to press her for more, the doorbell sounded, jolting us both into upright positions. The girl jumped to her feet and rushed toward her backpack. I hurried after her and took a gentle hold on her arm.

"Please, don't leave. No one knows you're here, right? Go to my room. If you get scared, there's a panel in the back of the closet. Slide it to the left. You'll have plenty of space." I had no time to reflect on my landlord's account of the survivalist nut who lived here before me and how his paranoia had come in handy.

Overcome by an irrational sense of panic—the person at my door couldn't be Mary's killer—I stopped halfway to my bedroom and the pepper spray tucked in my bedside table. It could be Rob. Maybe he misplaced the key to my apartment, except he never lost anything. Or it could be Mom, back from her trip down ancestry lane or Dad with news about her or even Jams ready to finish her story from earlier. Still, it wouldn't hurt to take a little precaution. I grabbed a bottle of disinfectant from the kitchen and tiptoed to the foyer. Careful to be as quiet as possible, so I might have the option of pretending I wasn't home, I leaned forward and pressed my eye to the peephole.

I blinked, looked again, then took a half step back. It was my trust-fall partner, Kevin Thomas.

14

At the sight of Kevin, a warm sensation filled my chest, immediately followed by a queasy flutter of guilt in my stomach. My fiancé and all his furniture were missing. My mother's daddy complex had her off chasing down leads like a detective from a black and white movie, and my grandmother emerged as a first-rate liar. I had a grieving teenage girl tucked away in my bedroom. And my initial reaction was a totally inappropriate tingle of pleasure.

Before I had time to dwell on the shallowness of my nature, the bell rang again, startling me into emitting a yelp loud enough to end any pretense of my not being home.

"Claire, it's Kevin, Kevin Thomas. I apologize for the late hour, but I need to talk to you. Please let me in."

The sound of his voice made me feel safe, as if opening the door and inviting him inside was the logical thing to do. I imagined multiple victims of charming serial killers felt the same way seconds before they disappeared forever.

But surely Kevin was no crazed murderer, and—armed with disinfectant that promised to kill ninety-nine percent of all bacteria—I was no hapless maiden.

I turned the key in the lock and opened the door but didn't motion for him to enter.

"Thanks." Rather than attempting to push past me, he remained on his side of the threshold. "Is it okay if I come in?"

When I stepped aside, he brushed by, close enough for me to breathe him in, a blend of pine and spice.

"I really appreciate you seeing me. I promise not to take up too much of your time."

We settled in the living room. I sat on the sofa; he took the chair across from me, his posture as stiff as his tone. Despite the late hour, the navy-striped shirt beneath his dark gray suit jacket looked freshly pressed, the crease in his trousers sharp and precise. If not for his wavy hair and deep-blue eyes, I'm not sure I would have recognized him as the man who rescued me from humiliation before tricking me into a fake trust-fall.

Reverting to my training, I mirrored his demeanor—uncrossing my legs, planting my feet firmly on the floor, and squaring my shoulders—refusing to be intimidated in my own home.

"What's so important it wouldn't wait until tomorrow?"

"I have to ask you some questions about the person you know as Rob Evans."

"The man I *know* as Rob Evans?"

"Sorry. I'm getting ahead of myself. Before we get into that, I need to make a confession."

"Get into what? What could we possibly get into about Rob?"

"Please, let me explain."

"Go on then. Tell me the whole story."

"When we met at the workshop, I didn't sign up to come with my girlfriend. Actually, there is no girlfriend either."

"No Judy?"

I bit my lip to remind myself I sat across from a man who had lied to me, one I had no reason to believe wasn't still lying. Unlike me, he understood the registration process for Dr. Sheila's big event. So, why make up a partner? There had to be easier ways to get a date. And who goes to a couples' seminar to pick up girls?

"I'm making a mess of this, aren't I?"

Although I suspected the question was rhetorical, I was sick of letting him control the dialogue. "How am I supposed to tell if you're making a mess when I don't know what the hell *this* is? You come into my house in the middle of the night telling me we met under false pretenses, asking about my fiancé when it's none of your business."

"Right. I've screwed this up from the start. But please. Hear me out before you throw me out, okay?"

I shrugged my consent.

"I didn't just mislead you about the girlfriend thing. I also wasn't forthcoming when I told you what I did for a living."

His line of work held little interest for me. It was those details about his past—his absentee father and distant mother, his fear of abandonment—that I cared about. But I didn't want to go there. Instead, I asked, "So you don't own a security business?"

"Not exactly, at least not in the physical sense. I help companies where there's been a breach in the system."

"You mean like hackers?"

"Sometimes, but our main area is with internal issues. Uncovering fraud, finding who might have leaked information to a competitor, those kinds of problems."

The muscles between my shoulder blades tensed. "I don't understand what any of that has to do with me."

"It doesn't. Not directly anyway. A few months ago, a private agency hired me to check out one of their employees concerning a data breach that occurred around the same time he left the company. In the process of our investigation, we discovered we weren't the only ones looking into him. What can you tell me about who Rob works for?"

"Rob? Are you saying he's involved with industrial espionage? Not only is that ridiculous, but it's impossible. He's been with Haderman and Associates for years as one of their top forensic accountants." I didn't mention my own unsuccessful attempt to contact his office.

Instead of answering, he shifted focus. "When did you last see him?"

Once again, he caught me off guard. But now I was pissed. "Why should I tell you anything? I haven't a clue about how you really ended up at Dr. Sheila's workshop the same time as me. You could be some kind of sick stalker. And what did you mean when you said *the man I know?*"

"I promise I'm not a stalker." He leaned toward me and I scooted farther back on the sofa. "I'll prove it. Ask me anything."

"Obviously, it wasn't a coincidence that we were at the same workshop. How did you find out Rob wouldn't be with me?"

He bit his lip before responding. "I didn't. Both of your names were on the registration form."

An irrational sense of disappointment overcame me. The flirting, the electricity, the way he connected to my desire to be a writer—all pretend. It was all an attempt to get to Rob. I swallowed my hurt feelings.

"And what would you have done if he had come? Picked us both up?"

"I wouldn't put it that way. More like I would have tried to establish a rapport with you."

His cell rang, leaving me with unanswered questions about Rob's identity. He stepped into the foyer to answer, leaving me alone with the depressing realization Kevin had played me—could still be playing me. But why?

I stood and moved closer to the hallway, hoping I might catch some of his conversation, but he must have been whispering into the phone. Frustrated with my failed attempt at eavesdropping, I decided to be more assertive with my line of questioning.

"I didn't mean to keep you waiting."

I jumped at the sound of his voice.

"Sorry, but I have to leave. I promise I'll be back and answer your questions. Maybe then you'll be able to answer mine."

I wanted to tell him he could take his questions and shove them up his ass, but he was gone before I got the chance. I locked the door and leaned against it for a moment before I remembered Emily.

I stopped at my bedroom and listened for sounds of life. If there was a prescribed etiquette for harboring a fugitive teenage girl who witnessed her mother's murder, I was unaware of it. Rather than barge in, I tapped on the door. When there was no response, I knocked louder and called her name. Still nothing.

Fearful my break-in expert was also an escape artist, I bolted into the darkened room where I found Emily curled up around her backpack in the middle of the bed. Resisting the urge to brush a thick strand of her dark hair from her face, I draped one of Mom's quilts over her and turned off the lights.

On the way to the guestroom, I noticed the curtain from which my guest had made her dramatic entrance was crooked. When I stopped to straighten it, it occurred to me I might catch a glimpse of Kevin's car. Not that identifying it would make a difference. But at least I would be doing something instead of waiting for something to happen to me.

There was no sign of my late-night visitor. I leaned my head against the glass and stared at Emily's now-waning moon.

I was midway into closing the curtains when a car rolled into view, hugging the curb. If it was Kevin, he'd either parked down the block or in the back of the complex. The darkened windows made it impossible to see the driver of the sleek white sedan as it glided away.

15

A little after six, I woke from a night of fitful sleep, wondering where the hell I was. Sunk deep into the too-soft bed, trapped under the too-heavy covers, I remembered I was a guest in my own home with Sleeping Beauty—or would it be Goldilocks?—encamped in my room. At least, I hoped she was still there.

This time Emily wasn't curled up on my perfect mattress nor was her backpack on the comforter. My heart raced at the idea she might have slipped away and slowed when I heard water running in the bathroom.

Surprised at the intensity of my reaction, it was more than being worried about not getting answers to questions connecting me to Mary's death. I feared the girl was in real and immediate danger.

After seeing the familiar white car outside my building, I suspected being with me might not be the best way to keep Emily safe. If the vehicle I saw last night belonged to Kevin, had he been parked beside me in the garage of Rob's apartment complex? Did that mean my workshop mystery man was connected to my boyfriend's disappearance or Mary's murder? Or both?

I knocked back a slug of strong black coffee, badly burning my tongue and reminding me I hated strong black coffee. The scorching pain snapped me out of my spiraling conspiracy theory.

Addressing my toaster-reflected image, I spoke firmly. "Settle down, girl. You can't be sure whether it's the same car. And even if it is, that doesn't mean it belongs to Kevin."

Shit! I mentally interrupted my lecture. It could belong to anybody.

"Talk to yourself much?"

"Jesus!" I shouted, sloshing hot coffee on my thumb and forefinger. "Sneak up on people much?" I turned on the tap and let cool water run onto my scorched digits.

Emily, wearing my fancy silk kimono with her hair wrapped in a towel, opened the refrigerator, and stood there staring into the bright, cold light.

I bit back my mother's warning refrain—*Shut the door! You're wasting electricity*—and watched as she took out a carton of orange juice and studied the label.

"With pulp," she sighed and returned the offending box to its place.

"How about coffee?" I asked, wondering how long it would take for the interior light to burn out.

She wrinkled her nose. "I don't drink that stuff."

I swallowed another one of Mom's oldies but goodies—*Beggars can't be choosers*—and began reciting a list of options fit for a no-pulp, non-coffee-drinking adolescent: milk, water, diet soda. At hot chocolate, Emily stepped away from the fridge and, finally, thank God, shut the door.

"Yes, please," she responded and sat at the table, looking and sounding less a haughty teen princess and more the lost child she was.

I opened a cabinet and plucked an envelope of cocoa from the box. To avoid an *I don't drink the instant kind* moment, I kept my back to her as I dumped the mix into a mug, tossed the empty packet into the trash, added hot milk, and placed the finished product on the table. While I watched her take a careful sip of the steaming liquid, an unwelcome sensation came over me. I recognized it: it was the weight of responsibility. Somehow, it had fallen to me to keep Emily from danger.

The coffee kicked in, offering me greater clarity on my earlier position that the girl wouldn't be safe at my place and not just because Kevin might show up again. I refused to accept Rob had abandoned me. That meant there was the possibility he, too, would pop in unannounced and at risk himself. I considered and dismissed the idea of taking her to work with me when Janis Joplin began belting out her demand to take another piece of her heart.

Emily snapped her head toward the counter, where my cell vibrated to the beat of the song.

"My grandmother," I explained as I picked up. "Hey, Jams."

"Morning, Sunshine. I've got some good news. Your dad found your momma at the Holiday Inn Express in Jacksonville. They've decided to spend a little quality time together and won't be home for a few days."

I winced at her announcement—not because I wasn't happy Mom was safe and sound with my father. Because I'd forgotten she was missing, which made me a crap daughter.

"Did she find *him*?"

"No, honey, she didn't. But if I know your momma, and the good Lord help me I do, she'll never give up."

"How about you? Are you okay? You seemed awful upset after that phone call."

"That? That was nothing. Just this jackass I've been haggling with about fixing the light switch in the garage. Honest to God, that man could throw himself on the ground and miss. I told him to forget about it, that I'd find somebody else."

"I can see why that would be so upsetting. Having someone that stupid rewiring your electricity."

After a brief pause, she said, "Exactly. I'm sorry for subjecting you to all that rough talk, but something about that man stuck in my throat like a hair in a biscuit."

It seemed the farther from the truth she got, the closer she was getting to her down-home roots. Since she had no intention of being honest with me, I might as well change the subject before she started blessing my heart.

Emily slurped the last drop of her cocoa, and I turned toward the girl with her chocolate mustache, realizing I had the perfect solution for both a topic shift and a safe place.

Emily's lack of enthusiasm about spending a few days with my grandmother hadn't surprised me. When I assured her she had reliable internet and a TV in the guestroom, she agreed to give it a try. Despite her professed annoyance, I suspected she was secretly relieved at the offer of a reprieve from the independence her mother's death had forced on her.

Push-back from Jams, however, was unexpected. I was vague about my connection to Emily and the nature of her distress. I told her a family emergency had left the girl without a place to stay until the authorities located her relative, thinking the less my grandmother knew, the less she would worry. Known for being the first one to provide sanctuary for the bruised, battered, or broken, she responded to my request with excuses and evasions. She had errands to run, might be coming down with a cold, desperately needed a haircut. Only after I revealed the girl's mother had died did she acquiesce.

"Why in God's green acres didn't you say so in the first place?" she demanded.

"Emily's a very private person," I said.

She answered with her own brand of genteel skepticism. "That's horseshit."

By the time we reached my grandmother's home, it was after eight. High-pitched yaps from the neighbor's backyard announced our presence. Jams opened the door before I rang the bell and threw her arms around me. The heavy aroma of cinnamon drifted from the kitchen.

Turning to Emily, she said, "Aren't you pretty as a peach?" Then she pulled her in for a hug, visibly startling the girl. "That thing looks like it weighs more than you do." She pointed to the backpack that had slipped from Emily's shoulders during Jams' enthusiastic greeting. "Claire will carry that for you."

As she ushered Emily down the hallway, I trailed behind, dragging the bag. Jams stopped at the door to the guest room. "Why don't you get situated, then come on into the kitchen. We can all sit down and have a hot cinnamon bun."

I expected a brief lecture on the negative effects of sugar, but the heady scent of Jams' creation must have worked its spell on the girl.

"Thank you," she said.

I shoved the backpack with my foot until it was over the threshold. Emily picked it up and hugged it to her chest before placing it in the chair next to the quilt-covered bed.

Seated at the table with coffee and bun, I thanked Jams for helping with our guest.

She kept her eye on the door and whispered to me. "That poor child is as lost as last year's Easter egg. And she has the aura of a much older person, someone who's given up."

Before I replied, Emily slipped into the room. With her hair slicked back in a ponytail, her eyes were more prominent. Unlike my grandmother, I didn't profess to reading auras; all I saw was a fifteen-year-old girl dealing with pain that knew no depth.

Jams scooted a chair out, scooped a roll from the pan, and plopped it on the plate in front of her. "How about some milk?"

I winced and waited.

"That would be great."

I resisted the urge to remind her she didn't like milk.

We ate the rolls in silence. Emily licked icing from her fingertips, and Jams grinned her approval. I drained the rest of my coffee and took my plate to the sink.

"I wish I could hang out, but I'm getting slammed at work. I'll check in after lunch." I kissed my grandmother on the head, patted the girl on the back, and grabbed another bun.

"Let me walk you out." I stiffened. The only people she walked out were guests or family members who needed private reprimands.

"I'm good. You two should relax and get acquainted with each other."

But she hopped up to accompany me to the door and said, "Honey, you ought to know by now I can always tell when you're bullshitting me. So, don't try to zip in and out when you pick her up. I want to hear the whole story."

"All right. But that's a two-way street, isn't it?" I scurried down the steps and got into my car without looking back.

16

"Lisa's in your office with some lady," the receptionist said.

My stomach dropped from immediate unease and possibly the second cinnamon bun. Lisa had worked for me long enough to understand how much I valued privacy, partly because of sensitive information, partly because she knew I hated anyone touching my stuff. She insisted visitors remain in her area until I cleared them for entry. If today's guest bullied her way in without me, something was wrong.

"Ms. Kincaid," she said when I entered. Her serious expression and formality dealt another blow to my sinking stomach. "This is Regina Atkins. She's with the Atlanta Police Department." She made no attempt to leave.

Instead of immediately acknowledging the introduction, I stepped to the corner of the room and hung my jacket on the rack, willing myself to calm down and steady up.

The woman rose and came toward me, hand extended. I offered mine and gripped hers tightly, hoping she wouldn't notice the shaking.

"It's Detective Atkins," she corrected, then turned to Lisa.

"Thank you for keeping me company while I waited, but I'd like to speak with Ms. Kincaid alone."

I could hear my mother's voice reminding the woman to say please.

Lisa glanced at me, and I gave her a quick nod.

"I'll be at my desk. Only a few steps away. Buzz me if you need anything, anything at all."

We didn't have a buzzer system, but I liked the way she made her point.

"Close the door," the detective said, then added, "please."

Jesus, was this woman reading my mind?

Only Atkins wasn't issuing a polite request. She was issuing a command.

My assistant hesitated and gave me another look. I smiled and spoke with an assurance I didn't feel. "Thanks, Lisa. I'm sure we won't be long."

On my way to the power seat behind my desk, I checked out this woman who had upended my day, possibly my life. She wore a camel-colored cashmere jacket and nicely tailored navy pants—more like real estate agent or insurance salesperson than a tough-ass cop. Her only makeup was a little mascara that accentuated her dark brown eyes and a hint of blush on her high cheeks. Even the severity of her hairstyle, a sleek black bun that rested low on her neck, and the presence of a few lines on her forehead did nothing to detract from her beauty.

But no way would I let her pleasant appearance fool me. As Mom said, *Pretty is as pretty does.*

I eased into my chair and sat as tall as possible. "I admit I don't get too many police detectives in my office." I smiled; she didn't. "So, how can I be of help?"

"It's come to our attention that you're in a relationship with Robert Evans."

I wanted her to explain how my love life related to her detective work. To demand she tell me who gave her that information. But it was useless to antagonize her, so I gritted my teeth and spoke softly.

"You want to know about my relationship with Rob?"

"Yes."

"Exactly how is this police business?" Louder and more forceful. But my earlier eagerness to placate this woman had died down, leaving righteous irritation in its place.

"Robert Evans's name came up in an ongoing investigation."

"What kind of investigation?"

"I'm not at liberty to discuss it."

I wanted to say I wasn't at liberty to fill her in on personal details—a semi-adult version of *I'm rubber, you're glue*. But something told me Detective Atkins wasn't the kind of person who played games. The best way to get rid of her would be to give her enough information to make me sound honest and innocent, which I was.

"Rob is my fiancé," I said, not sure if that was still true.

She took a small spiral notebook from her jacket pocket and began scribbling as she spoke. "Right. Can you tell me the last time you saw him?"

"He left town on a business trip Monday."

"Where did his *business* take him?" Her nostril curled as if she detected an unpleasant odor.

Wishing I'd been a better listener—a better girlfriend—I had to admit I didn't know. "He travels so much; I have trouble remembering details."

"But you would remember when he returned, correct?" She kept her eyes on the notepad and continued scribbling in it.

"Of course, I would. Except he hasn't. Gotten home, that is." If not for her snarky implication that Rob's return could have slipped my mind, I might have come clean about finding his empty apartment.

Atkins stopped writing and fixed her dark eyes on mine. "Are you saying you haven't seen him since last Monday?"

"Well, Sunday night, to be precise." The intensity of her stare was unsettling, as if she'd caught me in a carefully constructed trap. "He doesn't like to sleep over before a business trip."

"I'm sorry, Miss Kincaid, but I'm a little confused. We have information that suggests you and Robert Evans signed up for a couple's workshop on the Monday you say he was out of town."

"Oh, that." I sighed, releasing the tension that had been building in my shoulders. "That was just a big mix-up. When I registered for Dr. Sheila's conference, I didn't realize I was signing up for two."

"What was confusing about the *couples* part?"

Her tone had gone from slightly snarky to borderline nasty, and it pissed me off. "I don't understand how that's relevant."

"It's relevant because, according to the attendance record, both you and Rob were at the workshop. You even led some of the exercises. Dr. Nolan said she was impressed with, let me see." She flipped through the pages. "Here it is: 'The two of them had an impressive commitment to the trust fall.' Whatever that is. Do you still maintain Evans was out of town on that day?"

"Well, that's kind of a funny story," I began, doubting the woman in front of me would be in the least bit amused by my account of Kevin's appearance and our subsequent deception. Worse, she most likely wouldn't believe Kevin Thomas even existed.

Worst of all, I was beginning to question his existence myself.

17

At ten minutes until twelve, Lisa announced Judge Harrison was waiting in the conference room with his two bodyguards, who attached themselves to their boss like blood-fattened ticks. I had just returned from my fourth trip to the restroom where I'd thrown up what had to be the last of Jams' rolls. I told myself that intense, uncontrollable vomiting wasn't an unreasonable reaction to dealing with a police detective intent on connecting me to unnamed crimes involving my fiancé. Or was it crimes my alleged fiancé had *committed*?

Either way, I'd been too sick to concentrate on the upcoming meeting with Harrison. Thankfully, Lisa had stepped in. She compiled the information we had, secured Sarge's appearance, and brought a cold cloth for me to hold against the back of my neck.

Standing at the door, she said, "Before I forget, Sarge is tracking developments in the Saunders's case. Nothing yet, though. You still don't look any better. We can stall him if you need more time."

I unwrapped a peppermint from the candy jar on my desk and popped it into my mouth. "I'm way better now. I hate to ask you this, but there might be a little throw-up on my clothes. Could you double check, please?"

She circled me. "You look clean although you wouldn't be the first person to have vomit on you during a meeting with the judge."

Still unsteady, I held onto the edge of the desk. "I will take you up on that offer to stall a few minutes."

She snapped to attention and said, "Those who are about to die salute you."

I smiled as Lisa raised a fist and tapped it to her chest, but the thought of Atkins's grim face destroyed the moment. My prediction she wouldn't be amused at how Kevin rescued me from certain humiliation had been dead on. Without commenting, she closed her notebook and gathered her things. On her way out, she took one of her cards from her pocket and scrawled her home number on the back so that I could call the minute Rob got in touch with me. And although she didn't say it, the gravity of her tone and expression indicated dire consequences if I failed to do so.

Midway to the conference room, I could hear the judge shouting. Flanked by his bodyguards, the solid oak door muffled much of his rant, but words like *incompetent morons*, *brainless twits*, and *sue you assholes* broke through and exploded in the air.

I paused on my way in. I could almost smell the acrid odor of his fury. His vitriol wasn't surprising. In the past, I often required a pre-meeting Xanax to help calm my terror in the face of his rages. Atkins's appearance had not only made me forget to take a pill; it had left me so unnerved that the judge's raving was anticlimactic, no more impressive than a tantrum thrown by a two-year-old. After all, what was dealing with a nasty client compared to answering questions from a detective intent on harming the man I loved?

But did I even know Rob? Had I been too eager to find the right person and settle down the way Mom wanted? I convinced myself his frequent absences meant he was ambitious and hard-working. I cast him as the strong, silent type and imagined myself as the only woman who could reach him. He was Sleeping Beauty, and I was the one who would wake him from his emotional slumber. As Jams would say, I'd fallen for a load of horseshit.

I brushed by the thick-necked bodyguards who ignored me and went into the room where Harrison was haranguing my colleagues. Red-faced and trembling, Lisa leaned against the desk with Sarge towering behind her. As usual, he maintained a neutral facade.

"It's about goddamned time you got here," Harrison bellowed. "Another minute and I would have been on the phone with Barry."

Barry Gregory was the judge's high-powered attorney. I would have pitied him if he hadn't been an entitled jackass who was almost as obnoxious as his client.

"With what I pay you and your pack of thieving scum, I shouldn't have to put up with a second-rate Nancy Drew and that has-been GI Joe."

Lisa grimaced. Sarge's right eye twitched.

"Those two are as useless as tits on a nun. If you don't start moving your asses and show me how I'm going to crush that miserable sumbitch, I'm going to..."

He continued his diatribe, but I tuned him out and watched as he gestured wildly toward Lisa and shook his fist at Sarge before focusing on me. Normally, I would have retreated behind my desk and waited until he ran out of hateful insults and profane attacks. Then I would apologize for whatever perceived slight he had endured and gently maneuver him to the purpose of our meeting. But today, I was over coddling this rodent-like tyrant who was currently jabbing his finger at my face. I felt as if I were playing whack-a-mole, and I wanted to use a very heavy mallet.

So instead of backing away, I stepped into his negative force-field.

"Judge Harrison, you need to stop," I said.

Although he was close enough for me to see the occasional spray of saliva when he let loose a stream of profanity, he was so caught up in his own performance he seemed to have forgotten I was there. Whether from shock at unwanted audience participation or surprise that someone had interrupted his flow, he stopped.

"I can assure you there is nothing second rate about anyone on my team. Now take a seat, and we'll get started." He stared at me open-mouthed as I chose a chair at the conference table and motioned for Lisa and Sarge to follow suit.

The judge continued to stand, his scarlet face darkening into a frightening shade of purple. I wondered if he might be having a stroke and what I might or might not do if he was. When he resumed shouting, I experienced a twinge of disappointment.

"Who the fuck do you think you're talking to, you little bitch?" he hissed.

Sarge pushed back his chair. I shook my head at him and slammed my hands down on the table, visibly startling everyone including myself.

"Perhaps I wasn't clear." I enunciated each syllable. "I said take a seat. If you do not sit down and shut up, this meeting is over. And if you call me a bitch again, I will have you and your two thugs removed from the premises."

"Are you aware of how much money your firm makes off me? If I pull the plug on this relationship—"

"If you decide to cancel our contract, the information we collected no longer belongs to you. Termination of said contract would free us from any future confidentiality agreement. And I'm sure you know that means we would have the right to share our findings with whomever we choose."

I watched the judge fade from purple to pink, then shuffle to the table and sink into his chair.

"This better be good."

I ignored his remark and nodded to Sarge. "I think we're all set now."

"Nope," he said.

Lisa and I exchanged glances. Harrison's mouth dropped open.

"You do have the files, don't you?" I coaxed.

"Oh, I've got them all right—complete with photos, emails, and documents. But I'm not saying a word until this sleazy bastard apologizes for calling you a bitch."

Back in my office after Harrison had gone, I took out the bottle of bourbon Dad had given me to celebrate my promotion and filled plastic glasses from the break room.

"Woodford Reserve," Sarge said. "The woman's bringing out the good stuff."

"Nothing's too fine for my team." I raised my drink. "To Judge Harrison and his ever-loving sweet temper. Bless his tiny little heart."

He and Lisa laughed and tapped cups.

"I wish I had a picture of that blowhard trying to choke out the words *I'm sorry*." She smiled.

"I wish I'd choked the motherfu, uh, I mean the asshole." Sarge finished his drink in two gulps and refilled it.

"And his face when you started spouting all that legalese: priceless. Honestly, I can't believe he bought that bullshit," Lisa said. "Where'd you come up with it anyway?"

"Mostly from *Law & Order* reruns, which means it's one-hundred percent accurate." I topped off my drink, then added, "I don't know whether he bought it, but he definitely calmed down after I mentioned the possibility of sharing his info."

I thumbed through the papers on my desk, wondering what I was missing. According to Sarge's report, it was only good news for Harrison. Not only had he found documentation of Margolin's gambling debts, but he also discovered at three questionable instances where the judge's opponent ruled in favor of men who held his markers.

"Looks like you got enough on the guy to take him down, which means we scored a win for our asshole." I killed the rest of my bourbon and motioned for Sarge to pour me another.

"Maybe not," he said, then reached into his inside jacket pocket and took out a flash drive. "While I was digging for dirt on Judge Margolin, I came across some pretty interesting shit on *our* judge." He moved closer to the corner of my desk and swiveled the laptop toward him. "Check this out."

He connected the drive and clicked on a file before sliding the computer back to me.

The screen filled with photos: closeups, crowd shots, deserted streets.

I had trouble processing what I was seeing. "This looks like some kind of rally." I zoomed in on Harrison, peering out from behind a podium. The face of the man standing next to him was partially obscured. If not for his snow-white hair and portly build, I wouldn't have given him another thought.

"Him," I tapped my finger on the screen. "The one that looks like a dumpling in a suit. I've seen him before."

"His name is Delmar, Otis Delmar."

That was it: *Meeting with Delmar, October*—from the back of the photo Mary had sent me.

"Ever heard of Reconstruction Done Right, RDR?" Sarge asked.

"No, uh, give me a second." I minimized the window and searched my email for happyharrison69. "Here, I got this a few days ago." While they stared at the screen, I told him about the envelope from Mary with Delmar and Harrison's picture.

"What exactly is Reconstruction Right?" Lisa asked.

"Reconstruction Done Right," Sarge repeated. "Bunch'a old white guys pretending to care about urban development when they're just about a half-step from the Klan. And our boy there, he was a keynote speaker at their last meeting."

"I don't get it. Everybody knows he's a racist jerk. That can't be what the judge is worried about," Lisa offered.

"True, but there's a lot more to RDR." He returned to the photo file and scrolled down before clicking on what looked like a darkened gym.

I squinted at the screen. "What are all those boxy things under the canvases?"

Instead of answering, he swiped to another picture, a closeup of one of the rectangular objects with Harrison standing beside it. With the tarp removed, it was now clear what had gotten the judge fired up. It was a voting machine.

Still puzzled, I turned to Sarge. "Voting machines? Why would that miserable son of a bitch be involved with—"

"Hold on." He thumbed through more canvas-covered machines, stopping at the shot of Harrison and Delmar shaking hands in the foreground. "The guy behind Delmar on the left works as an assistant to the voting commissioner. I'm not sure who the others are yet."

He explained he'd gotten his guy to turn over documentation proving Delmar's people had reprogrammed the machines, making it easy to tamper with election results. The man also told him where the key players would be after the rally. Sarge had snapped the incriminating photos from the announcer's booth above the gym floor.

I only registered about half of what he was saying because I did know one of the other men in the group photo. He was the man who whispered in my ear, pretending to be my fiancé and tricked me into a fake trust fall. It was Kevin Thomas.

18

After discovering Kevin's connection to Harrison and Otis, the thrill of standing up to the judge dissipated along with my bourbon-fueled high. Knowing my mystery man could be part of a scheme geared to suppress minority voting further dampened the festivities. What should have been elation about having something to hold over Harrison's head became despair.

Sarge and Lisa must have sensed my sudden drop in mood. He finished his explanation of Delmar's vote-rigging plan, then admitted his uncertainty about the exact role Harrison played in it but would keep digging until he found out. She suggested we postpone making any more decisions until we had more to go on. After I agreed, they left me alone in my office, where I tried to make sense of all I'd learned in the last week.

Mary's death seemed to be the pivotal event. But as far as I could tell, Detective Atkins's visit had nothing to do with the murder of Emily's mom. She came looking for Rob and didn't believe my story. If Kevin hadn't turned up at the workshop, there was no reason for her to doubt my statement about not seeing Rob in over a week. Most likely, she wouldn't have barged in to question me at all.

It appeared Kevin was the common denominator in the unholy mess my life had become.

. . .

I spent the next hour or so attempting to concentrate on Sarge's report but kept returning to Kevin, trying to imagine how he fit in with Harrison and Delmar. Since we were in the dark about what their plan was or even who Kevin Thomas was, I gave up on connecting those dots and turned to Rob, the other man in my life with a questionable identity.

I went to the alumni page for Deluca, my fiancé's supposed alma mater, located his class photo, and searched for him. He was in the back row, third from the left. I hadn't wanted to admit, but Anna had been right about the poor quality of the picture. The man in it resembled what a younger Rob might have looked like. But so did any number of random strangers.

I clicked on the contact tab. My finger lingered over the information listed for J. T. Williams, President of the Deluca University Alumni Association. Then, without giving myself time to rethink it, I made the call. Expecting to be sent to voicemail, I did a mental run-through of what I might say. Midway through it, a woman answered.

"This is J. T. Williams. How may I help you?"

J. T.'s stern, sharp voice—one that reminded me of my high school principal, serious with little patience for adolescent or any other kind of silliness—startled me. I realized it would take more than plain truth to get past the gatekeeper of all things alumni. It didn't hurt that my background in PR had eaten away at my belief in honesty as the best policy. Whatever the reason, the resulting yarn I spun, while unplanned, was impressive.

"Good afternoon, Ms. Williams," I began. "This is Detective Regina Atkins with the Atlanta PD, and I'm looking for information on one of your graduates, Robert A. Evans."

The sound of shuffling papers filled the silence, while I considered the penalty for impersonating a police officer. Misdemeanor or felony?

J. T. spoke before I concluded how much jail time awaited me. "There's a limit to the amount of information I can provide without seeing your identification, but I'll try to help. Do you know the year of his graduating class?"

I gave it to her and added he majored in forensic accounting. Then she put me on hold where soft jazz flowed through me like a mind-numbing drug, making me forget what or who I was waiting for.

J. T.'s no-nonsense voice snapped me back. "I may have found the Evans you're looking for."

Still groggy from my music-induced trance, I perked up at her announcement. Knowing he was real validated our relationship. It meant the man I planned to marry was no more nor less than what I took him to be: a practical person who planned to marry me back. My optimism was short-lived as it occurred to me Rob's disappearance might be related to one of his forensic audits. Despite my ignorance about his job, I'd read enough headlines and watched more than enough movies to know it's never good news when accountants disappeared.

"Are you there, Detective?"

"Uh, yes. Sorry. Just making a few notes. Please, go on."

"Well, there's only one Robert Evans who graduated from that class." She cleared her throat and paused.

"And do you have any contact information for him?"

"I'm afraid that's a bit of a problem."

"I don't understand."

"I can't provide it for you because there isn't any. Two years ago, Robert Evans died in a car crash."

• • •

I vaguely recalled thanking J. T. for her help before ending the call, then sitting at my desk, trying to piece the Rob Evans puzzle together. The real Rob, of course, had been out of commission for some time. So, when Detective Atkins came calling, she had to know mine was a fake. Did she suspect me of being in on the ruse, an accomplice in whatever he'd been involved with? Or did she view me as a victim? If I were the subject of a romantic con, what did Rob plan to get from me? Had he been interrupted in his scheme and decided to disappear? Or had he been disappeared?

It was after three when I got to my grandmother's house. I have no recollection of deciding to go to there or of the trip itself. Parked out front, I pried my hands from the steering wheel and wondered if they had stopped the violent shaking that had begun shortly after I learned the truth about Rob Evans. They hadn't. Instead, the trembling had increased in intensity, causing my upper body to vibrate in sympathy. I closed my eyes and wrapped my arms around my chest.

Desperate to compose myself before facing Emily and Jams, I decided now would be a good time to use some of the meditation tricks from the class Anna talked me into taking.

Breathe in, breathe out. Clear your mind and concentrate on your mantra.

What the hell was my mantra? My friend insisted we go with something exotic, so we chose a Sanskrit chant. In English it meant some crap like being blissful or thinking about bliss or screw thinking and just exist. In Sanskrit it started with *chat,* or was it *sat* or maybe *chit?*

"Shit." I slammed the steering wheel almost the same second someone knocked on the window. Startled, I turned and saw Jams with her face close to the glass. I killed the engine, and she stepped aside so I could get out of the car.

"Honey, Emily and I have been waiting a good five minutes for you to come to the door. Are you okay?"

I threw my arms around her. Standing there holding her tight, I realized my decision to go straight to my grandmother hadn't involved logic. It was muscle memory of the soul. Whenever my world tilted and disaster slid toward me, I fled to Jams.

"Whatever it is," she crooned, "it'll be all right."

Of course, there was no way anyone could be sure there would be a positive outcome for the mess I'd gotten us into. But when my grandmother said it, I accepted it as fact.

Arm-in-arm, we walked to the porch. I assured her I was fine, just had a bad day, which was total truth. I added I worried about how she and Emily were doing and left work early to check in with them. Partial truths.

"We're doing great, aren't we, dear?" Jams looked at the girl, who was waiting for us in the hallway.

With her hair in a sleek ponytail, her face free of makeup and despair, she seemed younger, lighter somehow, except for her eyes. Removing her dark eyeliner and heavy mascara failed to erase their haunted look.

From the back of the house, Dolly Parton, with her clear, almost childlike voice, entreated Jolene to please not take her man. The singer had been Grandpa Walter's favorite and despite my grandmother's predilection for rock, she loved her, too.

Emily surprised me with a smile. "We are doing great," she said. And for that moment, I believed she was telling the truth.

Jams got us settled in the den, where she adjusted the volume on her CD player before heading to the kitchen.

"How are you really?"

Emily shrugged. "Not so bad. Your grandmother is pretty cool and all, but..."

But she's not your mother. I needed to remind her this was only a temporary solution, that eventually we would have to go to the police. Except I didn't want to spoil a single second of relief she might feel from being in the Jams comfort zone.

My grandmother returned, carrying a tray with tea and oatmeal cookies at the same time Dolly was promising she would always love us.

"Okay, honey, spill it. And please do not tell me it was just a bad day."

I gave a recap of Harrison's nastiness, omitting the part where he called me a bitch—more to keep Jams from taking him out rather than concern about exposing her to profanity. I left out the voter fraud since the man was still our client, and we weren't sure of his role in the scam. And I never told her about Kevin, so I made no mention of him at all.

When I finished, she peered over her glass of sweet tea, raised one eyebrow, but kept quiet. Her expression suggested she had more questions, and we would be returning to the subject.

"What an asshole," Emily said, sending cookie crumbs flying. She swallowed. "Sorry, I shouldn't talk with my mouth full."

Jams smiled and nodded, then changed the subject. "A little bird told me you had a late-night visitor, so I'm guessing things between you and Rob are good?"

Before I could set down my tea, Emily said, "I told her I was in such a crappy mood I didn't come out to meet him."

I grinned at her attempt to cover for me.

"We're great. Life is hectic right now since we've both been swamped at work, but everything will settle down soon."

"Uh-huh. Speaking of change, your momma called. She wants us to get together and hear about her trip. I told her I had a guest and wasn't sure when we'd be ready for that talk. Said you and I would come up with a time."

"I don't want to be in the way," Emily said. "I'll hang out at the mall or the library."

"No!" Jams and I said simultaneously.

"There's no hurry. Right, Claire?"

"Nope, none at all." The last thing I needed was to attend a reveal party for my mother's biological father.

"Besides, I like having somebody a little younger than my bridge ladies to hang out with."

"I'm about to get jealous." I was only halfway joking. Then, noticing what I took for a look of concern on Emily's face, I said, "Just kidding. I think you and my grandmother make a great pair. But try to keep her out of trouble."

"What would be the fun in that?" Jams laughed. "I'll be back with more tea."

When she rounded the corner, I turned to Emily. "I haven't learned anything more about your mom's case, but I still have someone working on it. Would you mind staying here another day or so until we have more information?" I knew the right thing to do was insist we call child services, but the way the two of them were getting along, I couldn't do it.

"I guess that would be okay." The brightness of her sudden smile indicated it was more than okay.

"I brought more cookies." Jams set the plate down and refilled our glasses.

"I didn't hear the neighbor's dog when I came in," I said.

Jams' hand jerked, sloshing tea onto her sweater. "The neighbor's dog?" She dabbed at the spot with a napkin. "I heard somebody drive by on a motorcycle, but a dog barking? No. How about you, Emily?"

"No. Actually, I think I saw them bring her inside." Emily stuffed another cookie in her mouth.

Neither of them looked directly at me, and I experienced one of those brain twitches like a rabbit must when hawk wings disturb the air.

My cell buzzed from within my purse before I had time to estimate the danger. It was Lisa.

"Sorry, but I need to take this. It's work." I walked into the hallway to answer.

"Claire, if you're not watching the news, tune into Channel 9 right now."

"Okay. Give me a second." I hurried to the kitchen, turned on the small TV Jams kept on the counter, and flipped to the local station.

A tall brunette with shoulder-length curls and a serious expression stood beside an ambulance where a stretcher was being loaded into the back.

"The police have confirmed the identity of the body found in suburban Marietta as Judge Paul Margolin. Cause of death has not been determined, but neighbors reported hearing gunshots earlier this afternoon."

"Holy shit," I said to Lisa.

"Holy shit is right."

19

Along with my team, Stan Reynolds, one of the firm's founding partners, sat at the conference table. Next to him was his attorney. Harrison either hadn't been invited or failed to show.

Reynolds cleared his throat and nodded at Sarge, who took his cue. "We don't know a lot yet, but Margolin's wife found him in his office at home before noon. The cops are saying it's a burglary gone wrong, but I'm not buying it." He thumbed through the folder in front of him and removed a few black and white photos. "These are from the crime scene. Take a look." He slid them to Reynolds, who closed his eyes.

"I won't ask how you got these *things*." Using the tip of his index finger, he pushed them back to Sarge. "Why don't you summarize your conclusions?"

He shrugged. "Sure," he said and held up the first picture. "As you can tell from the blood splatter pattern, Margolin fell forward."

Mercifully, the dead judge was not in the photo, but the outline on the desk blotter was graphic enough to elicit a gasp from Lisa and a visible shudder from Reynolds. By pretending I was watching a TV crime show, I managed to stay detached.

"That means whoever shot him came from behind. Coroner has the time of death fixed for earlier in the afternoon. Unusual for a break and enter since the judge's car was parked out front in plain view from the street."

He placed the photo face down and showed us a second one featuring a wide angle of the room. Somebody had tossed books from shelves and flung papers everywhere. A broken bottle of liquor, its contents spilling onto the carpet, lay on the floor beside them.

"The room's been ransacked like the intruder was searching for something specific. No way to tell if he found anything. As for the rest of the house, nothing seems to have been disturbed."

We might not have a solid clue what the killer had been so desperate to find, but I sure as hell had a strong inkling it pointed to the elephant not in the room: Harrison. My normal approach would have been to wait for someone else, anyone else, to mention the judge, but I was tired of tiptoeing around the issue.

"I don't mean to sound callous, but I guess this means the hanging judge will be running unopposed. Wouldn't this be a good opportunity to consider dropping him as a client?"

Reynolds winced for the second time in less than ten minutes, but I continued. "Let's be honest about this. That man is a weasel, and we all know it. And now he's a weasel whose opponent has been murdered. I'm not saying he had anything to do with Margolin's death. It won't take long, though, until everybody else does."

I was tempted to bring up the voting machine problem, but if Sarge wanted to involve management, he would speak up. I looked directly at Reynolds and added, "I suppose you could say it's ironic, you know, since we're a PR firm, but do we need that kind of publicity?"

"Believe me," he said with a sigh. "I'm well aware of the situation. Frankly, nothing would thrill me more than to drop Harrison like the hot potato he is. Unfortunately," he paused to nod at the lawyer, "there are legal issues involved that make it necessary to tread lightly. We're exploring our options. In the meantime, we need all of you to work on damage control. Draft a statement he can issue expressing his deep remorse about the loss of such a fine colleague, blah, blah, blah."

He pushed back his chair and stood, then reached into his pocket. "I had to bribe his intern to get me into his Twitter account. I changed the password to slow him down if he tries to tweet on his own." He handed me a folded index card and strode toward the door. Over his shoulder, he said, "Put something out there before he figures out something's wrong and changes it again."

I unfolded it and read: *Harrison Twitter: POMPOUSASS*

• • •

Sarge took off to see if his contact had any new information while Lisa and I worked on issuing public statements. I revised Harrison's upcoming speech, and she tweeted from his account. After a few hours, she came to my office to share what she called her "masterpieces."

"Read this one." She held out her phone, then pulled it back. "No. Let me." She cleared her throat.

I'm shocked at the loss of my esteemed colleague Judge Paul Margolin. His love of the law and fair administration of justice will be greatly missed.

"Pretty good, huh? Especially after Harrison's last tweet calling Margolin a shifty-eyed sonofabitch. Of course, I took it and quite a few others down." She scrolled to the next message. "And this one."

Men like Paul with his strong ethics and unquestionable sense of morality are few and far between.

"Shouldn't you slip in a few derogatory remarks?" I asked. "Something along the lines of *Despite his weak intellect, men like Paul, yadda, yadda.* Harrison supporters would expect nothing less than for our guy to insult a dead man."

Lisa shrugged. "Too easy. Here, listen. This might be the best of all."

I'm deeply concerned for Paul's lovely wife Eileen and their two beautiful children. I'm taking a break from the campaign trail to be there for them in their time of need.

"Didn't he call her a horse-faced nincompoop after suggesting his grown boys were so dumb they couldn't pour piss out of a boot with the instructions written on it?"

Lisa nodded, took a bow, and said, "You're welcome."

"You are good. You almost made me forget what a scumbag our judge is."

"Wouldn't you love to see the look on his face when he reads what he's been saying? Hopefully, he won't catch on too soon. This is fun."

"I especially like the part about suspending his campaign. There's nothing that blowhard loves more than a captive audience." I grinned at the image of an apoplectic Harrison confronted with the fact his roadshow had been placed on hiatus. My smile dissolved when I pictured the confrontation my team would most likely have with the judge.

"We've done about all the damage control we can for now. I'll email Reynolds with my revisions and warn him about the shitstorm, or should I say tweetstorm, coming his way. You go on home."

.   .   .

It was after eight by the time I stumbled into the kitchen. My rumbling stomach reminded me I hadn't eaten since a protein bar that morning. Standing in front of the refrigerator, I held the door open longer than Emily had while I rummaged for something to eat. After settling on cereal and milk, I took my bowl to the sofa, where I flipped on the TV. I wanted to see if there were any updates on Margolin's death, but the earliest local news wasn't until ten.

A sitcom rerun from the late nineties became white noise as I finished my little golden o's and drank the remaining liquid from the bowl, the way I had done as a kid. Then I ran through my missed messages. The voicemail from Jams was a brief command to call right away. Mom had texted a similar demand. Dad, who had recently discovered emojis, sent me four praying hands. I composed a group text to the three of them, explaining I wasn't sure how long I'd be at work dealing with the Harrison emergency. I promised to get in touch when I got a break.

Totally absorbed in lying to my family, I almost missed the last message. It was from a number outside my contact list. Thinking it was most likely an unwanted solicitation that had slipped through my system, I was ready to dismiss it but looked closer. It wasn't from an unknown source after all. It was from Rob.

As smart as you are, maybe too much for your own good, you've already guessed I'm not coming back. There'll be a lot of crazy stuff floating around about me in the next few weeks. Don't believe everything you hear. There are two things you can count on. In my own way, I did love you and you're better off not being with someone like me.

20

Rob's strange goodbye message devastated me less than I would have imagined. His use of the past tense when referring to his feelings for me hurt. But his more ominous statement indicating I would be better off not being with someone like him frightened me. Because, while I didn't understand it, I believed it. But I refused to accept it. Too on edge to lie down, I finished the last half of a bottle of expensive red wine he'd left behind. Instead of sleep-inducing, the Merlot increased my agitation, keeping me awake until after one.

I woke a few minutes after four with a serious case of dry mouth. On my way to get a glass of water, I retrieved my laptop from my bag and took it to the den. Curled up on the sofa, I returned to the Deluca alumni page and the picture of Rob Evans. When I clicked on the drop-down menu, I discovered their association published a newsletter and wondered why I hadn't noticed it before.

"It's because you'd rather run from the truth." The wine made it seem normal to be speaking out loud to myself in the darkest hours of the night.

I searched the site for any mention of Rob Evans in the years between his graduation and his death. Either he'd been extremely humble or had no interest in keeping in touch with his classmates because the only time he made the newsletter was in the memorial section. I skimmed his obituary, reprinted from a local newspaper in Chagrin Falls, Ohio and noted he had worked as an accountant for the county and was survived by his wife Sarah and both parents.

The notice came across as sparse and ordinary as his life seemed to have been. At first glance, even his final moments sounded tragically mundane. On his way home from a late night at the office, Rob had failed to make a turn and careened down an incline into the Chagrin River. What struck me as unusual was the omission of the details of the crash. Searching through obituaries where cause of death had been single-car collision gave me a ghoulish vibe.

Next, I searched for police reports on the accident itself. The spot where Rob died had claimed multiple victims over the years. The county's increase in signage and caution lights did little to protect drivers from the sharp curve and narrow shoulder. Additionally, the roads were icy that night, suggesting he could have lost control of the car. The part of the article that strayed from the ordinary was the mention that there were two sets of skid marks at the scene. The authorities found traces of paint not matching Rob's sedan on the rear bumper, advancing the theory of a possible hit and run. They were looking for a second vehicle.

After coming up empty for a follow-up article, I drafted a list of other options to pursue.

One: Call the Chagrin Falls police. Two: Get in touch with Sarah Evans. Three: Check with the classmates in Rob's photo.

It was too early to do any of those things and my head was pounding, so I took two extra-strength Tylenol and headed to the shower. While blow-drying my hair, I prioritized my options. Before I continued, I had to determine the difference between what I wanted and what I needed.

From a professional standpoint—if public relations counted as a profession—I had to work on damage control for Harrison. But I didn't need or want to think about that slimeball when I was at home.

My priority was to uncover as much as possible about my ex-fiancé. The real question was more important: was that information crucial for me? Whether Rob was a petty crook who stole people's identities or something more sinister, he abandoned me. Although he had wounded my dignity and broken—or at least severely bruised—my heart, I knew I was better off with him out of my life. In addition, my pride and ego had taken a serious hit. None of that, however, necessitated conducting my investigation unless I planned to find him and beg him to come back, which I most certainly did not.

Then why was it I couldn't let go? The answer was simple: While I no longer considered Rob as part of my future, he played a significant role in my recent past. I had to know who the man I'd taken into my bed was. Because if what I learned was something sinister, it wouldn't be so easy to dismiss him as an object in my rearview mirror. It could mean that not only had I trusted the wrong person with my heart. I might also have put my life in the wrong hands.

. . .

Rather than falling asleep, I descended into a state of unconsciousness. When the alarm sounded, I could have sworn it had been minutes, not hours, since I closed my eyes. After making myself a cup of coffee, I reconsidered the steps of my plan to find out more about the real Rob Evans. A phone call to his widow would be a terrible invasion into her grief. Tracking down his friends was a better option but would take a lot of time.

So, I dialed up the Chagrin Falls police department and asked to speak to someone who might know something about the accident. I gave them the number of the report. As expected, no one was there who could help me, but the officer who answered the phone promised somebody would get back to me. Despite his sincere tone, I wasn't going to hold my breath.

As soon as I stepped out of the elevator a little after 8:00. I heard the uproar.

"Where the hell is Kincaid?" Judge Harrison's voice boomed from the reception area.

"Shit!" I stopped inside the frosted glass door. I so did not want to deal with him first thing this morning, but it seemed he had adjusted my priority list. After smoothing my hair and skirt, I stepped into the lion's den.

One of the judge's bodyguards positioned himself directly in front of me. I thought the goon was going to body search me. If that had been the plan, the look I gave him caused him to reconsider. He stumbled out of my way.

Stan Reynolds and the judge stood in the middle of the open space. The second Neanderthal leaned against the back wall.

"Ms. Kincaid," Reynolds said. "I tried to call earlier, but I was sent directly to voicemail."

His reproachful tone irritated me. I wanted to tell him I'd been slightly unhinged by the discovery of my fiancé's obituary, written long before I met the man, and had forgotten to charge my phone.

"Well, I'm here now. How can I be of assistance?"

"How can you be of assistance?" he repeated loudly enough for the window washer in the neighboring building to hear. "How can you—"

"No need to shout. Let's take this to the conference room. Unless you have another idea, Mr. Reynolds."

He mumbled something I took for acquiescence, as I brushed past them, adding, "You two go ahead. I'll be there as soon as I stop by my office."

I tossed my jacket onto a chair, removed my phone from my purse and plugged it into the charger on my desk, then texted Sarge and Lisa to warn them before I began walking the last mile to the conference room. An ominous stillness filled the hallway, making it quiet enough for me to pick up Neanderthal One's thick nasal breathing as I approached.

I should have been relieved the obnoxious man had stopped shouting, but in this case, a silent judge was more worrisome than a howling one.

Harrison leaned back in his chair, tapping his sausage fingers on the table. His normally pasty complexion had reddened and was splotched with dark purple like a rotting plum. I glanced at Reynolds, who sat across from him, dabbing at his forehead with a white handkerchief. When he caught my eye, he bit his lower lip and shrugged.

I took the gesture to mean I was in charge. "First, Judge Harrison, I want to say how sorry I am for your loss."

He stopped the tapping and gave me a blank stare.

I continued. "Even though you and the honorable Judge Margolin had your differences, it's obvious you had a deep and abiding respect for each other."

He recovered. "Deep and abiding? What the fuck are you talking about?"

I imitated the tone and stance of my high school librarian and said, "Now, Judge. Remember what we discussed? Cut the profanity or Mr. Reynolds will have security remove you."

Then I turned to my boss. "Isn't that right, sir?"

I didn't wait for confirmation. "So, let's stop with the bullshit. If you want to survive this campaign, you have to show respect to your dead opponent. That means—"

"Are you kidding me?" Harrison hissed. "How the fuck do you think I made it this far without knowing when to kiss the right asses?"

"Beats the hell out of me. But if you're on board with how to deal with Margolin's tragic loss, what's the matter?"

He reached inside the briefcase by his side. "This. This is the goddamn problem." He yanked an unlined index card from a mailing envelope and slid it over to me.

With letters cut from magazines, someone had spelled out a colorful message.

People need to know the truth about you. And when they do, you're not going to like it, not at all.

Before I had time to ask questions, he dumped the contents onto the table. Considering the nature of the photos that lay scattered in front of me, I didn't bother to scold him for his inappropriate language.

. . .

"Dear mother of God. Harrison must have been shitting bricks." Lisa tossed the offending eight by ten glossies back on my desktop.

Sarge stood beside her, shaking his head. The two of them had arrived shortly after the judge stomped out of the conference, shouting threats about taking us down with him. I suspected we had no legal or professional connection to Harrison's latest debacle, but there would be no way our firm would escape the public scandal.

Mr. Reynolds followed him down the hallway, mumbling assurances we would do everything in our power to contain the matter. They left me behind with the disgusting evidence of Harrison's hateful bigotry.

Something about the note struck a chord, but the images strewn in front of me drowned it out. I captured them with my cell phone camera. When I was satisfied I'd gotten the best possible shots, I plucked a tissue from the box on the table and used it to slide everything back into the envelope, not because I was worried about contaminating the evidence. Because I was afraid it would contaminate me. Then I took it with me to my office where I sat with my team trying to determine our next steps.

Sarge picked up a blurry shot of a man in a white robe, matching hood draped across his arm. His back was turned, but the silvery crop of hair made it difficult to believe it was anyone other than Otis Delmar shaking Judge Harrison's hand.

He squinted at the other side of the photo, then handed it to me. "Some digital developers date their stuff. Whoever took these didn't, so we have no way of knowing if they were taken before or after the ones I got of the voting machine. That note, though, doesn't sound like somebody with his panties in a wad about election fraud. It sounds personal."

Sarge began rearranging the pictures until he had created a possible timeline of events. The first was of the judge standing on the porch of an antebellum home.

"This one." I pointed to the multi-columned structure. "That's the Delmar Plantation. I saw it in the Sunday paper when they did that series on Civil War homes. Pretty ironic, what with good old boy Otis living in a mansion built by slaves and renovated by members of the Central American invaders he's so hell-bent on keeping out of the country."

"Jesus, what was Harrison thinking?" Lisa tapped the image of the judge and Delmar shaking hands.

"Not much more than what all those assholes ever think about, the size of the check he was going to get from the racist bastard," Sarge replied.

"I'm sure he didn't expect anyone to document his encounter with good old Otis," I said. "Which brings us back to the question of who took these pictures."

"Somebody with a for-shit camera," he responded. "Or at least a crappy close-up lens. They're all out of focus."

Blurry—just like the shot of Harrison and Delmar at the restaurant.

"Give me a second." I dug around in my purse until I found my key chain, then opened my locked file drawer, and removed Mary's folder. "Check this out," I said, handing the photo to Sarge.

After taking his reading glasses from his jacket pocket, he compared the first piece of photographic evidence with the ones on my desk. "It's impossible to tell by looking. But the department has software programs that will determine if these were taken by the same device. If you're okay with it, I'll see if he can match the one Mary sent you with this batch."

I agreed, then picked up the paper and reread it, concentrating on the phrasing. The author of the note wrote that people would find out the truth about the judge and when they did, he wouldn't like it all. It was an echo of what Emily said to me about how people ask for honesty, but don't really want it. If she sent the damning photos and a veiled threat to Harrison, she obviously hadn't shared the whole story with me.

I wanted to tell Sarge about Emily, but if he knew I was harboring a witness to a crime, who was also a minor, he'd have to report it or risk losing his license. Even if he had been able to talk to her without putting himself in legal jeopardy, subjecting the frightened girl to my hulking investigator held no appeal for me.

But if Emily, as the note suggested, was out for revenge, she might not be the one I should worry about intimidating. Maybe she was less in danger and more the danger itself.

■   ■   ■

After giving Lisa and Sarge a vague excuse about checking on my grandmother, I tore out of the garage, calculating how far over the speed limit I could push it without the risk of being stopped by the cops. Mom said in for a penny, in for a pound. Dad maintained less than ten miles over was under the radar. Jams promised if I used them correctly, my boobs would get me out of a ticket.

That reminded me my grandmother was waiting, and I didn't have time to stop for a cleavage flash. I might have left the one person who loved me without reservation alone and helpless with a dangerous fugitive. Despite my sense of urgency, I smiled at the idea of Jams as helpless. I drove between ten and twelve miles above the limit, being careful to stay within the flow of traffic.

I picked the middle lane to keep a low profile, double checked my mirrors, and signaled when appropriate. A few cars back, a white sedan followed suit. Even though I was aware of the popularity of that model and color of vehicles on the road, I had the anxious sense it was the same car I'd been seeing for the past week. I fought against my urgent need to make it to Jams as fast as possible, slowed down, and eased to the right, hoping to see the license plate when he passed. The driver maintained his position and didn't speed up to close the gap.

My exit came too quickly for me to try out more action movie maneuvers. I held off until the last minute to leave the interstate, and this time I did it without using my blinker. Sometime along the way, the white car disappeared.

My self-congratulatory mood was short-lived when I saw another familiar vehicle parked in the drive, a 2014 Subaru SUV. And it belonged to my mother.

•　　　•　　　•

As soon as I entered the house, I heard Mom berating Jams from the kitchen.

"But why won't you tell me?" she shouted.

My grandmother spoke in a softer voice, making it impossible to make out her response. From the foyer, I saw the door to the guestroom was cracked and, deciding to avoid getting into the fray until the last possible minute, slipped into the room, where I found Emily sitting on the edge of the bed.

"How long have they been at it?"

"Not sure. I had my headphones on the whole time. Your mom has a really strong voice."

"That's one way to put it." I sat down beside her, deciding I needed to get directly to the point. "We need to talk."

"About what?" she asked, picking at a thread in her stylishly ripped jeans.

"Come on, Emily. You don't expect me to believe you've told me everything about Judge Harrison and your mom."

She focused the same laser-like stare her mother had directed toward me at our original meeting and said, "I don't know what you're talking about. I've never even heard of Judge What's-His-Name, and I can't think of a reason Mom would have either. She never, ever mentioned him to me."

Emily kept her eyes on mine during her denial. No shifty looks to the left or right. No hair twirling or other visible tells. And if she'd stopped there, she might have convinced me. But, like many rookie liars, she belabored the point. When someone assures you something never, ever happened, you can bet it did.

I kept staring at my teenage adversary while reaching into my purse to get to the offending pictures.

"And these? Please don't say you've never seen them before." I thrust the phone toward her, and she took it. Before I gauged her reaction, my mother burst through the door.

"What are you doing hiding in here with poor Emily?"

The girl made a sad face and hung her head.

"Hello, to you, too. How was your trip?"

"If you'd joined us in the kitchen when you got here, you wouldn't have to ask how things went. But let's not air our dirty laundry in front of our guest. In the den. Now," she said and marched from the room.

I sighed in surrender, took back my phone, and followed her, stopping on the threshold to give Emily what I hoped was an intimidating look. "We're not done here."

"As I was saying to your grandmother," she began. "My trip to Jacksonville was interesting but not particularly helpful."

She explained she visited a woman named Brenda Abernathy, whose DNA revealed she was a cousin of my mother on her father's side and lived in a mobile home community outside the city.

"It had a swimming pool and tennis courts, picnic tables and shuffleboard. If it hadn't been for those squatty little boxes they live in, no one would guess it was a trailer park," Mom asserted.

She and her newly discovered cousin had lunch at the Cracker Barrel where Brenda told her she was only five or six the last time she'd seen the Edgerton side of the family. Everyone had gathered to celebrate the eightieth birthday of Granny E.

Between bites of fried chicken, mac and cheese, and blueberry cobbler, Brenda said she didn't remember much about the event.

"I didn't say anything, but she should not have been eating like that. All that greasy meat and the carbs, my goodness." Mom continued her nutritional aside with a brief commentary on Brenda's weight and how baked chicken and a salad would have been a much healthier choice for her.

"Anyway, her mother, another relative I haven't met, said her older brother called the youngest a nasty name. And then, all H E double hockey sticks broke loose. Only Brenda didn't spell it out. Her parents got divorced about a year later—nothing to do with the birthday fracas. My aunt told my cousin one of many silver linings about getting rid of her husband had been never being forced to spend another second with his trashy family." She paused and gave Jams a pointed look. "Isn't that sad? Having a huge chunk of your history ground up like a rotten tree stump?"

When there was no reaction, Mom continued. "Brenda didn't see much of her father either when she was growing up. No one even told her he passed until six months after his funeral. Her mother's in a home now, too addled to offer any more information about what happened to the brothers. All Brenda remembered was the name of the two uncles: Frank and Bradley Edgerton. I looked them up. Bradley died last fall. There were no survivors listed in his obituary. As for Frank, not a trace of him online or in court records. Nothing. It's like he never existed. Don't you think that's strange, Mother?"

Jams shut her eyes for a few seconds. Opening them, she reached for the framed photo on the table beside her recliner. It was a picture of her and Grandpa Walter standing in front of the Grand Canyon a few years before he died.

"That sweet old fool hated heights. They scared the bejesus out of him. But he loved that big hole in the ground. He rambled on and on about how people had once lived way down there by the water. How John Wesley Powell lost four of his ten men on the Colorado River. Talked my ear off the whole trip. But he was a good man. Walter, I mean. Not that there was anything wrong with Powell, according to the pamphlets." She put the photo back in its place.

"For gosh sakes, Mother. I loved him like he was my daddy. But it's important for me to learn about my biological father."

Jams slammed her hand on the hard leather arm of her chair. "How the hell can you be so sure what you need and what you don't? I'm the one he lied to. And I'm telling you, you're better off forgetting about him."

Mom tried to speak but choked on sobs instead.

Jams leaned back, her flash of fury fading into resignation.

"All right, Janis. I'm going to tell you about your biological daddy. Or at least, as much as I know about him myself. And when I finish my story, I never want to talk about him again."

It turned out Jams' friend Nichole played a much bigger role in my mother's conception than I'd known. The free-spirited hippie who appeared in my grandmother's life had been the catalyst for the Woodstock trip.

"That girl was a hoot. She sneaked her grandpa's camper van out of the garage—the old fart hadn't been able to drive in years— and showed up in front of my house while my momma was at her Joy Circle, more like gossiping with God if you ask me. Nichole and I had been talking all summer about how much we hated living in Podunkville. How great it would be to take off. Then she read about this big ole festival in a place called Woodstock, and she went slap-ass crazy. If we made it to New York, our lives would be changed forever."

Jams stared out the window so long I got scared she reconsidered finishing her story. Finally, she sighed, turned to Mom, and smiled.

"It sure as hell changed mine. For the better, of course. Anyway, she didn't have to work too hard to convince me to pack a bag and jump in the van. I left Momma a note about helping take care of Nichole's sick aunt in Florida. Didn't expect her to fall for it but hoped we could buy some time in case they came after us, which they did. It took a while for them to find out there was no aunt in Florida or anywhere else and call the highway patrol. By then, we'd crossed the border into Virginia."

Mom interrupted. "My goodness. You must have scared poor Granny half to death."

"Hell, that old woman would have spit in the devil's eye and laughed in his face. Tougher than shoe leather, she was. And we checked in with Carol when we stopped for supplies, so she could tell everybody we were okay."

I wanted to scream at my mother. If she kept throwing in comments, Jams might stop talking. I didn't have to worry about that, though. It was as if something had broken loose inside my grandmother, and she had no choice but to set it free.

"I'd about given up on that stupid map, figured it had to be wrong. Nichole and I both thought the whole damn state was one big city. That's how dumb we were. When we kept getting deeper and deeper into farmland, my stomach dropped to my knees. That was before we got close enough to see all the cars and all the people. My daddy would have called them dirty hippies, bums. To me, they were exotic wildlife."

They drove as far as they could. Along the way, stragglers hopped in and out of the van sharing pot baked into brownies and strawberry wine. Eventually, everything came to a halt. Everybody started pulling over and abandoning their vehicles. The girls loaded up their backpacks with enough food and cheap booze for the day, then joined the group snaking away on foot in the direction of the stage area.

"Everywhere people were dancing and hugging. Friendliest bunch you'd ever hope to see. Course most of them were so stoned if they'd thrown themselves on the ground they would have missed. But I fell in love with it all. That's when I met your daddy."

A thick stillness sucked the air from the room. I could hear the faint ticking of the grandfather clock in the hallway and the soft inhaling and exhaling of my mother beside me.

When Jams resumed her story, we both jumped at the sound of her voice.

"He was the most beautiful boy I'd ever seen. Long blonde hair falling past his shoulders. Greenish gold eyes that bored into your soul. And his body, oh Lord, that body."

I felt my Mom stiffen.

"He looked like an angel. But I forgot old Lucifer once reined in heaven."

Mom gasped.

"I'm exaggerating, honey." Jams reached across to pat Mom's knee. "He wasn't the devil. Just a kid hellbent on taking me to bed. At least that's what I took him for."

I braced for another dramatic exhalation from my mother. Other than a visible tightening of her jaw, however, she remained impassive, and Jams continued.

"And boy, was I ripe for the picking. When he blathered on and on about peace and love, I thought I'd found my very own Gandhi. He told he came to Woodstock to encourage harmony between the races, to make the world a better place. Turns out his reason had nothing to do with peace and goodwill. But I didn't discover that until the end of the festival. It's why I left without telling him goodbye and why he could never be in your life."

"Mother, please, don't say you can't explain why he came. Please." Mom's voice broke. For the first time in forever, we were on the same page.

"I'll tell you. But only if you understand I meant it when I said I wouldn't speak of him ever again. Understood?" She set her mouth in a thin line and looked at us both.

"Understood," I replied. My mother nodded.

"That's not enough, Janis. I need you to say it. Say you understand."

Mom whispered she understood.

Jams took a deep breath. "Your daddy is Frank Edgerton—didn't find out his real name until later. He was a member of the Ivory Glove, a sick extremist group. They thought Woodstock would be a perfect spot to set a spark to all the racist bullshit spreading through the country. I never found out all the details, but the rumor was the Gloves planned to shoot one of the Caucasian performers and blame it on the blacks. Problem was black folk ended up going to their own concerts in Harlem at the same time. That festival was a sea of mud-splattered white faces."

"Momma, what are you saying?"

"Your daddy, that beautiful boy who filled me with thoughts of peace and love and a whole lot more, was supposed to be in the front row when the last act came on the stage. He was the man assigned to take out Jimi Hendrix."

21

If not for my mother's tear-stained face, I might have found the announcement that my biological grandfather had been an assassin commissioned to take out of the most popular guitarists of his generation ridiculous. And if Jams hadn't beaten such a hasty retreat to her room after making her shocking declaration, I would have questioned her about the veracity of her story.

Despite the ridiculous nature of the charge, however, there was nothing ridiculous about its effect on two of the most important women in my life. Shortly after Jams' door slammed, Mom stood, gave me a wordless hug, and left.

I sat for a few minutes, trying to understand her story. I had no trouble imagining a small-town girl falling for a hot hippie. It was easy to picture her being swept up in a youth movement that let her lose herself in the whirlwind of peace, love and rock 'n roll. But unintentionally becoming involved in a racist plot to sow enough hatred and confusion to stall, maybe even destroy, that movement and the country with it? That just didn't make sense.

My theories and questions were irrelevant. It only mattered that Jams accepted her story as truth. And the account devastated my mother.

I wandered into the kitchen and grabbed a Sam Adams from the refrigerator. Then remembered why I came to Jams' house. I took a long pull from the bottle before heading to the room where I left Emily after her denial of having any knowledge concerning Harrison's damning photos.

Expecting a less than enthusiastic welcome, I knocked softly on her door but didn't give her the chance to tell me to go away. Emily reclined on her side, engrossed in twirling and untwirling a loose lock of hair. I sat on the edge of the bed.

"I still want more than anything to help you find out what happened to your mom." She loosened another strand and weaved the two together. "If you cooperate with me, we can do that. But we can't do anything unless we trust each other."

Emily bolted upright and gave me a withering look. She transformed from an almost-child dealing with unspeakable grief into an entirely different creature, one I barely recognized. Although I'd never experienced her level of pain, I understood it had the power to morph her into both child and Fury at once. But the intensity of her expression, contemptuous and vengeful, vindicated my earlier need to rush to my grandmother's house.

"Why should I trust you? If you hadn't set up that meeting with Mom, she wouldn't have been in the alley at all. She would still be with me." She covered her face with both hands and sobbed.

"I'm so sorry." I reached out to pat her on the back, then thought better of it. Only the touch of a ghost would ease her suffering. Any attempt on my part would be useless. It might even reawaken the beast inside her. Despite the callous nature of going with logic, I gave it a try. "Remember, your mother set up our meeting. And I think she did it partly out of fear. Mostly, though, she did it because she was brave; she wanted to do the right thing."

She uncovered her face and wiped at her eyes. "Really?"

"Absolutely. And, above everything else, she wanted to make sure you would be safe. That's why it's so important you tell the truth about the note and the pictures. You sent them, right?"

She nodded. I waited for more information, but she remained silent.

"Why, Emily? What did you hope would happen?"

"Nothing, I guess. I meant to scare the douche bag. To show him someone was on to him and he wouldn't get away with it. I wanted to scare him the way he scared Mom."

"Well, you did a good job. Unfortunately, frightening him may be the best we can do unless we can come up with stronger evidence. If not, you may have put yourself in real danger."

Emily explained she found the pictures on her mother's phone and assured me there weren't any more. Not only did I not believe her, but I suspected she was hiding a lot more than blurry photos.

I remained surprisingly composed on the drive from Jams' to my apartment and attributed my lack of emotion to exhaustion from dealing with three distraught females, at least two of whom were not being completely forthcoming with me. However, I recognized that at any moment I might join the ranks of women on the brink of losing it and preferred to be at my apartment if that time came.

My biggest fear was that Harrison would eventually reach the conclusion Emily sent him the envelope filled with evidence linking him to something unsavory at best, criminal at the worst. He would be savvy enough to figure out the pictures alone wouldn't provide proof of wrongdoing but cunning enough to understand whoever sent them probably had more. Even if he didn't worry about additional evidence surfacing, he might not want to take a chance and go after anyone he perceived as a threat.

For that reason, I spent a good amount of time trying to convince Emily she should bring the police in. But she desperately wanted to stay where she was, and we both knew it would be unlikely the authorities would allow that.

And I had been honest when I warned her we didn't have enough evidence to tie Harrison to anything more than being a horrible person, what's less anything that would connect him to Mary's murder. Other than our collections of photographs and our combined instincts, we had nothing significant enough to share with the police.

The two of us agreed to sleep on it and to keep Jams in the dark about Emily's latest involvement with the judge. At least until my grandmother calmed down over her unresolved issues with my mother.

After pulling into my parking garage, I questioned my decision. I sat for a moment, remembering the look of pure rage on the girl's face when I asked for her trust. Had that been only raw emotion bleeding through or had it been the real Emily? Was she a tortured teen or masquerading as one? And did she blame me for the part I played in her mother's death? What if her desperation for revenge was so strong, she didn't care who got hurt in the process?

The girl I left lying in a fetal position seemed incapable of intentionally inflicting pain. And she would have to be quite the actress to fake her growing affection for Jams. Plus, my grandmother had a talent for judging a person's character.

Although I'd been oblivious to the possibility the man I was sleeping with could be capable of God only knew what, Jams never embraced the idea of Rob and me as a couple. No, regardless of how slick Emily might be, my grandmother was slicker.

By the time I reached my apartment door, my initial composure dissolved into what I recognized as stage one of a panic attack. My breath came in quick, sharp gasps, and my hands became increasingly unsteady. Struggling to get the key in the lock, I felt a hand on my shoulder and froze, certain that thoughts of my fiancé had conjured him.

"I didn't mean to scare you." Not Rob.

I whirled around to face Kevin. "What the hell are you doing here?"

"I'll explain everything but not here. Would it be okay if we went inside, please?"

If he wanted to kill me, he could do it just as easily outside my apartment as inside unless he planned to torture me first. With those dark circles under his eyes and his pale, drawn face, he looked too tired to rough me up, so I let him in.

"I'm having a glass of wine," I said, leading him to the kitchen. Before I could stop myself, I added, "Can I get you some?"

Mom conditioned me to be the perfect hostess, regardless of whether my guest was a potential suitor or a psychopathic killer.

"Do you have anything stronger?" he asked, settling himself on the sofa.

I took down the bottle of Maker's Mark—a gift from Jams—and two glasses. Without asking whether he preferred his over ice or straight up—take that Mom and Miss Manners—I poured the bourbon and handed it to him, then sat in the chair across the room. He took a long swallow and sighed.

"I can't tell you how sorry I am about running out on you the other night."

I wanted to tell him to try, but he did look sorry, and I felt myself softening. Seriously? This guy is not your friend. Do not let him fool you again. What did Jams say? Something about mules.

Ain't no education in the second kick of a mule.

I took the remembered advice and ignored the apology. "It's late and I'm tired. So, can we please get to it? Why were you lurking outside my door?"

"Remember I told you I consulted with big companies dealing with security breaches?"

"Stop right there. If you're going to tell me you lied about that, too—"

"No, no. That was the truth and so is the part about an investigation into Rob Evans."

I waited for him to tell me that the real Rob had been killed. And when he began, I thought that's where the conversation was going.

"I got some bad news today." He took a sip of bourbon, and I followed suit. "First, I should tell you about me and Detective Atkins."

"You and Atkins?"

"Yes. She and I have been working together on the Evans case. I mean on your fiancé's case."

No need to tell him Rob's death unengaged me.

"Well, things have changed—"

"Please be specific. How have they changed? Never mind; it doesn't matter. If you and Atkins are working together, why didn't you tell her you were the one with me at the conference instead of letting her grill me like that?"

"You're right; I shouldn't have let that happen. But I didn't want to clue her in on everything I'd discovered. Still, it was a terrible thing to do."

"Terrible doesn't begin to cover it. Letting me worry I would be arrested for being a part of whatever Rob had done. Wait, you must have given her the idea I held something back when we talked. You couldn't trick me into spilling my secrets, so you were turning me over to Regina to sweat the truth out of me. You're despicable."

Emily's furious face came to mind, and I realized I'd done the same with her. Only she did know more than she was saying. But I understood why Kevin had trouble accepting my innocence when it came to being involved in my fiancé's criminal activities.

Stop being so goddamned understanding. Showing empathy for the man who allowed his girlfriend or associate or whatever to cross-examine me in my own office made me a sucker.

"That's not true. Okay, maybe it's a little true. I didn't imagine you had anything to do with something illegal. But possibly you heard or saw something important and not realized it. That's why Regina and I decided she would question you. But you don't have to worry about any of that. She cleared you of any criminal involvement."

So, now instead of an accomplice, I had become a simpering fool.

"Isn't it wonderful you told Regina that I hadn't taken part in some criminal conspiracy to defraud or cheat or whatever else the two of you suspected me of." I tossed back my bourbon and waited for its warmth to spread through me.

"I wish I could go back and change all that. This thing has been out of control from the beginning. I know there's nothing I can say to make things better. But I didn't come to ask you to forgive me. And after I explain why I'm really here, most likely you'll never want to see my face again."

Despite the heat from the alcohol, a chill came over me. It seemed I had been right about the real purpose of his visit.

"Early this morning, the police found a car registered to Rob Evans. A shell of a car, I should say. It looks like someone set it on fire." He leaned forward as if he wanted to touch me. I shrank back into my chair.

"That's not all, Claire." He took out his phone, scrolled across the screen, then handed it to me. It was a close-up with two shots of a gold Rolex: one of its face, the other of the back with a familiar date engraved on its surface. The day Rob and I met.

⋅ ⋅ ▪ ⋅ ⋅

My reaction to this second death pronouncement of the man I'd planned to marry surprised me. Technically, it was the first since I had never even known the real Rob Evans. And in the strictest sense, it wouldn't count as an actual notification until the identity of the man in the car had been confirmed. And that might take a long time as the authorities hadn't a clue about him.

So, if Kevin expected me to fall apart at his news, he would be disappointed. I refused to show any emotion in front of him. I even considered calling him out on the picture I'd seen of him with the rigged voting machines. But it would be a waste of time. He'd either come up with some tall tale exonerating himself or tell me he wasn't at liberty to share that information.

So, I didn't ask him any questions. I simply rose from the sofa and walked to the door. He must have said something before he left because his lips moved, but the thick cotton gauze wrapped around me kept me from hearing him.

It created a silence between us, but not the soothing sort that gently descends as you fall asleep. This heavy quiet seeped into my brain. I feared it would fill my mind and make me forget to breathe. Curled up on the couch with a blanket draped across my shoulder, I stared at nothing for what might have been seconds or minutes. The insistent vibrating from my pocket brought me back.

Jams.

"First, don't get mad at Emily. She told me you insisted she keep her mouth shut about the judge, but when I saw how upset she was, no way I'd let her carry her burden alone."

I wasn't angry with the poor girl. When it came to effortlessly prying information from reluctant informants, my grandmother had her special brand of sly sweetness. The woman had cracked far more experienced liars than poor Emily.

"We weren't trying to keep anything from you. We just didn't want to bother you when you were so upset about Mom." I needed to know how much Emily had told her. If she stopped short of filling Jams in on the photos and the threatening note she'd sent.

"Emily has some, um, very interesting documents. We talked things over, and we think you should take a look."

Well played, Jams, I thought. Instead of sweating the information from the girl under hot lights, my grandmother had most likely plied her with pastries and blessed her little heart into submission before she knew what hit her. The poor kid had not only supplied my grandmother with much of what she told me, but she'd provided even more details to her compassionate inquisitor.

"Honey, I know it's late, but you should hear what she's got to say as soon as possible. Why don't you pack your pjs and a toothbrush and come on over? We'll have a slumber party."

I didn't expect to get much sleep and wasn't in the partying mood, but the idea of spending the night underneath a pile of quilts my grandmother's grandmother had made offered a comfort I hadn't known I needed. I packed my pjs and hit the road.

22

Sheets of paper covered the dining room table. A closer look revealed they were emails to various people from Happy Harrison. Emily had arranged them in chronological order.

The first was identical to the one good old Happy had sent me, the one announcing that the meeting of RDR had been rescheduled. I had never received the promised TBD time and date. The chain continued without me: suggested times for the rescheduling, obscure references to the esteemed guest speaker—never a mention of his name—and other vague comments.

"I don't understand how I was in this group one minute and out the next. Or how the hell I got on it in the first place."

"I'm pretty sure I know." Emily took another folder from her backpack and removed the original email, complete with all the recipient addresses and what appeared to be nicknames at the top.

"See that one, Clara Jones? I bet when Harrison put the group list of his asshole email buddies together, he accidentally clicked on your name, too. He probably confused Claire with Clara, and you're next on the alphabetized names. Since this is the only one you got,

I'm guessing he caught his mistake and took you off before all the good stuff started."

"Wait a minute," I said after reading through the addresses. "This looks like it came from happyharrison69's account." Had Mary gained direct access to the judge's computer? Not likely, since most of them had been sent after she was murdered. "How did you get a copy of his private correspondence?"

Emily shrugged. "It's not that hard if you know what you're doing. Let's say somebody needs to get into someone's account. Like a matter of life and death, but that person doesn't have the password. But he or she has the guy's email address and phone number, okay?"

Jams and I exchanged glances. "Go on," I said.

She continued. "So, the first person, the one who's trying to stop some terrible stuff from happening, goes to the login page and puts in the address. Of course, that person doesn't know the password, so he clicks on forgot password. And then asks to have the verification code sent to the other guy's cell phone. This is where things get a little shady." Emily paused to drink from her water bottle.

"This is where things get shady?" I asked.

"Well, if you don't want me to explain—"

"Hey, I'm in too deep now. Go ahead."

"Yes, go on, honey," Jams urged.

"Okay. This is where I, uh, I mean the person who's trying to catch a real asshole, sends a text to the asshole's cell pretending to be from Google. Masking your own number is a little complicated. First—"

"Why don't you skip that part? It sounds like advanced email fraud. Remember, Jams and I are in Hacking 101."

"Right." Emily nodded. "So, you give them some fancy language telling them Google has detected unusual activity, blah, blah, blah, and ask them to respond to the problem with the code they just received. Mostly only idiots fall for it, but luckily—"

Jams interrupted. "Luckily, our guy's so dumb he doesn't know whether to check his ass or scratch his watch."

"Nice." Emily grinned and repeated. "Check his ass."

"She's hilarious. But let me get this straight. You're saying the judge—or our guy, I mean—fell for it? Then what?"

"The good guy or girl uses the code to set a temporary password and boom. They've got control of the account. Even if the bad guy changes it later, we still get his private emails unless he messes with the settings. And most people are clueless about stuff like that."

"Jeez, Emily. This cannot be legal." I dropped my head into my hands and closed my eyes.

"Legal, smegal," Jams snorted. "If we're gonna run with the big dogs, we have to get off the porch."

"And get chased straight to jail," I moaned.

"Not necessarily, since I'm a minor, and you two don't have the skills to understand what I was doing."

"That's right." Jams nodded her head. "Who would ever think a sweet little old lady like me and a do-gooder-rule-follower like you could ever think about hacking into someone's email?"

I didn't know whether to be offended at the whole do-gooder-rule-crap or impressed with my grandmother's criminal acumen.

"What the hell," I said, holding my head high. "Pass me those emails."

"No more, please." I was referring to both the plate of caramel brownies and the ever-increasing pile of paper. Emily had only printed a few pieces of the judge's correspondence from the flash drive she'd kept hidden in her backpack. Jams and I wanted to read them all, but my grandmother preferred a hard copy. When we saw how many were on the drive—not to mention those she continued to have access to—we decided to print the ones from the weeks before and after Mary's murder and let her cherry-pick from the rest. As for me, I planned to look at all of them but hadn't counted on how disgusting they were.

Emily reached for her fourth brownie, then ignored my request and handed several more of the printed emails to me.

"This is from Clara Jones," she said before stuffing her mouth. "I highlighted the worst parts."

The worst parts included a racist comment about a low-income area in Harrison's district. She suggested installing the "brand new super effective" voting machines there to make sure the results were accurately represented. Playful Clara had added a dancing monkey emoji.

"I need a shower," I said as I dropped the email on the table.

"Pretty sickening. I didn't know people like that still existed." Emily finished her brownie.

"My grandmother used to say it wasn't their fault. That they just weren't raised right." Jams shook her head. "She was a sweet woman, but maybe she's part of the reason those folks have survived. Think about it. Most of those shitheads are so stupid if brains were dynamite, they couldn't blow their own goddamn noses. Without good Christian folk like my grandma to make excuses for them, there's a good chance Darwinism would have taken them out a long time ago."

I pictured a scene where a group of stuffy-headed halfwits followed each other off the edge of a cliff. Smiling at the image, I stood to stretch and caught a glimpse of the kitchen clock.

"I can't believe it's after midnight. This has been fun, ladies, but I have to work tomorrow. Would you be okay if I made a copy of your flash drive? I want to get some input on the best way to proceed."

She removed it from the computer and closed her fist around it.

"Please, Emily. You can trust my team. We all hate being associated with the judge. Nothing would make us happier than to see him get what's coming to him."

She hesitated, then motioned for me to pass my laptop to her. The three of us sat silently as she transferred files to my computer. I put them on a flash drive of my own for backup.

"I'm going to set it up so you can get into Harrison's emails, too," she said when the transfer was complete. Keeping her eyes focused on the screen as she worked, she added, "I've read through this shit at least a gazillion times, and all it proves is that the judge is a racist douche. But he's a smart racist douche. He never says anything that couldn't be taken as a joke. He doesn't come out and say *Yes, please. I'd love to cheat to win my election.*" Her voice broke. "And he never mentions Mom, not one single time."

I didn't say it, but the same thought had occurred to me.

"No, but it's a beginning. And your mother, well, she—" I stopped myself from pointing out that Mary had been dead when those emails have been sent, so they couldn't have been part of what she'd planned to share in our meeting.

I reached for her hand and held it. "Emily, I need you to think hard about this. The night your mom was coming to meet me, was she carrying anything like files or folders with her? Did she maybe drop them when she fell?" I hated taking the girl to the worst moment of her young life, but we were missing something, something that had cost Mary her life.

"I didn't see her when she left. And if she had anything like that with her, it was gone when I got there." The teardrops that had been pooling in her eyes water-falled down her cheeks. "He's going to get away with it, isn't he? People like him, rich and powerful, they always get away with it."

"Your mother was a very smart woman. There's no way she wouldn't have made a copy of whatever it was she might have been bringing to me that night. We'll find it and when we do, we'll make sure he gets what he deserves."

I wanted to have faith in my optimistic declaration, but Emily was right about rich and powerful people. It was a hell of a lot easier for them to get away with everything from fraud to murder. But just because it was harder to catch them didn't mean it was impossible. All we had to do was locate the missing evidence and figure out how to use it.

Which was what Mary had been doing when someone—maybe someone I'd let into my bed and my heart—had shot her in cold blood.

23

I hadn't expected to get much sleep, but the comfort quilts on the daybed in Jams' office combined with a shot of bourbon did the trick. Except for the barking of the neighbor's dog sometime in the middle of the night, I was dead to the world. If not for the smell of sizzling bacon and baking biscuits coming from the kitchen, I might have slept through my alarm.

My grandmother stood at the stove, spearing thick slabs from the cast-iron skillet.

"Coffee's ready," she said, plopping the strips on a paper towel covered plate. After draining the grease, she cracked eggs and whisked them together with cheese and butter, then dumped the mixture into the hot pan. Expertly dodging rising steam and scalding droplets, she continued stirring until the liquid dissolved from the fluffy concoction. She scraped the contents directly onto our plates, and I blew on them as she brought the bacon to the table. While I poured my coffee, she took the biscuits from the oven and coaxed them into a wicker breadbasket that she placed in front of me.

"No Emily?" I asked, picking up a piece of bacon with my fingers.

"Not this morning. It's just you and me. I peeked in to check on her. The poor girl was tangled up in the covers with that laptop of hers still in her arms. She must of stayed up half the night going over those emails. I bet she's slap out."

We ate in easy silence for a few minutes before Jams spoke.

"Did you believe what you said about Harrison getting what he deserved? From what I've seen, the sonofabitch is slicker than owl shit."

"I want it to be true." The words stuck in my throat. And the buttery eggs became too rich, the bacon too thick. I laid my fork on my plate and sipped at my coffee.

"You eat like a bird. I'm fixing you a doggy bag."

"Speaking of dogs, I think the neighbors are home."

"Why would you think that?" Jams dropped the basket on the counter hard enough to dislodge the top biscuit. She scooped it from the floor, blew on it, and returned it to its place.

"Yeah. That dog barked forever. Didn't stop until at least after two."

"Sorry, but I sleep like a log these days. The neighbors must not be finished moving out."

She turned her back on me and opened the Saran Wrap drawer.

After arriving at the office, I put Jams' carefully wrapped biscuit and bacon sandwich on my desk, next to a pink sticky note from Anna.

Luis dug up some info for you. With a client until 1:00. I'll be there as soon after as I can.

With all the high-level drama in my life, Anna's offer to see what her husband could find out from the district attorney's office slipped my mind. I even forgot about those FBI agents who visited

Anna. When they never materialized, I assumed they decided I wasn't worth the trouble. Unless one of them had shown up, pretending to be someone else. Someone like Kevin Thomas.

What a fool I'd been, falling for his second—or was it third—big lie. Was his story about going after Rob for stealing information just that—another tall tale to keep me from figuring out who he was: an FBI agent? I racked my brain trying to remember what I said to him the night Emily had been hiding in my bedroom. Had I revealed something that might have led to Rob's death if he was actually dead? And if Kevin had been lying to me from the start, why trust him to tell the truth about the man in the car? Or anything else.

Or what if he had nothing to do with the men who questioned Anna about my whereabouts? They could have been impostors, which made it seem even more plausible that they were involved with the burned-out car and Rob's body.

"That doesn't make sense. Who would go to that kind of trouble to get to a hacker?" I asked myself, then answered, "That would depend on the value of the information and the person who wanted it back."

If the data Rob accessed was important enough for someone to murder him, and that someone had been looking for me, was I next on the killer's list?

"Hey," Lisa called from the doorway. "You okay? Sarge and I were worried about you. You left so suddenly."

"Sorry about that. I forgot I had to run an errand for my grandmother. Some medicine she needed picked up."

I hated lying to her, but I promised myself I'd make it right later, would tell her and Sarge all I knew about Emily and her mother. Except for the Rob as killer part. I wasn't ready to share that possibility.

She wrinkled her brow before relaxing it and smiling. "I'm glad that's all. And I have some good news. Harrison won't be coming in today for a follow-up meeting. His assistant called and said the poor judge has come down with something nasty. I asked how she could tell the difference. Didn't get an answer."

"That is about the best news I've heard all week." This time I told the whole truth and nothing but.

"Of course, he'll turn up again when he's out from under the weather." She grimaced. "Then Reynolds and the big bosses—thanks to the judge's swollen bank account—won't be able to resist his charm. And we'll be forced to sit in the same room with him and his hairy nostrils. Unless maybe he gets thrown under the jailhouse." Lisa grinned before walking away.

The idea of helping shove the judge into the pokey was appealing enough to send me to my computer with Emily's instructions for logging into Harrison's account. If someone told me two weeks ago, I would be hacking into the email of a state official, I would have been too appalled to entertain the thought.

And now, I was entering a whole new realm of crime: digital eavesdropping. Overwhelming, yes. But there was an awesome power in sneaking into someone's personal correspondence, invading the private thoughts they had shared, never imagining those thoughts could be hijacked by an outsider. How might possessing that kind of dark magic affect me?

I let my hands linger over the keys for a minute before my first attempt at entering the password. My fingers stumbled, and I had to type it two more times before I got it right. Once I was in, a sense of elation replaced my apprehension. I was breaking the law but for an honorable cause. I was fighting a terrible evil, one cloaked in the robes of righteousness.

I was also full of crap, but I didn't care.

I entered the letters RDR in the email's search bar and watched as the screen filled with matches. The longest thread began with the email I received with about thirty responses, most of them taken from the suggested replies at the bottom of incoming messages and, therefore, useless: Looking forward to it. I can't wait. Great! Thanks!

Skimming through them, I averted my eyes when I came to Clara Jones's vile remarks. Then I landed on an interesting one. Unlike the lovely Clara, the sender provided no clue to an actual name, going only by WhiteBeach. The person's identity might have been disguised, but there was nothing obscure about the message.

Delay reeks with the stench of cowardice. True leaders move quickly and decisively.

We have too much invested to let victory slip away. If you're not up to the task, get the fuck out of the way before someone does it for you.

Whoever WhiteBeach was, he wasn't pleased with Judge Harrison's rescheduling of the RDR meeting. I hit print and continued reading the rest of the emails, this time focusing on locating more communications from the angry sender. I was halfway through the first page when Anna burst into the office.

"Que hijo de puta!" she exclaimed, shutting the door behind her. "I spent the entire morning trying to convince Mayor Bailey it would not be wise to sue his opponent for calling him 'saco de mierda mentiroso.' I told him it would only call more attention to the fact he was a lying sack of shit." She cracked up at her own joke and plopped onto the chair in front of my desk.

"You did not say that." Bailey was a third-rate political hack whose father had bought the mayoral seat for the son he wished he'd never had. Now the younger Bailey ran a small municipality a few miles south of Atlanta. He stayed in the news for his outlandish comments on race, poverty, and immigration, while being investigated for embezzling from city funds.

"Not in those exact words, but I finally managed to get the point across. Why do we keep representing these sleazy hijos de burros?"

"First, that's an insult to donkeys everywhere. Second, I'll put my son of a donkey up against yours anytime."

"And you would win. Lose, I suppose, is more accurate. I say screw the both of them."

She reached inside her purse and removed a silver flask embossed in hot pink letters: And yet, despite the look on my face, you're still talking.

The old Claire would have waved off her offer for such early day drinking. The new and improved version, destroyer of corrupt politicians, opened my bottom desk drawer and brought out two small tumblers.

She poured the pale golden liquid, her favorite brand of aged tequila, the kind made for sipping, not mixing, she'd explained the night she introduced me to it.

She held up her drink. "Salud!" Then she touched her glass to mine.

"Salud!" I responded. We tossed back our drinks, and I took a deep breath to cool the fire traveling down my throat.

Anna pushed my hand away when I tried to stop her from pouring another. "Please, the news I have for you is at the least the two-shot kind."

We repeated the ritual. The heat filled my almost empty stomach before spreading upward throughout my chest.

"Luis uncovered some very disturbing facts about your Rob Evans."

"I'll save you some time," I interrupted. Her inclusion of *your* gave me the impression her husband had found out my Rob Evans didn't exist. I told her I knew about Rob's fake identity.

The tension lines on her forehead relaxed for a second, then returned as her frown deepened.

"Worse than his deception regarding who he was," she continued, "is his story about what he was. According to the information Luis discovered, your Rob was not a forensic accountant. He wasn't an accountant at all. If the FBI has the right information, and they usually do, your fiancé is a contract killer."

I don't know how Anna expected me to react to her statement, but she seemed surprised when I said nothing, did nothing, didn't even move.

Finally, she asked, "Did you get that, Claire? A contract killer. A thug who commits murder for money. That puts you in danger. You must come and stay at my house until they catch him."

"Yes, I heard you. The FBI thinks Rob was a contract killer, a hit man, a murderer." The expanding lump in my throat threatened to choke me if I kept talking. The fiery sip of tequila scorched my windpipe and instigated a coughing fit.

Anna grabbed a bottle of water from the mini fridge, patted me on the back until I caught my breath, then said, "So why are you so calm?" She paused as my words sank in. "Oh, my God, did you say he was a killer?"

I took a swallow. "I did, and I don't think we have to worry about him being a danger to me because the police found Rob's burned-out car. There was a body in it."

"My poor Claire." She leaped to her feet, rounded the desk, knelt beside me, and cradled my head to her breast. I breathed in her expensive cologne, something floral with a hint of spice, then extricated myself from the awkward position. She leaned back on her heels.

"Are they sure it's him?"

I shrugged. "They don't have a positive id, but who else would it be?" I had, however, been thinking the same thing. Burn victims—I shivered at the thought—can be hard to identify. And did they even know who they would be identifying? Certainly not the real, long-dead Rob Evans.

There was no reason to mention my doubts to Anna. Mostly because I didn't want to hide out at her house or anywhere else. I'd spent a night in her guest bedroom after one of their wild parties, trying not to listen to her and Luis's boisterous lovemaking on the other side of the thin walls. That time, I had been between boyfriends and the couple's passion made me envious. Now, the thought of lying in my lonely bed with a pillow over my head just made me sad.

"I suppose you're right." She stood and leaned against the desk. "But I still want you to stay with us. I want to keep you close until they have a positive id on the—until they know who was in the car."

That was another reason I didn't want to hole up at Anna's. I wasn't ready to deal with being wrapped in compassion and concern like an antique vase.

"I promise I'll be fine. Even if Rob wasn't the one in the car, I can't think of anything that would make him want to hurt me. I'm pretty sure I haven't pissed anyone off enough to warrant them taking out a contract on me. Besides, if my Rob was the dangerous killer the FBI says he was, I'd already be dead."

"Danger or not, you should be alone now. And remember how much you love Luis's breakfast empanadas?"

Luis was one hell of a cook but being coddled and fed would only give me time to chew at the problem my life had become as if it were an annoying hangnail and I didn't have a nail file.

"I promise if I feel anxious or sad or scared, I'll head straight to your place. Right now what I need is to take my mind off the whole thing, at least for a little while. The only thing that will do that is to keep busy here."

We had often discussed how throwing ourselves into our work had helped us with past catastrophes.

"I guess I understand. I don't like it, but I understand. And just so you know, you can expect to see more of me at the office." She hugged me again, then walked to the door where she stopped to add, "You better check in with me as well, or I will come looking for you."

I smiled and promised she would hear from me every chance I got. A mix of relief and regret came over me as I watched her leave. How easy would it have been to walk into the sunshine of Anna's thoughtfulness, to eat spicy Mexican food served to me by her hot husband, to wallow in well-earned self-pity?

And maybe I would take her up on that offer later. But not now. Because I hadn't been lying when I told her work was the cure for my disease; I'd only been a little deceptive. I expected she would assume I meant taking meetings or working on campaigns or cleaning up the judge's messes. What I had in mind, however, was different.

Yes, it did relate to the judge, only I wasn't planning on a clean-up job. I intended to go back to my plan before dad's frantic call about Jams losing it. I was going to that boutique employment agency, the one with the silly name.

After removing and opening Mary's file, I found it: Temp of the Town. I would use my well-honed persuasion skills to extricate information about the places Mary had temped.

What had Sarge said about the place? I closed my eyes and imagined our investigator sitting in front of my desk. He called it fancy pants and then—what word did he use? Fishy. That was it. He said it smelled fishy. He'd also said something about discretion. I ran a search and got a fast hit on the agency. Temp of the Town, written in one of those pretentious flowing fonts, shimmered into view. Underneath the logo, in a smaller version of the same annoying font, and above the list of all the amazing duties their temps could perform, was the line I'd been looking for.

Our personnel are efficient and discrete.

What company hiring a temp wouldn't insist on efficiency? But discretion? How secretive could billing shipments or catering assistance be? Yes, attorneys and accountants might expect this criterion although I couldn't imagine they would assign a confidential issue to someone they hadn't properly vetted. Even politicians like the judge weren't stupid enough to trust someone they barely knew with sensitive information. While Harrison might not be a genius, he couldn't have made it as far as he had without being shrewd and cunning. But he was also greedy and arrogant. The headiness of power combined with his love of money could have made him careless. And Mary might have died because of it.

24

Located in Sandy Springs, a city with a population of around a hundred thousand people, Temp of the Town was in a multi-storied building with darkened windows that gave me an uneasy feeling. I hated the idea that all those unseen worker bees had a clear view of me on my trek up the walkway. I imagined them chuckling as I checked to make sure my dress wasn't hiked up in the back or judging my choice of lingerie when I adjusted a runaway bra strap. It made me want to contact the office manager and demand to know what was going on behind that creepy glass.

Today, I planned on finding out what at least one of them was hiding.

I blew into my hand to check my breath, then popped a wintergreen mint before approaching the entryway. The automatic revolving door, also dark, was out of order. The sign taped on the side of the building instructed me to use the manual entrance to the right. When I leaned my shoulder against it, I caught sight of a white sedan gliding by. I stepped back and dashed to the curb in time to see the vehicle turning out of the parking lot. I fought to shake the irrational thought that this was the same one I saw in Rob's garage and, later, at my house the night Emily arrived.

Don't be an idiot, I told myself. How many freaking white sedans are there in the Atlanta area? Forget about the damn car and find out what happened to Mary.

Despite my best intentions, my apprehension remained. However, I talked myself into getting back to work. I checked the directory, then rode the elevator to the top floor, which was entirely dedicated to the temp agency.

Almost directly in front of me, the glassed-in reception area looked more like the lobby of a small but elegant hotel. A twinkling of crystals on the three-tier chandelier announced my arrival. Shiny leather chairs in a light shade of mauve lined one wall. Bronze accent tables created space between every other seat. In the middle of the room, a pair of navy love seats faced each other. An enormous glass coffee table completed the arrangement.

My heels sank into the plush beige carpet as I walked toward the willowy brunette sitting behind a polished rosewood French desk. She wore her dark hair in a super chic pixie. Her low cut but tasteful black blouse called attention to the creamy pearls around her ridiculously long neck.

Other than a navy-blue leather notebook, a fake quill pen, and an antique candlestick phone that I doubted was functional, there was nothing else on the surface. A small glass-topped table sat beside her. It, too, was bare except for a thin silver laptop that cost more than the furniture in my house. The brunette stretched her thin red lips into what, from my vantage point, was a practiced professional smile.

She welcomed me in a low-pitched voice that sounded as phony as she looked. "How may Temp of the Town be of assistance to you?"

The thick sweep of hair covering most of her left eye distracted me. Wouldn't the blockage obscure her view or constantly throw her neck out of alignment? I suppressed the urge to tilt my head to the right and told her who I was without telling her the name of my company. Then I explained I had come to see the person in charge about one of their temps.

"Our manager is extremely busy at the moment. If you would fill out this form regarding the identity of the employee, including a description of the problem and your contact information, someone will get back to you at our earliest convenience." Other than a slight twitch of her upper lip, the smile remained in place.

"Extremely busy?" I looked pointedly around the empty room, then turned to the pixie queen. "I'm afraid later is not convenient for me. This particular temp worked for my company when some confidential information about one of our clients was leaked to the media. This is a very serious and time-sensitive issue. So perhaps you can tell him I need to see him immediately." I gave her my version of a fake smile.

Hers slipped a notch as she held the white and gold receiver to her ear and inserted a slim finger into the rotary dial. I masked my surprise that the phone actually worked. Striking what I hoped was a nonchalant pose, I leaned on the desk and fluffed my hair while staring at the painting of lily pads floating in muted shades of blues and greens. I stretched forward and strained, trying to make out what she was saying to the person on the other end.

"Yes, sir." She ended the call loudly enough for me to hear. "Mr. Petit will see you now."

Petit, huh, I thought. Sounded French, which would explain all the ornate furnishings.

She rose from her desk and admonished me. "Keep in mind that he has only a few minutes to spare before his next meeting, so you will need to be brief." I followed her down the long hallway, and she added, "Walk this way, please."

She teetered on her stilettos, as her hips, tightly encased in a black pencil skirt, swayed from side to side.

"Like this?" I said under my breath, then slung my own hips in an exaggerated imitation.

We stopped at a polished wooden door with Petit's name on it. Miss Pixie Cut knocked lightly, then opened it.

"I explained to Miss Kincaid that you have an extremely tight schedule."

"Thank you, my dear Denise. I'll take it from here." He spoke in the slightly nasal style my high school French teacher had insisted we emulate. Instead of sounding like sophisticates gliding past the Right Bank of the Seine, we honked like the geese on the shore.

The portly man watched Denise's impressive hip swivel before pressing his hands on his rectangular rosewood desk and pushing himself into a standing position. His pale face pinked, suggesting that even the small amount of exertion was taxing. He produced a lacy handkerchief from his jacket pocket, swiped his oily forehead and dabbed at the sweat pooling in the indentation below his nostrils. After stepping over a round cushioned stool, he walked toward me and extended his hand.

"Victor Petit at your service." He spread his lips, revealing crooked yellow teeth with oversized canines. The imitation smile morphed into a grimace as he tightened his pudgy fingers around mine. His grip was surprisingly strong. Too strong, like cement sucking you in as it hardened into concrete. I tugged free of the fleshy vice and flexed my hand, puzzling over his need to apply so much pressure. Was he trying to establish dominance through pain or did his grasp imply something more sinister, a threat maybe?

More likely, he was a jerk who enjoyed using a social convention to bring women to their knees. Either way, I didn't like it or him.

"Please, have a seat." He motioned to the small chair slightly to the right of his desk. I sat on the throne-shaped one to the left and waited for him to return to his spot.

"Since neither of us has a lot of time, I'll get straight to the point. I need to know all the places one of your employees worked last year. Her name—"

"I must stop you there. You see, it is impossible for me to reveal confidential employment records."

"I understand that, but in this case, I think you'll want to make an exception. The person I'm inquiring about is Mary Saunders." I looked directly into his red-rimmed eyes. Other than three rapid blinks and a phlegmy throat clearing, he showed no reaction.

"I'm sure you remember Ms. Saunders," I urged and waited a beat before adding, "Mary Saunders, the woman who worked for your agency off and on for the last two years. The woman who was murdered outside her apartment a few nights ago."

In seconds, his face went from deep pink to ash gray and his emotionless expression darkened.

"That was a terrible tragedy," he said through clenched teeth. "But it has nothing to do with this agency or anyone who works here. And as I mentioned before, I cannot help you. Perhaps you would show yourself out."

Feeling as if I'd been dismissed from the principal's office, I held my head high as I turned the doorknob. "I hope you'll reconsider your decision. If not—what is it the French say? Que sera sera? Or is that Italian? Beautiful language, Italian." I wriggled a goodbye with my fingers and didn't bother to close the door behind me.

My linguistic insult had been childish, but that overblown bully had it coming. Rising fury increased my pace as I walked to the reception area, and I almost collided with the woman who stepped into the hallway as I passed by. Before I could register my surprise, she grabbed me by my arm, pulled me inside her office, and shut the door.

Small with a stylish brown bob, she had that ageless quality only well-groomed women who take advantage of necessary cosmetic surgery have. With her dove gray suit, crisp, pale peach blouse, and diamond pendant, she could have stepped off the cover of Working Woman's Digest, had there been such a magazine.

"I hope I didn't startle you." She held out her hand. After my bone-crushing experience with her boss, I wasn't eager to extend mine, but Mom's basic training kicked in, and I followed suit. Her handshake was confident, firm, and painless.

"Please, have a seat. I'm Vera Wilson, head of accounting." She laughed and added, "Actually, I'm the whole accounting department."

I sat on the well-cushioned chair beside her desk. Rather than retreat behind it Petit-style, she took the matching one and moved it closer. Before I could introduce myself, she said, "And you're Claire Kincaid. I would say I couldn't help hearing your conversation with Mr. Petit, but that wouldn't be entirely true. I couldn't help hearing it because I was standing outside his office, listening in. I hope that doesn't offend you."

"I'm not offended, but I am curious. I mean, do you eavesdrop on all your boss's conversations, or was mine special?"

"If you'd ask me that a year ago, before Mr. Petit became manager, I would have been shocked at the question. My former supervisor was a gentleman. He cared about his employees and the integrity of the agency. It never crossed my mind that I should keep track of what he was doing. Mr. Petit? Not so much. When I heard Mary's name, I had to find out what he would say."

She stiffened at the sound of her boss shouting for Denise, then whispered, "Poor girl tries her best to ignore his bellowing." She reached for a thick document folder on her desk. "I'm sorry I can't give you a more detailed explanation. But I do have this."

Petit roared again, closer this time. Vera jumped to her feet and motioned to a door by the bookshelf. "You should go out the back way, so he doesn't get suspicious. My phone number is in there if you have questions. Unfortunately, this is all I have." She led me to a narrow hallway and pointed left. "That exit will take you to a service elevator."

"I appreciate your help."

"I wish I could do more. Mary was a wonderful person and a hard worker. We weren't as close as I would have liked, but I considered her a friend."

She stepped back into her office and shut the door.

Still reeling from Petit's hostility and my hasty exit, I didn't notice the white car behind me until I exited the parking deck.

25

Winded from the sprint from my car to the elevator, I breathed a quick greeting to the receptionist and raced to my office. By the time I was settled in at my desk, I had halfway convinced myself that I wasn't certain the sedan had been the same one I'd been seeing or that it had been following me.

"What you need to do," I said aloud, "is to stop thinking and start taking action." And I did.

First, I left a voicemail for Sarge asking him to find out who owned Temp of the Town. I spent the rest of the afternoon going over the documents Vera gave me. I started with the eleven pages detailing Mary's schedule. The records included place of employment, duties performed, hours worked, and her comments about the company. The earlier entries were varied: a few management companies, the occasional real estate brokerage group, and several legal firms.

I ran my finger down the list and stopped when I noticed a familiar name, Barry Gregory, the judge's jackass attorney. His was the last before Mary began exclusively working for Harrison.

Her comment about Gregory didn't reveal much: Very particular, has special requests.

Was the review Mary's way of sending a message to Vera telling her to send only their most meticulous temps? Or had the mention of the special requests been a warning? Had Gregory insisted on using a version of the Dewey Decimal System to organize his clients by areas of criminal involvement? Or were those requests more demands—possibly of a sexual nature?

Although I spent almost no significant amount of time with her mother, Emily demonstrated determination and a strong will, positive traits that didn't happen by chance. They were most likely developed and encouraged by a woman with those same qualities—someone like Mary, who sleazy Gregory wouldn't be able to intimidate.

I suspected she'd grown tired of dealing with his lack of character, dropped him, and gone to work for someone else. Except her next assignment included working for Judge Harrison, a man with even less moral fortitude than Gregory. Our guy was willing to pull out all the stops, no matter how disgusting they might be, to win reelection. But was he capable of murder?

After Mary started her work with the judge, all her comments were the same: No problem. Sometimes, when someone says no problem, they mean there were too many problems to mention, so why bother? In Mary's case, her employment had been more than a problem. It became a death sentence.

I was still puzzling over the material, trying to connect dots that weren't there when Anna appeared, hands behind her back.

"I came to make sure you're okay. And I do not come empty handed." She whipped her arm around and dangled a white bag over my desk. My stomach growled when I saw the Sublime Donut logo, a winged donut soaring high. "Two Dulce de leches and two dark chocolates with raspberry filling. Plus, two iced mocha lattes."

"You are the best friend in the entire universe," I said, unwrapping the first pastry I came to, a dark chocolate. I took a bite and moaned. "This is better than sex."

Anna grinned. "You haven't been with my husband. A good thing, as I would have to kill you. But this is a close second."

I finished my donut and washed it down with a sip of latte. "Thanks again for the donuts and for being such a great friend."

"I should be thanking you for giving me an excuse to load up on these delicious calories." She brushed powdered sugar off her jacket and stood. "Take the rest to your beautiful abuela."

Her mention of my grandmother got my attention. I glanced at my watch and was shocked to see it was after six, over ten hours since I checked in on my grandmother and the potentially dangerous guest I dumped in her lap.

I worried that taking Emily to Jams' house hadn't been such a great idea. At the time, I'd been confident the police would never think to search for her there. Only a handful of people were aware of my connection to Mary. And none of them had any reason to suspect I had her daughter stashed at my grandmother's house. Unless someone was following me in a white car.

I grabbed my purse and double-timed it out of the building.

*   *

Emily smiled shyly as she twirled around in the new outfit she and Jams bought on what had turned out to be a massive shopping expedition. The skirt was a floral spray of deep purples, bright pinks, and pale yellows. She paired it with a white peasant blouse and finished it off with Doc Martin boots—a combination that worked only for the young.

She wore her hair in a bun that sat low on her neck. Wisps of dark tendrils framed her face. Without the heavy eyeliner and thick makeup, her resemblance to her mother was uncanny. It was also a reminder she might be in the same danger as Mary.

"Isn't she lovely?" Jams asked when Emily left to change.

"Yes, incredibly beautiful."

She returned wearing slim jeans, a white t-shirt, and a pale peach denim jacket that made her skin glow. Black sandals replaced the Doc Martins.

"Wow. That color is fantastic on you."

"You think so?" she asked. "I thought it might be a little girly for me, but your grandmother said I'd be crazy not to get it."

"She was right. You look great."

"I got two more pairs of jeans, tennis shoes, and some underwear." She smiled and turned to Jams. "If you don't mind, can I use your machine to wash my clothes? Even the clean ones are super wrinkled from being shoved in my backpack."

"Of course. Put them in the laundry room, and I'll do them for you."

"No, you won't. Not after all you've been doing for me." She gave Jams a stern look, then turned toward me. "I made her promise she'd let me pay her back for the clothes and everything as soon as I get a job. And I've been in charge of my own washing and drying since I was a kid, so it's no big deal."

"She's a different girl," I said when she was out of hearing range. "Hope she didn't wear you out."

"Are you kidding? I was up for two more stores when she started complaining about her feet hurting." I believed her because my grandmother's shopping stamina was legendary. "I have to come clean, though," she added.

"Come clean? You're not going to tell me you guys shoplifted all this stuff." I laughed, expecting her to join in. When she stayed solemn, I grew worried. "Please tell me you didn't."

"Don't be silly. It's nothing like that. It's just that, well, all those pretty new things aren't the only reason for Emily's good mood.

Most likely, it has more to do with the young man who went shopping with us. Pierce, Pierce McEvoy."

It took a second to register he was the boy who lent Emily his delivery shirt, to trick our receptionist into giving her the address. The same one the police had questioned about Emily's whereabouts. And if the cops knew about him, who else did?

"Oh, my God, Jams. You let her meet up with a boy from her school? What if the people looking for her have been following him?"

"Hold on, missy. I didn't let Emily do anything. We walked into Abner and Fitch, and there he was. I couldn't tell him to buzz off, now could I?"

"I think you mean Abercrombie and—never mind. I'm sure he is absolutely wonderful, but it's not a good idea for him to be hanging out around Emily."

"Please. I'm not an idiot. I told them this had to be a onetime event. At least, until everything gets settled. But it was such a joy watching them together, seeing her looking so damn happy."

"It's terrific you two are having fun, but you know she can't stay here forever. Sarge is keeping up with her mom's case, but if Emily's telling the truth, she doesn't have anybody. Eventually, she has to go back to school. It may not be safe for her at her old one, which means she'll have to register in a different district. For that, she has to be in state-approved care."

"I'm sure you're right, honey. But we don't have to deal with that now, do we? Can't we just let her enjoy wearing her new clothes and being part of our family for a few more days?"

Being part of our family might not be all Jams was making it out to be, but Emily did seem to be coping. If I was sure having her there wasn't putting Jams in danger, I would have agreed. But I couldn't.

"I wish that was possible."

"Then wish granted." She cut me off. "Unless there's something you're not telling me." She fixed her bullshit detector stare at me.

I squirmed in my seat, searching for a way to tell her I suspected the judge had been involved in Mary's murder and that he could suspect Emily had incriminating information on him, which meant he was coming for her, too.

Jams refused to break eye contact. In about a half a second I would have spilled my guts. But I didn't get the chance.

26

Emily stood in the doorway holding a ten by thirteen-inch envelope. Unlike the first one Mary sent to me, this was packed tight, with two thick rubber bands keeping it together. "I found this in my backpack stuck inside my calculus book. Mom must have put it there."

Her face was as pale as the sheets Jams used to hang out to dry in her backyard. "This has to be what got her killed." Clutching the envelope to her chest, she leaned against the door frame and slid to the floor.

My grandmother jumped up and rushed to her side. She knelt beside Emily, who slumped against the wall. I grabbed a clean dish towel from the counter and ran cold water over it. Then I sat next to them, pressing the cool cloth against Emily's forehead. The poor girl shook so hard I gave up on trying to keep the compress in place. Jams wrapped her arms around her, while I murmured inane assurances that everything would be okay and wondered how long I should wait until I ripped into the packet.

Eventually, she stopped shuddering, and Jams released her. When my grandmother stood, she nudged the envelope, and it slipped from Emily's lap. I swooped it up. On the front, written in the same bold print Mary inscribed on the previous one, were instructions:

If you find this and I'm not around, do NOT open. This does not concern you. Give it to Claire Kincaid.

She included my number and email address.

The message was matter of fact, clinical even. Probably, she hoped to stifle her daughter's curiosity, not provide a foreshadowing of her own death. Regardless, the torn flap proved it hadn't been successful.

I trembled now as I struggled to restrain myself.

"I didn't mean to. Really, I didn't. But since it had to be the last message she wrote, I had to read it. I'm sorry." Braced against the wall, she stood. "But Mom was right. I shouldn't have."

"Why don't you and I sit in here and let Claire go in the den and take a peek for herself?"

I was halfway to the door when Emily spoke, loud and strong now. "No! Please. I've seen the worst or, at least, I hope so. And I have to find out why she had a picture like that."

The way her voice shook when she said like that made me question my eagerness to open the envelope. One of the many areas in which teenage girls can be unpredictable is their definition of and tolerance for grossness. Anything from a bad haircut to attention from an unwanted suitor can be deemed disgusting beyond belief.

Emily seemed too mature to fall into this category. If, however, the photo she'd seen was remotely associated with her mother's sexuality, no level of maturity would protect her from the gross-out factor. But what possible reason would Mary have for including a picture like that in a packet her daughter had access to?

I'd been so caught up in my own thoughts about the nature of the photo, I didn't notice the two of them staring at me, presumably waiting for an answer to Emily's request.

"I guess it's your right to be here. We'll open it together, but only if you agree to let me check out each item first. If the picture is too upsetting or something with legal complications, you don't come near it."

An expression of annoyance or relief flitted across her face. Someone more experienced with adolescents might be able to discern the difference, not me. When she nodded in agreement, I decided it didn't matter.

Jams cleared her throat. "I shouldn't be here while you two do this." She started to stand, but Emily grabbed her forearm.

"Please, stay," she said, then turned to me. "It's okay if she's with us, right? I want—no, I need—her to be here."

I was torn between being touched by how deep the bond between them seemed to be and being fearful that seeing the contents of the envelope would harm my grandmother. It occurred to me I'd done that by bringing Emily to her house.

"You should stay," I said, then added, knowing full well not even wild horses could have dragged her from the room, "unless you feel uncomfortable." I was confident her main motivation for staying by Emily's side came from genuine concern.

But there was more than that. Science doesn't recognize curiosity as a hereditary trait. Yet both my grandmother and I hated being kept in the dark. The ability to ferret out lies served me well in my line of work. In my personal life, however, not so much. For some reason I would explore in the future, I refused to employ my ferreting gift to Rob. If I had, I probably wouldn't have gone out with him at all or, at least, bailed way earlier in our relationship. But where my hitman boyfriend was involved, my skills abandoned me. Or had I been so desperate to be in love, I abandoned them? Now, instead of setting us free, the truth might put us at risk.

"Claire, stop your woolgathering and open the damn envelope," Jams said.

"Sorry. But once we see what's in it, we'll never be able to unsee it. And there may be something in there that other people—maybe not-so-nice people—want to keep secret."

"If they even suspect we can access the information, do you think they'd give two shakes of a hound's tale whether we looked at it or not? We're better off knowing what we're up against." The determination in my grandmother's voice told me it was useless to argue.

I had an inkling of what lay ahead, but why say anything? That would mean explaining the bad guys would be coming for Emily, and we might very well become collateral damage. The time to address those concerns was long past. Jams had welcomed the girl into her life, and now she was ours.

"Okay, then. Let's get started," I said.

Rather than emptying the contents onto the table, I began with the photo that undid Emily. I peeked in, where I discovered the loose picture and the rubber-banded group I presumed it had come from. I slipped my thumb and index finger inside and grabbed them both.

When I dropped them on the table, the offending shot landed face down. I paused to glance at Emily. Her mouth was set in a grim, straight line, but she didn't flinch. I reached forward but froze an inch from the questionable object.

"Oh, for God's sake." Jams pushed my hand away and flipped it over.

It was not a compromising shot of Mary, nor an image of the judge accepting money from a shady thug. Because of the poor lighting and dark background, I squinted to bring it into focus. I was looking at two men—one standing, his silver hair illuminated by a flash that cast light over the outline of a body sprawled on the ground in front of him.

A second glance affirmed my first impression that the upright one was Otis Delmar. The man at his feet faced away from the camera, leaving only his smooth-shaved head visible. I identified a few specific details but remained unable to comprehend the bigger picture. To understand what was going on, I needed to examine it better, but the idea of touching it turned my stomach.

Jams had no such difficulty. She snatched it up and narrowed her eyes.

"I've seen the guy who looks like ten pounds of mud stuffed into a five-pound sack. Wasn't it on TV? Isn't he some big wig with some crazy ass right-wing nut group? But what the hell is he doing?" She removed her readers from the top of her head and slid them onto her nose. "And what's going on with the other guy? Sweet Jesus. Please, tell me he's not—"

"Dead," Emily finished for her.

"Surely not," I said. "Let me see." I reached for the photo, still tightly gripped in Jams' fingers. She studied it again before handing it over.

Like most of the pictures I'd seen involving the judge and Delmar, the quality was poor. With this one, the glare of the flash made it difficult to tell colors other than the snowy white of Delmar's hair and the coal-black of the other's skin.

Rust-colored smudges on that man's torn white t-shirt could have been streaks of Georgia clay, or they could have been blood. A jagged line on the shiny surface of his head might be a scratch or a gash. He was either unconscious, or, like Emily said, dead.

"Maybe the others will give us a better idea." I removed the rest from the packet and arranged them on the table.

None seemed to have any definitive connection to each other. Several featured Delmar schmoozing with an assortment of men I recognized as local politicians. Three of them included Harrison. The locations varied: an outdoor barbeque, an auditorium—possibly from the voting machine photos—a few political events.

One was a rally for our candidate. I cringed at the image of our judge wearing a campaign cap with the words Hang 'Em High emblazoned on the bill. Printed on the front, the judge had replaced a popular western action hero from the seventies with his own cowboy-hatted face. The object dangling from his gnarled fingers was a noose.

My team had not approved this obnoxious piece of swag. As far as I knew, we weren't aware of its existence. And, as Harrison had never tried a capital case, the juxtaposition of him and the noose was as ridiculous as it was grotesquely intimidating.

Overcome with disgust at the judge's weaselly face grinning beside the rope, I didn't notice details of the crowd surrounding him. Emily jolted me from my reverie when she snatched the picture off the table and held it up to the light.

"It's him," she whispered, releasing her grip.

I watched the photo float to the floor and let it lie there a few seconds before bending to pick it up.

"No!" Emily shouted, then more softly, "Please, don't touch it."

Startled by her outburst, I froze in my seat and stared helplessly as she wrapped her arms tightly around her torso and began rocking from side to side.

Jams scooted her chair closer to the girl and squeezed her shoulder. "There, there, honey. Look away if you need to. But please. Who is him?"

Emily shook her head so violently her ponytail whipped across her cheeks.

"Trust me. We won't let anyone hurt you. Please, tell us who you saw, so we can help." I picked up the picture before she could answer.

She stopped rocking but kept her arms wrapped around herself. Keeping her wild, wide eyes on me, she spoke so softly only I could hear.

"You know."

She was right; I recognized the man in the photo. I also understood from her look of terror she was certain he had killed her mother.

It was Rob.

27

Emily's identification of Rob sent her running to her room, where she locked herself in and refused to come out. Jams demanded to be told what the girl whispered to me. I insisted the words had been unintelligible. Of course, she didn't buy it, but her concern won out over her need for the unadulterated truth. After giving me a look of disgust, she hurried to the guestroom. I could hear her pleading with Emily to open the door.

While she was gone, I pocketed the photo that terrified the young girl and thumbed through the rest, hoping to distract my grandmother with another one that would explain Emily's panic without revealing its real source.

I needn't have worried about diverting her attention. When she returned to the kitchen, she opened a cabinet drawer and began rummaging through it.

"Dammit. Where the hell is that screwdriver?"

"What in the world do you need a screwdriver for, right this minute?"

"What do you suppose I plan to do with it? I can't leave her in there all by herself. I'm going to take off the doorknob."

"Are you sure that's a good move? I mean, sometimes girls her age overreact to the strangest things. She needs to process whatever it is she thinks she saw."

Jams narrowed her eyes. "And exactly what is that?"

I handed her a decoy photo featuring a blurred crowd shot. "No idea."

She shoved her reading glasses down and frowned before glancing up.

"See?" I shrugged. "Leave her alone for a bit, and she'll probably calm down enough to explain."

I rose from my seat, grabbed the photos, and stuck them back in my purse.

"I'm going to take another look at these when I get home." Before she had time to ask questions, I kissed her cheek and made a dash for the door.

Preoccupied with coming up with an acceptable excuse for Rob to be in the picture—he had done accounting work for someone at the event, he had attended with a friend, he had wandered in by mistake—I didn't register the rumble of distant thunder as I backed out of the driveway. The problem with all those logical explanations was that the rally took place long after we started dating. If there was an innocent reason for him to be hanging out with fans of the judge when my former fiancé knew how much I hated him, why hadn't he mentioned his being there?

And why was it the men in my life kept showing up in compromising photographs? First, Kevin and the rigged machines; now, Rob in a crowd of Harrison supporters.

Fat, lazy drops of rain spattered my windshield, but when I turned on the wipers, dusty smears clouded my view. I squeezed the washer button, and a weak spray thickened the mess into an oily smudge.

Fearful of running off the road, I checked my mirror. No one behind me, so I slowed to a crawl. An unexpected clap of thunder vibrated throughout the vehicle, followed by lightning that ricocheted off clouds and streaked the night sky with white-hot rivulets of fire.

Wind and rain powerful enough to bring tree branches to their knees cascaded over the front of the car. I slogged through puddles that had become ponds with the depth to sway the car. As I crept along, I sent up several prayers filled with promises to do better if allowed to make it home. Since it wasn't the first instance in which I'd negotiated deals with God, it surprised me when I made it home unscathed.

Torrents of water spewed from overworked drainage pipes into my apartment garage. When I got out of the car, I stepped into a puddle of it, soaking my second-best pair of work flats. I took them off and proceeded barefoot through the nasty flood, which was possibly filled with everything from used needles to jagged metal.

I should have listened to Mom when she reminded me to update my long-expired tetanus shot and wondered if God had spared me from the storm only to take me out with lockjaw. Once inside my apartment, I dropped my purse on the foyer table, then dashed to the half-bath in the hallway. I took a washcloth from under the sink, scrubbed my filthy feet until they turned a deep pink, and dried them with a fancy guest towel, which I tossed in the laundry room on the way to the kitchen.

My stomach rumbled, but I couldn't think of anything I wanted to eat. I opened the refrigerator door and stared into it. Settling on a hunk of Gouda that was only a month past its best-sold-by-date and a Blue Moon, I stood at the sink cutting the cheese into thin slices. After removing an unopened box of gourmet crackers someone had given me in a Christmas basket, I popped the beer cap and swallowed a third of the bottle before I noticed the frantically blinking light on the corner of the counter.

"Shit," I said. Now I would have to reset every freaking clock in the apartment thanks to that stupid storm. Normally, I would have put off the annoying task and used my phone as an alarm for work. Tonight, though, anything that offered a reprieve, however short, from thinking about Rob at the judge's rally was welcome.

I stuck a cheese-laden cracker in my mouth before picking up the flashing cube. A horn bleated from the street below, jolting me so that it slipped out of my hands and slammed onto the granite counter. Something clattered to the floor, but when I examined the face and back, nothing appeared to be broken. So, what had I heard hit the tile?

Kneeling, I scanned the area for a clock-related piece of debris. I located a black plastic object slightly bigger around than a quarter but thinner. I placed it on the counter before examining the clock again for jagged edges. There were none, but there was a sticky substance on the backside of the cube.

I held the dot in the palm of my hand, went to my desk, and opened my laptop. When I searched for small listening devices, I found two similar to the object I discovered. Neither was an exact match, but it seemed more than likely the disk from my clock was in the spying-device family.

It was difficult to believe someone planted the tiny dot to spy on me. Other than frequently talking to myself or bursting into choruses of "Hit Me with Your Best Shot" or "Bad to the Bone," there wasn't much to listen to in my apartment. Even when Rob was staying over, the conversation was pretty ordinary, downright dull. As for sex talk and accompanying sounds, we were a quiet couple. Whoever had been spying on us must have been disappointed.

That led to the question of how the thing had gotten there. Emily proved breaking into my apartment was child's play. But it still didn't make sense why anyone would have wandered through my place looking for the perfect location to plant them.

Unless that person had come under the pretense of ridding my home of a different kind of bugs: the exterminator I hadn't requested.

It was a little after ten, too late to call Sarge. I called him anyway.

Within the hour, he was standing in my foyer.

"I brought some traps, cruelty free," he said in a loud voice, then put a finger to his lips before whispering, "Follow my lead."

I nodded and responded, "Thanks. The little creatures are nasty, but I can't stand the idea of snapping their tiny necks. And that sound. Ugh." Maybe I made a mistake when I abandoned my acting career.

If Sarge was impressed with my mouse monologue, his face didn't show it. He got straight to business. His first step was to examine the little black dot, then pinch it between his thick thumb and forefinger. He held it up to the light for several seconds before easing it back onto the counter beside the clock.

"I see where they're getting in," he said as he opened the sliding glass door to the balcony and motioned for me to join him. Once we were outside, he spoke at a more natural volume.

"Definitely a bug. I don't recognize this specific model, but it looks military. And there's no way that baby is the only one. I'll sweep the place, but we need to talk about what to do once we find them all."

"I know exactly what to do. Yank them out and flush them down the toilet. What else would we do?" The idea someone was listening to my spoken thoughts, to my phone calls with friends and family, was almost worse than not realizing they were there.

"That's one way to go. But if you do that, we might never figure out who put them there or why."

"So, I should leave them?" I shivered at the thought of the continued intrusion, but Sarge was right. If I didn't find out the who and why, how would I ever be comfortable in my own home again?

"Unless we find cameras, too."

"Cameras? Holy shit." I slumped into the mini-size patio chair.

"Yeah, video equipment is a game changer."

He reached into his jacket pocket and removed a cell phone, except it wasn't.

"This sucker is the best RF detector on the market. Not cheap, but you get what you pay for. You ready?"

The plan was for Sarge to sweep the area twice. My assignment was to trail him and jot down the exact location of each bug or— please, God, no—camera. We found a total of five, counting the kitchen clock. Two were in the bases of lamps: one in the living room, one by my bed. The third was in the guest room. There were no cameras.

The one in the spare bedroom reminded me of the night Emily showed up. Everything about the traumatic events in her life had been recorded. Kevin's visit and our conversation about the workshop and Rob—all fodder for some creepy stranger to replay and enjoy.

Unless it wasn't a stranger at all. I thought of all those questions I never answered. Would he have resorted to spying on me to get those answers? And if he killed Mary, didn't that mean he knew where Emily was? But he had easy access to my place. He wouldn't have needed to impersonate an exterminator. And what did it matter anyway? He was dead, or was that what he wanted me to believe?

Regardless, whoever he worked for had to be alive. Rob must have decided not to share Emily's whereabouts with his employer because if he had—

No, he had no reason to suspect I was more than a babysitter for the judge. He could have planned to handle Emily himself and gotten burned up in a car fire before he had the chance. But that seemed too convenient.

That left Kevin as a strong possibility. He'd been looking for Rob and most likely hadn't believed me when I told him I had no idea where he was.

When Sarge was satisfied there were no more listening devices to catalog, we returned to the balcony.

"So when are you gonna tell me what's going on? No way I can protect you if you keep me in the dark."

I was growing more certain Kevin was my eavesdropper and found the idea less worrisome. Whether it was naïveté or stupidity, I didn't think he posed a threat to me. Sarge was right, though. I had to come clean with him.

Except for the part about Mary's envelope—I wanted to check that out myself before I showed it to anyone else—I told him everything. By the time I finished, he and I had gone through a third of my bottle of Maker's Mark. He spoke little during my account, but he jotted down notes in a small spiral notebook. After killing the last of his drink, he stood to stretch. Outlined against the sprawling lights of the city below us, he resembled a comic book hero—one who used his hulking power for good.

"Might not be a bad idea for you to get your grandmother to take the girl on a little trip. Say, the beach or the mountains, just for a week or so."

"That would be a great, only Emily's set on solving her mother's murder. And Jams, well, you know her, right?"

"Tough old bird, that woman."

I winced at the thought of her reaction to being called an *old* anything.

He suggested he get one of his guys to drive by several times a day to watch the house. Then he explained if I left the bugs in place, I could mislead whoever was spying on me.

"You and grandma can set up phone calls saying they're going on a trip. Call me and say you're headed to Bumfuck, Whatever. Keep 'em running in circles."

I hated the idea of remaining a central broadcasting center but acknowledged it would be fun messing with the asshole or assholes spying on me.

And I had enjoyed the experience of baiting eavesdroppers. Singing snippets from *The Sound of Music*—intentionally off-key or possibly on-key since I've never understood the whole key thing. Faking a conversation with Jams talking about where she planned to take Emily. Positioning the blender as close as possible to the clock bug and loading it up with ice before pressing the liquify button. Running the vacuum by the light in the guest room over and over. Blasting cable news into the device in the living room lamp.

But it was also extremely tiring. After the second chorus of "My Favorite Things," I moved the show to the bathroom. Although Sarge had assured me there were no hidden cameras in the apartment, I took the quickest shower of my life, then tugged my gown over my towel-draped body.

Despite my exhaustion, I discovered sleeping next to a listening device has its drawbacks. Every time I closed my eyes, the image of some featureless thug with headphones loomed over me. Like a reverse of the Cheshire Cat, who fades until only his grin remains, the star of my private horror show gained facial characteristics. A rustle of sheets drew raised eyebrows on his doughy face. The thud of my fist into my lumpy pillow teased narrow-set eyes into existence. An unexpected edge-of-sleep-snort opened and extended a slit of lips into a sneer. An exhalation of my breath brought about the eruption of a piggy snout. Before I could visualize that nose trying to sniff my scent through the airwaves, I jerked upright and turned on the light.

On my way to the living room, I snatched the comforter off my bed and grabbed a towel from the bathroom. I draped it around the base of the lamp and pushed the couch as far away from it as possible. Wrapped in the blanket, I dropped onto the sofa, fluffing the fattest of my many decorative pillows. Although I knew the bath towel wouldn't do much to muffle the transmission of my sleep sounds, it had a calming psychological effect on me. When I closed my eyes, my night stalker didn't appear, and I fell into a dreamless black hole.

28

On the way to work, I checked in with Jams.

"I'm fine," she said. "Worried about Emily, that's all. I coaxed her out of her room and fixed her a bagel with peanut butter like she wanted. How on God's green earth she can eat that unholy combination is anybody's guess, but at least she's eating. When I asked her why the picture got under her skin so bad, she gave me that epic shrug of hers and stuffed a cookie in her mouth."

I exhaled, glad Emily kept her suspicion about Rob being a killer to herself. Despite my relief, I wondered why she hadn't shared that detail. Was she questioning herself or planning her own form of revenge—one she didn't want my grandmother involved in or me to know about?

Stop overthinking everything, I warned myself.

"She insists she's okay," Jams continued. "But I don't buy it. Not much I can do until she decides to tell me what's going on. Unless you're holding back on me."

Thankful we weren't face to face, I said, "Hey, I'm as in the dark as you are." My lie contained a kernel of truth. While I knew more than my grandmother, I remained clueless as to how it all fit together.

"Right. Anyway, Emily is about to die waiting to see what you found out. So, did you check out the rest of that stuff?"

"Something came up, and I didn't get a chance to examine all of it. I've got it with me. I'll go over it at the office."

I expected her to ask me what happened and should have been pleased when she didn't. Oddly, her preoccupation with her house guest hurt a little.

True to my word, I began sifting through the contents of the envelope as soon as I reached work. I ignored the photos and removed a stapled packet of bank statements.

"You look like you could use a cup of coffee." Lisa startled me and I dropped the papers onto my desk before turning toward the door with a wild raccoon-in-the-headlights expression.

"On second thought, maybe coffee's not the best idea. Are you okay?"

I stuffed everything back into the envelope. "I'm fine, thanks. You're right about the caffeine. I've had three cups already. Imagine what I'd be like if I had anymore. Come, sit. I could use the company." My invitation for her to join me was more about delaying my foray into the contents of Mary's evidence than the desire for companionship.

She eyed me with an expression I took as either curiosity about my furtive behavior or concern over how dreadful I looked.

"If you're sick, I can cover for you."

Concern seemed to have trumped curiosity, which made me feel better.

"I appreciate the offer. But I'm okay. Just went a few rounds with a bout of insomnia. I lost. Anything new on the judge?"

"He wants to meet later this week to talk about how we'll spin Margolin's murder. That's a phrase I never thought I'd be using."

"Me neither." I considered telling her the whole story but decided it was bad enough that I might have put Sarge and my grandmother in danger. No reason to add Lisa to the list.

"Well, I don't have the faintest idea how we're going to make it look like Margolin's death wasn't good news for the judge. Can we steer clear of the subject altogether? Better yet, let's get Harrison to issue a statement asking for the election to be postponed."

"And give somebody else a chance to throw their hat in the ring? We are talking about the same Judge Harrison, right?"

She laughed, and we spent a few minutes chatting about inconsequential stuff. When she left, I realized she hadn't asked about Rob, which wasn't unusual. We shared a tacit agreement not to get too much into our personal lives. What should have been odd was that I hadn't told anyone about the burned-out car and the person inside it. Was reluctance the same as denial, the first stage in the grieving process? If I didn't say it out loud, that body would belong to someone else.

Hiding from reality wasn't my style. Instead of ignoring a crappy situation or trying to wish it away, I go with it. Only how could I accept his death when my senses told me he was alive? Our relationship might not have been perfect, but we'd been together long enough for me to have some internal indicator he was gone— an emptiness in my heart, a crack in my soul.

Possibly this lack of emotional connection resulted from the frequency of his out-of-town trips. I was used to his being away and, despite the message he sent explaining he wouldn't be coming back, I hadn't dealt with the finality of his departure. Definitely final if I was wrong and he died in the car fire.

That reminded me of a bigger issue. My disbelief in Rob's death should have brought some level of comfort. He might have intentionally abandoned me, but where there's life, there's hope.

Except it wasn't hopefulness residing on the edge of my consciousness. It was a darker sensation, like dread or fear.

Emily's insistence Rob killed her mother was a good reason for my fearfulness. But how much substance should I put in a terrified young girl's judgment, one who had witnessed her Mom gunned down in an alley?

And even if I accepted her version of events that the man I once planned to marry would want to hurt me didn't compute. The real murderer, however, would be obliged to tie up loose ends, and Emily was the loosest one of all.

I removed the bank statements. Instead of finding Mary's name at the top of the first page, I was surprised to discover the account belonged to the Wade Harrison Election committee.

After thumbing through them, I learned the paperwork dated back six months. A few pages were crooked, as if they were hastily printed copies. If Mary made them in the judge's office, she had to realize the risk involved in smuggling them out. That raised the question of what she considered important enough to place herself in such jeopardy.

Someone, most likely Mary, had highlighted lines and scribbled notes in the margins. I jotted down the names of people and companies and carefully copied the notations, many of which were dates and times that made no sense to me. Several of them sounded familiar. I added asterisks by those, planning to run searches on them later.

The first such entry was a contribution of $3,000 from neither a name nor a corporation, just a set of initials: RDR, now expanded to RDR and Associates. Scanning through the pages, I found three more from the mystery company. The notation *OD 9/28*, in what looked like Mary's handwriting, was by a check written and deposited two days later. Delmar's association with RDR was too much of a coincidence for me not to assume her OD was the same man. I added a reminder to have Lisa track down where Delmar and Harrison had been on that date.

Below the 9/28 message, another payment to Temp of the Town was inscribed with *Financing for project* in parentheses by it. I jotted down the info on my growing list with a note to talk to Sarge about his progress identifying the owner of the agency.

I suspected there might be issues with campaign donations, but I lacked the experience to deal with bank records and understand financial violations.

I didn't miss the irony of my situation: I needed a forensic accountant to investigate my forensic accountant's possible involvement in a murder. Unfortunately, mine was missing or dead.

Anna was an option since she often dealt with people whose sloppy record keeping put their reputations and possibly their freedom in jeopardy. But if I consulted with my friend, I would have to give her information that might endanger her. Even with her help, the task of sorting out all the asterisks and cryptic notations, combined with my regular workload—clients to contact, prep for the dreaded meeting with the judge—would be overwhelming.

Desperate for a way to farm out some of it, I took a mental inventory of possible resources. I'd asked too much of Sarge. And I didn't want to put Lisa at any more risk. We assigned overflow work to the receptionist but giving her instructions without revealing the significance of the job would take more time than doing it myself.

Jams and Emily were eager to help. My grandmother was hell on wheels when it came to online research, and Emily might shed light on her mother's notes. But the image of her collapsed on the floor after seeing Rob made me question the wisdom of involving her. I did, however, want to talk to her alone to ask why she hadn't shared our secret. If I skipped lunch, I could catch up and leave early enough to get there before dinner.

I reached a stopping point at a little after four—emails answered, an agenda for the meeting with the judge set, proposals for two new clients ready to submit. Normally, I take work home, but I planned to dedicate the evening to Mary's case. The photos and bank statements weren't the only pieces of evidence in the envelope. My obsession with closure, however, dictated I tackle one item at a time. The pictures didn't count since we could only speculate on their relevance. Wading through the documents might provide enough clarification to solidify our speculations over wrongdoings.

It struck me that having an extra copy would be a smart idea, so I spent the next half hour lining up page after page of records and photos for the Xerox machine.

After securing the material in a sealed envelope, I stuck it in the small safe in my office, then texted Lisa to let her know I was leaving early. I put the original copies, interesting oxymoron, in my briefcase and headed to the parking deck. I was the only one in the elevator, and although it made sense because of my irregular departure time, it felt weird. The eeriness transformed into an uneasiness as I passed rows of quiet, empty cars.

Shadows of larger vehicles spotlighted by the position of overhead lights increased the creep factor. "Don't be ridiculous," I whispered to myself. "No one even knows you've got the stuff."

If I were lucky, nobody else had a clue the copied paperwork existed. Mary didn't strike me as being careless. Despite her caution, someone considered her a big enough threat to murder her. Had the envelope I carried been the killer's motivation?

I was unaware of the evidence Mary left behind before I discovered someone had turned my apartment into broadcast central. Of course, I helped hide the person most likely to have had that information, the victim's daughter.

I unlocked the car and tossed my bag in the back. A flicker of movement outside the passenger side startled me. Seconds later, the door flew open, and somebody hopped into the seat.

A scream caught in my throat as a hand clutched my wrist.

"We need to talk." The voice was barely a whisper, but I had no trouble recognizing who it belonged to.

29

"You're starting to piss me off." I snatched my arm from his grasp. "And don't bother apologizing."

He did it anyway, then insisted what he had to say was crucial to my safety. I agreed to hear him out.

"I've been looking into the death of Mary Saunders." He paused. "Were you aware she had a daughter?"

I tried not to show surprise or any other emotion. My first question was about the reason for his interest in Mary, but I bit it back for fear the answer would connect Rob to her murder and confirm Emily's identification. He might even guess I was hiding her. So, I remained silent, and he resumed his story.

"This girl, Emily, may have witnessed the shooting. If so, she has important information for the police, possibly a description of the killer. Whether she saw the shooter isn't the issue. What matters is if he got a look at her. If he did, she and anyone who's with her could be in serious danger."

I stared at the car parked across from me, trying to decide how much to tell Kevin. Even if Rob was dead, whoever hired him could still be after the damning evidence on Delmar and the judge. It would be a relief to have someone more qualified than a PR person and a senior citizen to secure Emily's safety.

"Surely, the police are searching for her."

"They went to her school, talked to her teachers and some of her friends. One of them, a kid named Pierce, said Emily had borrowed a shirt from the delivery service he worked for, but he claims he didn't ask why and has no idea where she is now. I thought maybe your investigator..." He took his cell phone from his pocket and scrolled through it. "Here it is, Alberto Alphonsi. My guess is he turned up something on the girl, might have learned where she is."

"If Mr. Alphonsi has information that should be shared with the authorities, I'm positive he would do so."

"Not before sharing it with you first. And that's what I propose he did: He found her and told you where she is."

"I can assure you he did not find the girl and has nothing to add about her current location." Instead of guilt over my deceitfulness, I experienced a pleasant jolt of self-righteousness. I might be misleading, or as Mom would say, *lying by omission*—which, according to her, was the same as outright lying. Technically, however, I was telling the truth. No one found Emily. She came to me. And, since I reached the conclusion there was no reason I should trust Kevin, I had no intention of sharing that information.

"Why is this poor girl so important to you? Aren't you investigating industrial espionage? Unless you haven't been telling me the whole truth."

"All I can say is I did work for the FBI for ten years. These days I'm more of a consultant. I wish I could give you more, but I promise, once the case is settled, I'll tell you everything I know."

"For God's sake." I slapped the steering wheel. I wanted to shout that I already discovered the FBI's supposition Rob was a contract killer but held back to see if Kevin would volunteer the truth. "After the way you weaseled into my life, you owe me more than that *once the case is settled* crap. The least you can do is explain the real reason you're investigating Rob. And do not give me that bullshit about classified information going missing."

"I'll say this much. The FBI suspects Evans of stealing data but not for the usual reasons. He isn't selling secrets to competing companies or dealing in intellectual property. The government maintains he's been breaking into systems to target specific individuals. Mary Saunders was one of them. Three other names surfaced: two of them are dead; one's missing. They don't see any of it as coincidental."

"When you say FBI, are you including yourself? Never mind. It doesn't matter. So, the FBI thinks Rob killed Mary and the others?"

"They consider him the main suspect in the murders."

"Weren't you convinced Rob was in the car when it burned? So, what's the big deal?" My stomach dropped. "Are you saying it wasn't him? Why? Has someone seen him?" My voice rose in what should have been excitement that my fiancé might be alive, but it wasn't. It was panic.

"Nothing like that. I've just got one of those brain itches like when something's off, but you can't scratch it away. I shouldn't have said anything since it's still too early to tell." He reached for my hand but stopped before making contact, and what should have been relief became disappointment. "Regardless, we want to find out who Rob or another unknown suspect worked for when he carried out the killings."

His nonchalant delivery gave the statement an uncomfortable ordinariness. Carrying out killing could have been picking apples, as in who were you working for when you were carrying out the apple picking. Or whose taxes were you preparing or any number of ordinary everyday things. Murder made mundane.

"Are you okay?"

"I'm fine. I just need a little time to process."

"Take as long as you want." He gave me a light pat on my shoulder.

"I get what you're saying about finding out who paid for the killer's services." I unintentionally mimicked his matter-of-fact tone by referring to the act of shooting someone the same way I would when talking about writing copy or shining shoes. "But that doesn't explain why you've been following me."

I'd never seen his car, but it made sense. The white sedan had been my unwelcome escort off and on shortly after I met Kevin.

"Someone's been following you? Because it wasn't me. Scout's honor." He held up the three-fingered salute before his expression darkened. "But if somebody's tailing you, it could be a problem. What kind of car is it?"

"You go first. What do you drive?"

"A brown Ford Escape. Now you show me yours." His open grin reminded me of our trust fall and the gentle way he held me before yanking his hand away, leaving me at the mercy of gravity.

"It doesn't matter." I attempted to quash the warmth of that memory. If he had been the one behind the wheel of the white car, it would be easy for him to lie. After all, I warned myself, the man was a natural liar. "But this is important. You said they're working on identifying the body in Rob's car."

"They are. But when we confirm who it is, we can't be certain if he was the guy pretending to be Rob Evans."

"Which means we might never be sure if he's dead."

"The FBI is good, Claire. It may take a while, but they won't quit until they solve it. And when they do, I'll give you your answers. You have to believe I couldn't be cruel enough to leave you in the dark."

"Why should I trust you?"

"Because the last thing I want is to see you get hurt more than you already have." He covered my hand with both of his, and for a moment, I believed him.

Then I remembered those bugs scattered around my apartment. Initially, I suspected Rob, but while Kevin might not have planted them himself, it was more than a little possible he'd been involved. And his presence in the sketchy voting photo loomed over us.

So, when he asked me if I would swear to him that I had no clue where Emily was, I swore to him I didn't. He raised his eyebrows and told me to call him if I found out anything about Emily's whereabouts. I promised I would.

There was no guilty twinge, nor did my earlier self-righteous glow return. I refused to rationalize my actions. And there was no equivocation about whether I'd mislead him about the past because it made no difference. I had committed to lying to him in the future.

I drove out of the parking deck and checked my rear-view mirror to make sure there was no white sedan or brown Escape behind me. Then I relived my encounter with Kevin. I reminded myself of his lies and deceptions and how he tricked me from the very beginning. With casual cruelty, he set out to gain my trust with his stupid stories about his difficult relationship with family. And that whole nice-guy routine. Pretending he cared about me when all he wanted was for me to help him gather evidence on Rob.

While I didn't regret my decision to treat him with distrust, I had trouble accepting that everything he'd done had been part of an act. Or was I setting myself up for another kick from that damn mule? Regardless, to stay focused on finding the people behind Mary's death while keeping her daughter safe, I had to put aside my conflicting emotions about Kevin.

I made it to Jams' without an escort and stumbled from the car as quickly as possible. I tried to steady my shaking hands, but when I reached for my purse, the strap slipped from my hand, and everything dumped onto the floor behind the driver's seat. I crawled into the back and scrambled around, tossing lipstick, pens, hairbrush, a screwdriver, a notepad, a mini high beam flashlight, and grocery coupons into my bag. The envelope landed upside down, but if anything had fallen out, I couldn't tell. I tucked it away, then used the flashlight to check under the front seat for something I might have missed.

So small I almost didn't see it, a rectangular-shaped device not much bigger than a quarter was caught between the middle compartment and the driver's side. It was too far back to reach with my fingertips, but I dislodged it with a pen.

Turning it over in the palm of my hand, my first thought was that it was another bug. But it didn't look anything like the ones Sarge removed from my apartment. It reminded me of a mini flash drive, so I put it in my pants pocket and darted up the walkway.

Jams and Emily were seated at the kitchen table with a carton of butter pecan ice cream between them.

"Hey, there, honey. Pull up a spoon and dig in. This is my side. And that's Emily's. You can start in the middle."

Shafts of afternoon sunlight settled into the lines of her face. Seeing her there brought back all the times we'd sat at that table, the two of us sharing ice cream straight from the carton. Had those creases been there last year? The year before? How had I not noticed? But I knew the answer. Acknowledging their presence was the same as admitting my grandmother had fewer days ahead of her than behind. So, I refused to see them, not unlike the way I ignored the warning signs in my relationship with Rob.

Despite having skipped lunch, I wasn't particularly hungry. Nevertheless, I grabbed a spoon and dug in—as much from the need to slow the passing of time as from my love of butter pecan.

"Get this. Miss Emily here has never, ever had pecan ice cream?" Jams gave *pecan* the deep South treatment: *pee-can*.

"Pee-can," Emily repeated and giggled. The same sunlight that exposed my grandmother's mortality made the girl look even younger as it flickered across her face.

"Hells bells," my grandmother moaned, scrunching her eyes shut. "Ice headache." She dropped her spoon and pressed her fingertips against her temples. "Hate those sonsabitches."

Emily laughed again, then shoveled in a few more spoonsful. "No more." She sighed and slid the carton to me.

"Me neither." I took another bite before closing it up and sticking it back in the freezer.

I wanted to extend the cheerfulness only ice cream can bring and rejoined them at the table. We chatted about normal things for the next few minutes: a celebrity breakup that shocked Emily to her core—Jams and I hadn't heard of either member of the couple but faked outrage anyway; a recipe for lemon cookies; Mom's two calls asking when would be a good time for us to meet and the way Jams stalled her both times.

As much as I wanted to hold on to the comfort of our normalcy, eventually, we had to return to trying to make sense of our new reality. I sensed there was a direct correlation between the documents Vera had given me, the bizarre photos, and the reason Mary had been killed. I also had a strong feeling Petit and his fancy agency might be the key to connecting the dots.

"Emily, you said you weren't sure where your mom had been working, but does Temp of the Town ring a bell?"

"Maybe, but like I told you, we hadn't been spending of a lot of time together. And when we did, we ended up arguing."

The light in her eyes from our butter pecan moment disappeared. I glanced at Jams, whose upturned lips morphed into a thin grim line. I'd succeeded in destroying the mood only to confirm Emily knew nothing about Temp of the Town. Feeling like the world's biggest party pooper, I remembered the tiny object I discovered and removed it from my pocket.

"I found this when I accidentally emptied out my purse in the car. It must have slipped out of the envelope with the pictures. I've never seen one this small, but it looks like a miniature flash drive. What do you think?"

Emily brushed a strand of hair off her forehead and held out her hand. "Wow. Pierce had one of these. They're pricey for what they are. Hold on and I'll get my laptop."

She returned and inserted it. I worried that what we were about to see would put us all in greater danger, then decided simply having possession of the damn thing would be a threat to Harrison or Rob or Delmar or all three of them. Not to mention the trouble we could face by hiding information from the FBI.

The video opened with another blurry crowd shot of what looked like the same group we'd seen in the photo. After a few seconds of background noise, the images began to come into focus, and I held my breath. If Rob was front and center in this one, there was no way Jams wouldn't recognize him.

Luckily, the videographer zoomed in on the two men from the picture. Party lanterns hung from trees, casting beams of light that bounced off the judge's bald head. Delmar leaned in close to the judge's ear. Whatever he said sent them both into gales of laughter. Their joviality was unsettling, chilling, even.

"Can you turn up the sound?" Jams asked.

Emily shook her head. "It's as high as it goes."

The camera panned to the right where heavily muscled men were holding on to a struggling man. A dark hood covered his head. Delmar and Harrison entered the frame, and the thugs who held the man looked expectantly at the grinning duo.

Delmar nodded and one of them yanked off the covering, revealing a young black man—more a boy—wearing a white t-shirt splattered with the same rust-colored spots we'd seen in the earlier photo, only this time I would have bet my life the stains had nothing to do with red Georgia clay.

The judge stuck his hand in his pocket. When he removed it, he offered up a tight fist to Delmar, whose face split with an evil clown grin. Harrison opened his palm and tossed a coin in the air. It landed on the ground, and they stared at it before the judge broke into an Irish-style jig.

The screen flickered before coming back into a close-up of the two buddies, who looked much less jubilant than before. The camera tilted down to the young man lying motionless in front of them. Then the scene faded to black.

We sat for a long time, staring at the space where the horror had played. The video clarified the ambiguity of the previous picture. The unnatural angle of the boy's neck was the main clue. Whatever had happened between the coin toss and the final shot resulted in death.

30

Jams spoke first, startling me with the sound of her voice. "Who in the world is that poor kid?"

As usual, my grandmother dove deeper into her thought process. While I'd been trying to restore order to my muddled mind, hoping to build a case against the judge, she'd gone straight to the human aspect. Somewhere there was a mother wondering why her son wasn't answering his texts or hadn't come home for dinner. Where I focused on bringing the men down, Jams worried about comforting the people who would soon be grieving.

Before I could tell her I would get Sarge to run a local search for missing persons, she commandeered Emily's laptop.

"The bridge ladies and I went to one of those author talks at the library. I can't remember her name off the top of my head, but she was a mystery writer." Jams continued to type while she talked. "I bought her book. It's pretty good. Anyway, she talked about how she got the idea for her story by looking at missing persons cases. She gave us some websites that list people who've disappeared by location and length of time they've been gone."

Despite the grim mood, I was impressed with my grandmother's skills. But I had other pressing issues on my mind. Like what we should do with the video and who might come knocking down our door looking for it.

"Before you start, we need to talk more about what we saw on the drive. I think it's time we got the police involved." Detective Atkins was the likely choice, but if I delivered the file to her, it would mean exposing Emily. They would keep her physically safe, but it was her emotional state that worried me.

If I expected resistance from my grandmother, I didn't get it. She simply removed her glasses, closed her eyes, and rubbed her temples.

Emily chewed a thumbnail and stared into space.

"Any thoughts on the best way to do that?" I coaxed.

"You mean without having the cops haul me away?"

"Nobody is hauling anyone away. Right, Claire?" Jams put her hand on Emily's shoulder.

"Of course not."

But that was what they would do when they discovered where she was. Unless we got the video to them anonymously. Sending it through the mail would take too long. I might be able to drop it at the station but not without being caught on camera. Even if we successfully snuck it in, it was after eight, which meant Atkins had probably gone home. And she was the one I wanted to see it first.

"The only way they won't put me in foster care is if I'm not here. I can hide out at a friend's for a few days."

I suspected the friend was Pierce and started to explain the police were aware of their friendship. They might even be watching his house. And if they weren't, somebody else could be—someone like Rob. So, going to his place was out. But that didn't mean Pierce was.

"Emily, did you say he worked for a package delivery service?"

"For a few months, why?"

"And that shirt he lent you. It wasn't the only one he has, was it?"

"I'm pretty sure he kept at least three. But how does this help?" She slapped her palm to her forehead, then said, "I get it. Pierce can deliver it for us."

"See, I told you Claire would come up with something."

I didn't remember Jams saying any such thing and, from the puzzled look on her face, neither did Emily. If she registered our expressions, she ignored them. "You girls work out the plan while I check out the missing persons lists."

We decided it would be better to ask Pierce to take the video to Atkins's home but didn't have the address. I interrupted Jams to find out if she had any ideas. She began a search on the detective. There were newspaper articles celebrating promotions and commendations but nothing of a personal nature. Then Emily came across a picture of Atkins with her husband and a daughter who had a different last name.

She checked Facebook and found the girl. After scanning through a multitude of photographs featuring her in too many places to count—none of them standing in front of a clearly marked mailbox captioned *This is where I live*—she employed another tactic. She messaged her.

Hey, this is Emily. It's been a while, but I'm in town for a few days. Let's catch up. Also want to pay back the money I owe you. Are you and your mom still living in that apartment on Auburn Avenue?

"Do you expect her to say you've got the wrong person and give you her address?" I asked.

"She might."

Although I seriously doubted it, I didn't voice my opinion. Instead, I stared at the screen along with her before asking Jams if she was having any luck finding information on Regina's husband.

"I found a few mentions of him on Google but nothing with his address. I'm still looking."

The computer pinged, and I snapped my head toward the sound.

"She answered." She clicked on the message.

Sorry, Em. You've got the wrong girl. I've never lived any place but good old Lilac Lane in Atlanta.

Emily thanked Regina's daughter. Then we shared a high-five.

Before we asked, Jams ran the street name through a site that provided estimates of property values.

"And here it is," she shouted.

Next, we spent the better part of an hour on the phone with Pierce coordinating the best way to get the video to him without alerting anyone who might be watching his movements. He explained he was at the CVS where he worked and suggested I stop by there. I could buy a candy bar or something and slip the flash drive to him when I paid. Then he'd go home, pick up the shirt, and head to his friend Brent's house to change. They would swap shirts and cars. Pierce would make the delivery, return to Brent's, and unswap.

I wasn't keen on involving yet another teenager, but both Emily and Pierce insisted Brent was chill.

"We're on," Pierce said. "Should we synchronize watches or some cool shit like that?"

I assured him we did not need to synchronize anything and wondered if I'd made the right choice bringing in a James Bond wannabe. If the boy even knew who Bond was.

"Okay." He sighed. "But what about a code word, so I'll know who you are? Or what if you wear a hat and a bright red scarf or something cool like that?"

He sounded so disappointed about the watch I agreed a code word was an excellent idea but suggested we keep it simple. I proposed we use *Emily.* He worried someone might hear her name and be on to us and insisted on a more exotic choice: hummingbird or Jacksonville or patio.

We compromised with *night,* as in *It's a nice night, isn't it?*

I repeated the importance of his not being seen when he delivered the drive.

He replied, "Duh," and asked Emily to take us off speaker.

While they chatted about whatever it is teenagers talk about, I gathered my things in preparation for the CVS run.

"I found him," Jams whispered.

"Him?" In the flurry of activity around Project Pierce Delivery, I'd forgotten about the poor kid pictured with Delmar and the judge. "Oh, him."

Emily finished her conversation and joined me, where I stood looking over my grandmother's shoulder at a photo of a boy in full football attire. Below the picture, the caption read: *Missing high school student Tanner Alexander.*

"Of course, there's no way to be sure, but the day he disappeared lines up with the timing of the video."

The brief article described a bright young man who was not only a stellar athlete with a full scholarship to UGA but also a talented actor who had racked up credits from roles in several movies shot in Georgia. It ended with agonizing pleas from his family, begging anyone who knew anything about the boy's disappearance to contact the police.

"I'll make sure Pierce gets this to Atkins, too." I opened a kitchen drawer, removed a sticky note, and wrote his name on it. Then I wrapped it around the tiny drive.

I asked Emily for a description, even though he was supposed to be the only one at the register. She showed me a picture, and I gave her instructions to text me as soon as Pierce made the delivery.

"Call me if anything goes wrong—anything at all. No matter what time."

They both promised.

"Okay, then. It looks as if all we can do now is wait," I said, and Jams walked me down the hallway.

"I don't like leaving you alone like this, but someone could be watching me. We need to behave as normally as possible."

She stepped over to the closet door and stood on tiptoe to retrieve a long leather case from the top shelf. Grandpa Walter's shotgun.

"I've always hated having this damn thing around, but I swore I'd keep it for protection. Sweet man is still looking after us."

She put the weapon on the floor and took down a box.

"Ammunition."

31

Pepper spray in hand, I unlocked my apartment door and eased my way inside. I stepped into the foyer and held my breath, waiting for the sound of footsteps. It had only been a little over a week, but it seemed like years since I entered my home without fear. I wondered if I would ever do it again.

After walking through each room, turning on every light in the place, I assessed the conditions and decided I was safe. I grabbed a carton of yogurt from the refrigerator and ate it standing in front of the sink.

My encounter with Pierce had been smooth. When I arrived with the disk clutched in my fist, the aisles were empty except for a gray-haired lady at prescription pickup and a few blue-vested employees. I spotted a tall, slender boy with clear skin and dark blonde hair at the counter and walked close enough to check out the *dreamy brown eyes* Emily told me to look for. Unsure if a teenage girl and an almost thirty-something year-old woman would agree on the definition of dreamy, I confirmed his identity by reading his name tag, and his eyes were pretty darn dreamy.

I didn't hear her describe me to Pierce, but she must have done a good job because when he saw me, those eyes widened, and his mouth fell open. After giving him my most reassuring smile, I surveyed the candy display and selected a giant Kit Kat bar.

"It's a nice night, isn't it?" I asked.

"Yeah, uh, sure." He stumbled over the words and shifted from one foot to the other, reminding me of an anxious gazelle about to take flight. But he stood his ground, cutting his eyes to the left, then right before pivoting his entire body to the rear and back around. "Now," he whispered between clenched teeth.

I cupped my hands over the disk wrapped in the sticky note, dropped it on the counter, then covered it with the candy bar. I kept smiling as I slid it across to him. His eyes continued their frantic left-right survey of the room as he scooted the chocolate to the scanner and palmed the tiny package.

I paid up and thanked him for his help. He grunted, then nodded. Once again, I worried he might not be up to the task of delivering the drive, but it was too late for doubts. And he was our best, maybe our only, bet.

Around four in the morning, I gave up on sleep. Planning to catch up on several much-neglected projects, I made my way to the shower, dressed, and headed to the office. By six, I sat at my desk drinking a second cup of black coffee, trying to concentrate on our latest client: a local school board member who wanted to rebrand himself after homophobic comments from a private meeting were leaked on Facebook. I doubted he would lose any of his shit-kicker supporters but enjoyed making a list of suggestions that might help to restore his good name: host a PRIDE party; submit a request to be on *Queer Eye for the Straight Guy*; winter in Key West.

In between my useless effort to rehabilitate the man, I checked for a text from Emily on Pierce's progress. A little after seven, my phone pinged.

The eagle has landed. LOL. Jams told me to put that in, so you'd know everything was okay.

I replied with two smiley faces and three thumbs up before returning to my errant board member. I debated whether to send my recommendations for salvaging his reputation to him when my phone rang. I didn't recognize the number.

"Yes," I answered with my coldest *If you're selling, I'm not buying* voice.

"This is Sheriff Joe Jankowski of the Chagrin Falls Police Department. This is a return call for Claire Kincaid."

"This is she. I appreciate your getting back to me."

"I understand you called with information on the Evans accident."

"I'm not sure information is the right word." I explained my connection to the case and that I wanted to find out if Peter Thornwall might be my Rob Evans.

"Afraid I can't help you with that. The FBI stopped by last week. They took over the investigation. Guess there's no reason not to share what I've got. It's been years, but I could never get that poor fella out of my mind. He'd be close to forty now. It was my first case. Damn near drove me crazy. We never came up with anything solid on Thornwall, but there was something funny about that guy.

"He was a classmate of Evans. One of the folks we interviewed said they had a run-in before graduation, but nobody would talk. Either they didn't know, or they were afraid of Thornwall. I still remember interviewing him. A real cool customer, showed no emotion at all. Just answered my questions with a smile on his face. Like he was sure we had nothing on him. We traced the other car to its owner, who told us it had been stolen the day of the wreck.

"Eventually, it turned up abandoned on the side of a back road. It had been wiped clean. Thornwall disappeared about a month after the accident. My chief said good riddance, that he was somebody else's problem. I'm guessing you might be that somebody else."

Rob's cold smile came to mind, and I shivered. "I might be."

"I'm not surprised. I had a feeling he'd turn up again."

"Can you tell me what he looked like?"

"Sorry, but he was average looking. A little under six feet, brown hair. I'll never forget his eyes, though. Dark, no emotion. If the eyes are supposed to be windows to the soul, his house was empty."

I thought of all the times I gazed into those eyes, searching for something, anything, that might give me a clue what lay behind them. I looked for confirmation of his love, sadness for the loss of his parents, happiness at being with me. Every time, I came away as empty as the sheriff's description painted them.

Without commenting on his assessment of my ex-fiancé, I told him the authorities suspected he was dead but were having trouble making an identification. I said I thought that was the reason the FBI requisitioned the files.

"The Feebs aren't so good at sharing, but if I had to guess, I'd say you're right."

I thanked him for his time and information, even though he hadn't been able to give me any solid leads.

"Wish I could help you more. But I can tell you this. If your guy is Thornwall, I wouldn't put anything past him. I'd advise you to stay clear of him."

I didn't bother to explain the obvious: What we had was a case of trying to close the barn door after the horses got loose.

Instead of formalizing my list to our homophobic client, I did the next best thing. I sent the info to Lisa with instructions to log into the Twitter account the agency had set up for him and launch a pro-tolerance campaign. I might not get his blubbery butt to a PRIDE parade, but I could make sure he encouraged others to attend.

She responded immediately with a meme of Batman twerking with Robin.

Satisfied the client was in good hands, I texted Jams and Emily to confirm they were okay, then turned to Google to search for Peter Thornwall, Chagrin Falls and found a Peter Zachariah Thornwall who died at the age of eighty-two in 2001. I was still looking when my news alert sounded.

Lisa and I both kept a running list of clients and their associates on our notification setting so that whenever their names popped up on breaking updates, we would find out fast.

This one had picked up on an item regarding Otis Delmar's arrest for questioning about the disappearance of a local high school student. There was a closing reference to his being under investigation in connection with faulty voting equipment.

Pierce's delivery had been successful, and Atkins got right on it. The mention of those booths had to tie in with the photograph Kevin was in, suggesting it was possible my ex-trust-fall partner might have been the one doing the investigating.

There was nothing about Harrison, but the notice was brief. There would be plenty of time for reporters to expand on it. When they did, I fully expected it would include details that the police had hauled our ferret-faced judge in to share a cell with Delmar because that old saying about there being no honor among thieves was even more accurate when applied to thieving politicians.

I picked up my phone to call Sarge, but before I had a chance, he and Lisa came barreling into my office.

"Did you hear?" She dropped into a chair. "My sweet Lord, Mellie, I think I've got the vapors." She did her best Scarlett O'Hara imitation, while he leaned against the filing cabinets.

"If you're talking about good old Otis, I just read he'd been picked up in connection to the missing football player. They didn't mention our judge, though."

I rolled over to my mini fridge, grabbed two bottles of water, and passed them out. Lisa opened hers immediately and drank a third of it in one long swallow.

Sarge said, "Rumor around the courthouse is that Harrison has gone missing. That shitass must have gotten wind the cops were on to him and took off. Man like him—somebody used to people doing everything he tells them to—won't get far on his own."

The idea the judge might escape punishment enraged me. But Sarge was right. The only way he could outrun the law would be on a private jet, and he didn't own one. With all the money he'd been funneling into his campaign, his finances indicated he would barely have enough cash on hand to rent one. That meant he couldn't afford to fly to any upscale non-extradition countries.

"Has anybody checked to see if Reynolds knows?" I asked.

They both shook their heads, then Lisa volunteered. "I want to break it to him. Since you said he should get rid of Harrison, it might be too tempting for you to say I told you so. Coming. from me, as in *Claire told you so*, might not sting as badly."

We both knew it wouldn't matter who delivered the news. Reynolds would freak out and chaos would reign until the next scandal hit the papers. The upside was that the only person who would have to listen to Harrison rant and rave would be his cellmate. Unless he somehow weaseled out of prison. In that case, I would have to keep Emily from going after him.

Thoughts of the young girl reminded me I needed to check in with my grandmother. With the judge on hold, we were at a slow point, except for the unpleasant school board member. Lisa told me she'd emailed suggestions for his Twitter account and was in the process of setting him up with some easy interviews on a Christian radio station.

"There's no rush on that," I told her. "It won't hurt to let our guy sweat it out for a bit. How about you, Sarge? Anything juicy to report?"

"Not sure if I'd call it that, but my buddy verified the photos were taken by the same device. I'm guessing it was the Saunders woman and taking them is what got her killed."

"I agree. Too bad that's not enough to have the cops to look into it."

"I may have something that could help get us closer to having some hard evidence. I've been digging for info on that temp agency. And guess who two of the silent partners are?"

"You don't mean—"

"Yep. I do. Our good old buddies Delmar and Harrison."

32

Sarge's news about the temp agency increased my anxiety about the safety of Emily and Jams. The video offered powerful evidence Delmar and Harrison were involved with the boy's disappearance, but they might be able to explain it away. Emily was the link between Harrison and Rob. The judge was smart enough to realize that and dangerous enough to do something to shut her up.

When Sarge and Lisa left my office, I cleared my desk and headed out. My anxiousness about Harrison worried me more than ever about the possibility I was being followed, so I remained on the lookout.

"What if the judge hired someone with a different car to follow me?" I muttered, then slapped the steering wheel. Why the hell did I have to go there? Now I would stay on high alert for any suspicious vehicle to make sure I didn't lead anyone directly to Jams and Emily.

I sped past the exit to my grandmother's home. Nobody rode close behind me, but I stayed in the middle lane until the next one was in sight. Then I zipped to the right, without using my blinker, and whipped off the expressway.

After heading in the opposite direction from Jams' house, I meandered through unfamiliar neighborhoods, periodically checking my rear-view mirror. Gradually, I reversed my course. When I'd driven for fifteen minutes without a tail, I decided to head to my destination.

I slowed to make the final turn, my grandmother's house within sight, and realized things were far from okay. On the curb near her driveway in broad daylight sat a white sedan.

Fear should have been my immediate reaction, but my first emotion was relief because Kevin told the truth when he swore he hadn't been following me. Then came the fear.

I parked a few houses down and took out my phone, keeping the motor running. I considered dialing 911 or the police, but what would I tell them?

There's this white car outside my grandmother's house, and I have a bad feeling about it.

Most likely, they would explain my situation didn't qualify as an emergency and hang up. And if they somehow took me seriously and sent someone to check it out, they could discover we were harboring a runaway. I wasn't ready to do that, not only because of the damage it would do to the grieving teen but also the danger it might put her in if the judge found out where they placed her.

Besides genuinely caring for Emily, I had to factor in Jams. My grandmother wrapped the girl in love and drew her into both her home and heart. And Emily, unless she was an incredible actress, enjoyed the warmth of being loved by her.

If there was a hostage situation going on inside my house, one in which the driver of the white car wanted to hurt me, not my family, the police might make things worse.

An image of Jams holding intruders at bay with Walter's ancient shotgun added to my concern about involving the authorities. From a distance, the cops might not be able to tell the difference between my gun-toting grandmother and the bad guys.

Sarge was another possibility, but if I called him, he would urge me to call the police. That led me back to my original conundrum.

There was one person who knew the story—not the part about me hiding a key witness at my grandmother's house—but enough to find a way to keep everyone safe. I opened my contacts and tapped on his number.

Kevin answered on the first ring. "Claire, is everything all right?"

"I don't know. The car that's been following me is here now," I whispered, even though I remained too far from the house for anyone to hear me.

"Are you at your apartment?"

"No, outside my grandmother's." I gave him the address although I suspected he already had it.

"I'm on the way. Should be there in less than ten. You stay put. I mean it, Claire. Don't go in."

I wasn't surprised he didn't suggest I call the police. From the little knowledge I possessed—mostly gleaned from the movies—federal law enforcement had a superiority complex when it came to their local counterparts.

While I waited, I remembered Emily's assertion Rob shot her mother. I fought against the notion my then fiancé was a cold-blooded killer. I lost that fight. Now the realization of what he was capable of became more terrifying because it increased the likelihood he would come back for the girl.

That threat would be eliminated if he were dead, as the police and Kevin seemed to believe. I refused to accept that premise. Whether it was a gut feeling or perverse wishful thinking, I didn't think Rob died in a car fire. That conviction relieved some of my fear. If the authorities were correct, he had been enjoying a successful career as a hitman for years. So, why would a professional killer risk everything to return to kill a terrified young girl whose testimony might easily be challenged?

My theory was both better and worse. Better because it didn't involve Emily being next on the hit list, worse because it meant I'd been sleeping with a sociopath. And not only that. My sociopath had been working for another sociopath. In my scenario, someone hired Rob to get rid of Mary because she discovered something damaging to some very powerful people and that it went beyond politics. I imagined the contract included destroying any evidence she had gathered, which put him in a difficult situation.

He'd taken care of Mary but hadn't been able to complete the transaction. It was obvious I was no expert on the man, but it made sense that someone as cold and thorough as Rob would be a perfectionist when it came to his work. Failure to finish the job would ruin his reputation as a professional killer, and that would matter to him. But keeping his freedom would trump accomplishing his mission. A person with his taste and style would not thrive in an orange jumpsuit and a roommate named Bubba.

My guess, supported by Rob's farewell email, was that he decided to disappear. The best way to vanish would be to fake his own death. A fiery death, where it would be nearly impossible to identify the victim would be an excellent choice. Even if the authorities determined who died in the crash, it would be a lengthy process, giving him enough time to be long gone. It would also provide the chance to take care of the business of Emily.

The curtain in the guest room fluttered, and I slumped down to avoid detection. An unnecessary move considering my darkened windows and the distance to the house. I stayed low and peered out the window. Another flutter and a glimpse of the young girl's face. She appeared and vanished so quickly I wondered what she might be looking for. Was it my car? Did she want to warn me? Or was she only admiring the scenery?

It had been at least five minutes since I'd spoken to Kevin, which meant I only had to sit tight a little longer. But something stopped Emily from completing whatever brought her to the window. And if that had put her in danger, I didn't have the luxury of staying still.

I kept my head down as I opened the door and eased out, then squat-waddled around the car. Sprinting for the neighbor's backyard, I hoped their dog wouldn't sound the alarm. There was no reason to worry, though, because Jams had been right about the neighbors moving. Mounds of trash spilled from the back porch onto the dead grass, creating a makeshift obstacle course that slowed my approach. I skirted by a dilapidated kitchen chair, almost tripping on a rusty saw blade, handle end up like some demon-plant straight from hell. I dashed past the sad little pen, now empty except for a plastic bowl coated with grime.

Once on Jams' property, I scurried low to the ground from one azalea bush to another. The last few steps to the basement were in the open, so I bolted from my flowered cover. When I reached the door, I flattened myself against the house. The windows Grandpa Walter kept spotless were covered in grunge. I used my sleeve to wipe off enough dirt and cobwebs to get a look inside.

When I was little, I loved playing down there. I hid behind furniture with foreign-sounding names like chifforobe and armoire, pretending to be a princess fleeing from an evil king. Most of those pieces were gone, victims of Mom's ongoing campaigns for Jams to purge before moving. I couldn't remember the last time I'd been in the cement-floor room. I also had no idea if the spare key was still hidden underneath the jolly fat gnome Walter had bought when they broke ground on their garden.

The statue was there, not so jolly anymore with his peeling paint and cracked cap but still fat and much heavier than I expected. I pushed him aside and had to scrape off several layers of mud before locating the rusty key. I jiggled it into the lock and maneuvered it around, unsure if it would work. When it clicked, I turned the knob and opened the door a third of the way before it landed against something solid. I might squeeze through if I pried it halfway, but less than that would be doubtful. I leaned my back against it and braced my feet on the bottom of the gnome and shoved hard. It gave a few inches. So, I sucked in my stomach and went for it.

After several harrowing seconds of fearing I'd done permanent damage to both boobs, I squeezed through, banging my knees against the bookcase that blocked my entry. Squelching a shriek of pain, I backed into the room and waited for my eyes to adjust to the dark.

Mom had been right when she'd said *nothing hates a vacuum more than Nature and your grandmother.* Jams replaced the missing furniture with an assortment of clutter: a porch swing with a broken chain, an upside-down two-legged stool, the mirror that had graced the vanity set of Jams' mother, and a multitude of mysterious items draped with dusty sheets.

I picked my way through and around the discarded treasures, still holding the key. Dad had urged Jams to change the locks for years, or at the very least, install a bolt lock for the inside door. Both Mom and I agreed the place needed tighter security. Now, climbing the wooden stairs to the interior door, I hoped Jams had ignored us. I inserted the key and sighed in relief when it worked.

After cracking it a few inches, I held my breath and listened. This entryway opened onto the hall leading to the garage. When I didn't hear a sound from the nearby kitchen, I tiptoed inside. I dropped to all fours and crawled to the cabinet under the sink where Jams kept the roach and ant spray. I grabbed the can, scrambled to the wall, and pressed against it. Sitting as still as possible with a mega-dose of adrenaline coursing through my body, I strained to hear the voices coming from within. I identified Jams. The other was a man's. He spoke too softly for me to be sure, but it wasn't Rob.

I stayed in a half crouch, bobbed toward the den, and eased to my knees, craning my neck. Whatever I might have imagined to see, it would never have been Jams on the sofa with her back to me, her head leaning against the shoulder of a man with silvery gray hair. Not the posture of someone being held against her will. But knowing how easy it could be to be taken in by a psycho, I kept my guard up.

Holding the canister with both hands, I rushed from the corner to face them and shouted, "Let go of my grandmother or I'll shoot."

Jams jerked her head upright and pushed away from her seatmate. "Holy mother of God, Claire. You scared the bejesus out of me."

Her stunned companion blinked behind gold-framed glasses. A memory struggled to swim its way through the hazy waters of my mind as I took in the salt and pepper hair. It was longer, and he was dressed in casual slacks and a short-sleeved polo, but that didn't stop his identity from surfacing. He was the man at the restaurant where Kevin and I had eaten, the one I thought had been waving at me from across the room.

"Honey, put down that damn bug spray. There's someone I want you to meet."

When he stood, the lens of his glasses magnified greenish-gold irises. I could see my own eyes reflected in those lenses. His full lips relaxed into a smile, and I reacted immediately with a grin of my own.

"Claire, this is Frank Edgerton. He's your grandfather."

My first thought was that the mild-mannered-looking man next to Jams didn't appear to be a vicious white supremacist. My second was why was my grandmother sitting so close to any type of white supremacist.

"Hello, Claire," he extended his hand. "I've wanted to meet you for a very long time."

Like my smile, extending my own was an automatic reaction. The weightlessness of our combined hands surprised me. It was as if together we were somehow lighter. I didn't break the grasp.

"Your grandfather and I have a lot to tell you. But first, how about something to drink?"

Before I could request tea, not bourbon, the doorbell rang, reminding me of Kevin and my promise to stay in the car.

"I'll get it," I half-shouted before bolting from the room. I planned to take him aside and explain I'd been mistaken. That it was an old friend of the family who'd dropped in unexpectedly and that I was sorry to have dragged him out for nothing.

I might have pulled it off, too, except in my haste to beat Jams to the door, I failed to notice my new granddaddy trailing behind me.

"Kevin." I took a step toward him.

"What the hell are you doing here?" he responded.

"I know I was supposed to stay in the car, but—"

"I think he means me." Although his voice was soft, it resonated with authority. Then Frank Edgerton stepped past me and said, "Good to see you again, Mark. It's been quite a while."

33

Less than an hour later, we were still sorting out the situation. Kevin's real name was Mark Parrish. He used Kevin Thomas when he did investigative work, like pretending to be an expert in catching hackers. His background in computer fraud and industrial espionage served him well during his time with the FBI, until two years ago when he started his own consulting firm, which frequently assisted the bureau.

Grandfather Frank, as I referred to him in my head, had also been with the agency. He and Mark worked together on several cases.

"What about Woodstock?" I interrupted. "I mean, uh, it seemed to me that, um." I searched for a polite way to accuse my new granddaddy of being a member of a racist organization.

My grandmother came to my rescue. "I got that all wrong." She turned to Frank and squeezed his arm. "I should never have doubted you."

"It's not your fault. I'm the one who involved you, who had to lie to you. But you were just so damn irresistible." He took her hand and pressed it to his lips.

From his moony-eyed expression, I saw he still found it impossible to resist her charms. The blush spreading up her throat and across her cheeks made it clear she enjoyed her continued status of irresistibility.

"I couldn't tell your grandmother about my undercover assignment. We spent months trying to infiltrate the Gloves and longer to determine what they had planned for the festival. The day we met, I was supposed to be scouting the area for a black kid to take the fall for shooting Hendrix. I discovered we were out of luck in that department. There may have been a few at the start, but most were gone pretty quick. Didn't matter since I never intended to follow through with the plan."

"Wait a minute," I interrupted. "Are you saying the Gloves were going to shoot Jimi Hendrix? And frame a *black* man?"

"Yes, but that's not exactly what they wanted. They were there to create chaos. In their tiny little minds, making it look like an African American killed him would cast doubt among the black activists. And all the ruckus would give them time to get away before the cops arrived. Part of the scheme included having members standing on the outskirts firing random shots into the crowd to keep the pandemonium going. I know it sounds insane, but the Ivory Gloves weren't the sharpest tools in the shed."

He continued his story, explaining the FBI had other undercover agents shadowing specific individuals. The second they saw any sign of weapons they would spring into action, arresting everybody on arms charges.

"While I wandered around pretending to be searching for a victim, I came across a bevy of dancing girls. A lot of them were pretty, even if they were muddy and stoned. But none compared to Sarah. She took my breath away."

For a moment, I blanked when he said Jams' name. Not that I forgot it. More like I failed to reconcile my funny, irreverent grandmother cavorting with hippies and captivating a handsome stranger.

"And you're still a smooth-tongued devil." She flushed with obvious pleasure. "But these kids don't need all the details. Suffice it to say, we hit it off real well."

The legend of the rocking van from the annals of my family's origin confirmed that they had indeed hit it off well.

"I spent as much time with your grandmother as possible, but I couldn't have her close when Hendrix took the stage. So, when she fell asleep, I slipped away."

He explained the original schedule had the musician playing Sunday night. But rain delays and other complications threw everything off. The supremacist group found out Jimi might not go on until Monday morning and aborted the mission.

"I went looking for your grandmother to explain why I came to the concert without blowing my cover. But we got our signals crossed."

"Frank's being gracious. Truth is I'm the reason things didn't work out. I woke up and saw him sneaking out of the van and thought he'd run out to meet up with another girl, so I followed him."

Instead of two-timing her, Jams discovered—or thought she had, anyway—the boy she'd fallen so hard for was a member of an extremist group. She overheard them discussing how they might still find a way for Frank to kill Hendrix. Terrified and heart-broken, she fled back to the van and insisted she and Nichole leave at once.

"I couldn't break away until late Monday morning. By then, Sarah had disappeared. I knew her name and that she was from a small town in Georgia and nothing else. Since we failed to catch the Gloves in the act, I had to stay under. It took over a year to track her down. And when I found her, well…"

"Walter and I were married."

Shortly after the girls returned home, Nichole's mom decided the life of a country girl didn't suit her. She and her daughter relocated to Atlanta. Jams had been so naïve she didn't understand her condition until they'd been gone a month. Rather than tell her parents, she took a bus to the Andersons, who had been happy to take her in.

Over in Macon, her mom and dad were frantic. Suspecting she might be with Nichole, they asked Walter, a childhood friend of their daughter, if he would venture to the big city and bring her home. He had wanted to be more than friends for a very long time and put aside his shock about finding the woman he'd loved since kindergarten great with child. He didn't hesitate, nor did he ask questions. He professed his love on the spot and begged her to marry him. After several weeks of Walter's persistence, Jams agreed. Walter found a job in Atlanta, and they stayed there for over a year after my mother was born.

"Janis was a tiny little thing, so we fudged on her date of birth. When she started school *early*, we let them believe our girl was a genius."

"Speaking of Mom, does she know about, uh…" I tilted my head in Frank's direction.

"Not yet. We meant to invite everyone over later. Then you came tearing in trying to exterminate us."

Frank patted her shoulder. "She worries because she loves you, right Claire? And who can blame her? I tried to let go of your grandmother, but I never got her out of my heart. I kept track of her, telling myself I just wanted to make sure she was okay. It wasn't until Facebook came around and I saw pictures of Janis that I started getting suspicious. I did some digging and figured it out. I called years ago and again this week, but—"

"But I was too pig-headed to listen to him."

"You had good reasons not to talk to me."

The phone call that sent Jams into a barrage of full-on swearing must have been from Frank. I swallowed hard as I watched the two of them. Were they silently mourning all the lost time between them or quietly celebrating their future together? Either way, I was close to bursting into tears.

"And I might have given up if not for Mark." He smiled at the man formerly known as Kevin. "We worked some pretty long hours driving around the country. I ended up telling him all about your grandmother—not all, but enough that when he got assigned to this case, he made the connection you were the granddaughter from my story. That's why I came to Atlanta. It's the reason I've been following you for the past few months. To protect you from Rob Evans."

Meeting my biological grandfather—Walter's face would always be the one I associated with Grandpa—had driven thoughts of Emily's plight out of my mind. But when Kevin-Mark suggested we celebrate our reunion with a drink, Jams and I looked at each other at the same time.

"Emily," we said in unison.

Mark's eyebrows shot up, and I immediately regretted our outburst.

"So, she is here after all."

I sighed, then gave him the sternest look I could muster. "Yes, she is here. And she is too fragile for you to be grilling her before you ship her off to some place where no one will understand what she's going through and where she'll run away anyway because she won't trust anyone and—"

"Whoa." He held up his hand. "What kind of person do you think I am? I would never *grill* a fifteen-year-old girl. And the FBI has no interest in sending her to a foster home. They're concerned with making sure their key witness to a murder stays alive. And your grandmother's home won't meet their qualifications for a safehouse—no offense intended, Mrs. Davis,"

"None taken, young man."

"I only want to ask her a few questions before we discuss how to provide adequate security," Mark said.

"I'd be happy to stay over with the girls. On the sofa, of course." Frank smiled at Jams, who had turned a deep shade of pink. "What about posting some men outside?"

"My boss would probably go for that, but I need to talk to the girl first."

"Normally, I wouldn't trust you, but this time I have witnesses. So, I suppose that would be all right. I'll get her."

Emily's door wasn't fully closed. I tapped lighted, but it opened on its own.

"Honey, are you awake?"

She didn't respond, so I entered. A gentle breeze floated through the curtains. The same window where she stood while I kept watch on the curb was now open. But she was gone.

34

We texted Pierce to see if he had any idea where Emily was, but he didn't answer. I prayed that meant the two were together. The buzzing of my phone dashed that hope.

"I just got your text," he said. "I haven't seen Em since the mall. Has something happened to her? Because if somebody hurt her, I'll—"

"I'm sure she's fine," I interrupted. "If you hear from her, let us know, and we'll do the same."

I stared at Jams, who sat pale-faced beside Frank. He kept his arm around her, occasionally whispering in her ear.

Then I watched Mark pull the same spiral notebook out of the same jacket as he'd done before but almost didn't recognize him. Not only had his name changed. His entire demeanor was different. He exuded a relaxed confidence in the face of the panic Jams and I showed. I resented him for deceiving me, and I had accepted the actions I'd taken for genuine interest were part of his plan to extract information from me, but I admired his calm self-control as he flipped through the pages of his notes.

"Here it is. Pierce McEvoy, 2530 Peacock Trail. Sometimes people remember more when you talk to them face-to-face." He looked directly at me. "Don't worry. I promise I won't *grill* the kid."

"I've got it covered," Frank said. "The girls and I will stay hunkered down until you contact us."

The idea of hunkering down with Jams and her long-lost love was not the least bit appealing to me. I suspected it was even less appealing to them. But I agreed.

"I'll be in touch as soon as I find her." Mark stood.

"Claire, why don't you walk our guest to the door?" Jams suggested, smiling as if it were a tea party breaking up. My look of annoyance went unnoticed as she stargazed into Frank's eyes.

I stepped in front of Mark and led the way without speaking.

He stopped in the doorway. When he began talking, I stared at the floor.

"I know you think I'm the worst kind of asshole. A liar who tricked you to get information, but it's not true. The part about me lying, well, that's true. But I cared about a lot more than just finding out what you knew." He placed an index finger on my chin and gently tilted it upward. "I still do."

I closed my eyes, unsure whether to be relieved or disappointed when the kiss didn't come. When I opened them, I watched him walk away.

I leaned against the dark wood, trying to sort out my feelings. I hadn't gotten far when my cell buzzed from inside my jacket. It was Emily.

Before I greeted her, she began speaking.

"Claire, I need you to meet me at your office. And bring Mom's envelope with you."

"Slow down, sweetie. We don't have to go there. You can come home. No one is going to put you in foster care."

She didn't respond, and I feared she'd decided not to trust me.

"Please, Emily. All we want to do is keep you safe."

I heard what could have been muffled laughter in the background and waited. When the response finally came, it wasn't from Emily. "Oh, Claire. I'd say it's entirely too late for that." It was Rob.

"Come on, come on." I drummed my fingers on the steering wheel and craned my neck. A long line of cars, trucks, and SUVs stretched far into the distance ahead of me. A quick look in my rear-view mirror confirmed the situation was as bad behind.

"What the hell are you doing?" I asked myself. Then I thought of the shriek of pain after Rob insisted I come alone.

"If you hurt her," I'd hissed into the phone. He stopped me with his laughter.

"What exactly will you do if I hurt her?" His question was followed by another cry from Emily.

"Stop it, please. I'll be there as soon as I can."

"That's what I love about you. You're so pliable. But enough sweet talk. All I want is that envelope and the video. Bring them and don't tell anyone where you're going. Follow my instructions and nobody has to get hurt."

I didn't buy his reassurance for a minute. So, I checked under the bathroom sink for some debilitating cleaning products. I shoved a canister of super-hold Oh So Beautiful hairspray and a spray bottle of ammonia-based shower cleaner into the canvas overnight bag I'd left at Jams. Hopefully, Rob would take it for an over-sized purse. That he would assume a woman as useless as me would blindly follow instructions.

I debated telling Jams and Frank I needed to go to the office, but slipping out without alerting them made more sense. The way they were looking at each other, I suspected it would be quite some time before they noticed I was gone.

Then I texted Mark—I still had trouble calling him that. I gave him an abbreviated account of the situation, emphasizing Rob's demand that I come alone.

The car in front of me crawled a few feet before stopping. At this rate, I was afraid Rob would start getting antsy.

"Call Emily," I commanded Siri and reached her voicemail. "I'm on my way, but traffic is terrible. I'll get there as fast as I can."

I imagined Rob's face as he listened to my message, a look I had finally determined meant he was irritated: a slight scowl between his eyebrows and the compression of his lips into a straight line. It usually passed so quickly it had been difficult to interpret its significance. It might not pass so quickly at the news of my delay. I'd never seen him lose control, but I'd never really seen him at all.

Jams' ringtone startled me; I started to answer, then wondered what I would say when she asked why I left without telling her goodbye. I could say I was going to pick up Emily, but that would only lead to more questions I would have to respond with half-truths and lies. I let it go.

Traffic began a slow roll. At this snail's pace, it could take another forty-five minutes for me to get to the office. How long would it be before Rob—?

I didn't want to think about what he might do when his patience ran out.

My cell chirped and Kevin's name popped up on the screen.

"Where are you?" he asked.

"Stuck in traffic," I said, even though I was now close to hitting the speed limit and would reach the office at least ten minutes under my estimated time. "What about you?"

"Same as you. Must have been a serious accident somewhere, but I'm getting off at the next exit. If the back roads aren't clogged up, I should be at your building in half an hour according to Google maps. I'll meet you on the second-floor parking deck. And whatever you do, do not go in without me. Do you understand?"

"Got it." I didn't tell him it looked as if traffic was clearing up in both directions. As long as it kept moving, I would be there in time to see Rob before Mark arrived. Because, despite everything, I believed I was the only one who might get through to him.

I took the corner too fast and announced my appearance with squealing tires. Other than a few scattered vehicles, the area was empty. I backed into a spot, then reached for my phone to text Rob. I planned to give myself enough time alone with him without having too much of a gap until Mark joined us, in case I was wrong about being able to cajole him into letting us go.

Before I finished my message, the phone chirped. Emily's name came on the screen.

"Where the fuck are you?"

Rather than offend me, the profanity sent a shock wave of terror over me. Always in control of his emotions, he never let loose with the hard stuff. Originally, I took his priggish attitude toward cursing as a result of a strict upbringing. Now I understood it came from his lack of interest. He hadn't been invested in anything—including me—enough to lose his cool. But that had changed, and I doubted it was a positive development for me or Emily. I gave up on having a civilized conversation. Nor could I wait for Mark. I had to get to the girl before Rob became more unpredictable.

"I just got here. I'm on my way up now." I dumped the contents of my bag on the passenger seat. Then I stuck my cans of makeshift self-defense spray along with Mary's envelope back inside. The canisters clanked together when I picked up the satchel, so I slipped it on my shoulder and tucked it between my elbow and side.

In the elevator I rehearsed how the scene should go. I would give him the documents, photos, and video with one hand, grab the hairspray with the other, and blast him in the face. Emily and I would race down the stairs while he flailed around the office, writhing in pain.

After all he'd put me through, the writhing part sounded especially good.

If she wasn't there, or he had her tied up or handcuffed to my desk, I would improvise. Maybe empty the cleaner in his face, then hit him with the hairspray and hope he stayed in place long enough for me to free her or for Mark to arrive.

The closer I got to my floor, the less confident I was about relying on aerosol products to take down a killer, not one as angry as Rob. Stepping from the elevator, I saw the reception area was dark. Even on weekends and holidays, management left the space partially lit. Switches had to be manually adjusted to turn off all the lights.

My hands shook as I inserted my key into the double glass doors. Within seconds of opening them, a slight glow from the hallway transformed the seating arrangement into shadowy mounds—perfect spots for Rob to crouch behind. Expecting he might pounce any second, I stayed far from the sinister shapes, which caused me to knock my shin against the corner of the reception desk. I stifled a cry and stood there, trying to regain my composure.

He hadn't specified where he would be waiting for me. I assumed it would be my office. I forced myself to walk forward at a steady pace. Once I reached the passage to the interior, I leaned against the wall and waited for my eyes to adjust to the increasing darkness. Creeping down the corridor past closed doors, I hit a dead end at the entrance to the conference room, then turned right toward my office. The blinds were drawn, but a slice of light escaped from underneath the frame.

Despite my comfort flats, my legs wobbled the way they had when I was little and tried to walk in Mom's high heels. Then, nothing had seemed more wonderful than the prospect of being all grown up—doing what I wanted, when I wanted to do it.

As Jams would say, "What a load of horseshit." Because here I was, all grown up, having to do the last thing in the world I wanted to do: face the crazy person I had planned to marry.

I hesitated as I reached for the knob. Should I tap lightly to announce my presence or barge right in? What the hell was the protocol for going head-to-head with a professional hitman? Screw it. I wasn't about to knock on my own damn door. I pushed it open.

"Finally," Rob said, taking my arm and pulling me inside. "Now we can get this party started."

Without releasing his hold, he jabbed me in the back with what felt exactly the way I imagined a gun would feel.

"Sit," he commanded. Only when I was securely seated at my desk did he loosen his grip and turn away from me. "You," he motioned with what was, indeed, a gun. "Move over there so I can see you."

Emily rose from the corner where she'd been sitting. Her hair hung in thick tangles over her shoulders, and she was unnaturally pale, but she appeared uninjured.

"Are you okay?" I called out, halfway rising from my chair.

"Did I tell you to get up?" His playful tone chilled me more than his earlier outburst had.

I no longer had any hope of reaching him. The weapon he pointed in my direction emphasized that point. I dropped into my seat.

"That's it. There's my Claire. We were worried you weren't going to show, weren't we, Emily?"

Fearful she would say something to cause him to erupt, I held my breath. When she didn't respond, I exhaled in relief, then feared her silence might provoke him. But his only reaction was to glance at his watch, one identical to the scorched version Kevin showed me— found on the body in the burned-out car.

"I wish we had more time to play, but I have an appointment with a very unpleasant judge. Seems he's in a hurry to leave town and wants me to bring him all the evidence in case he doesn't get far enough for them to drag him back. Well, what he doesn't know won't hurt him, until it does."

I trembled at the sound of Rob's low-throated laugh, a sound unlike any I ever heard from him. Not that I'd heard many outbursts of joy where he was concerned: a few chuckles from time to time, a derisive snort. But really let go and howl with hilarity? Never. Now I understood why. His idea of amusement involved someone else's pain.

"That slug is the reason we're here. Cheap bastard. Oopsie. Sorry for the language, ladies. Anyway, the tightfisted moron hired me to make sure he won the election. Wanted me to level some threats here and there. Then that sick perv got me into his stupid campaign kick-off. They were going to have one of those absurd reenactments or some shit like that to fire up all those old white fools. He and Delmar paid that black kid to play the part of a runaway slave. Nobody was supposed to get hurt, but the boy panicked when all those crazy suckers started chasing him. When they couldn't find him, Harrison insisted I track him down. When I found him, the situation escalated, and he took a nasty fall. Broke his neck."

He shrugged as if the boy's death was merely an annoyance, a fly touching down on a ham sandwich. He moved closer to Emily. "That thing with your mother wasn't personal. I wouldn't have had to get rough with her if she'd just turned over the documents and photos. Hell, we didn't even know she had the video. Harrison got wind of that from some cop he pays for information. God, I hate amateurs." He sighed and sat on the leather chair in front of us.

She stared at him with an intensity that frightened me.

"So why do you need the recording if the cops already have it?"

"I could ask how you know what they have isn't the original, but that would be silly, wouldn't it? A copy might not stand up in court. It could have been manipulated or faked. We've got to have the real deal, the one you've got, I'm guessing." He nodded toward my bag.

Please don't let him look inside, I prayed. Thankfully, he was too wrapped up in his dramatic monologue to check it out.

"Taking out the immediate threat would have been enough for most people but not for Harrison. No, he said the job wouldn't be complete until he destroyed everything your mom had on him. Insisted I bug your apartment. And you were a naughty girl, weren't you? Practically panting over that Kevin dude when you were supposed to be all mine. Other than being a shameless flirt, you were basically clueless."

He paused to shake a finger in my direction. I clenched my fists and forced myself to remain quiet despite my indignation over both his intrusion in my life and his insult about my intelligence.

He gave me a humorless smile and continued. "When I couldn't get my hands on what the judge wanted, I did the next best thing. I took out his opponent. And do you know what that ungrateful miscreant did?"

He looked at me as if expecting an answer. When I didn't offer one, he provided his own. "The smug jackass used some very inappropriate language to express his displeasure at the initiative I'd taken and refused to pay me until I brought him the envelope your mother had. He had the nerve to say he would take steps to ruin my reputation unless I complied, as if anyone who matters would listen to him. But I am a professional, and I hate loose ends almost more than I despise the judge. So, I agreed to meet him, deliver the evidence, and hang out. I'll stay until he transfers the funds to my account. And then, guess what I'm going to do?"

He looked from one of us to the other. "Here's a hint: I think you'll really like it quite a bit, Claire."

I had a sick feeling I knew what he intended to do. An even sicker one that he might be right—that I would like it.

"No guesses? You ladies are no fun at all. After the money transfer goes through, I'm going to shoot Judge Harrison in his empty old head."

Hearing it out loud, I realized I didn't like it so much after all.

"Are you sure that's such a good idea? Do you think he set up the meeting in a place he could ambush you when you get there?" It didn't matter to me who got shot, but if Mark arrived in time, I wanted to be able to tell him the judge's location.

"Why Claire, that's so sweet of you after all I put you through. You've always been loyal, one of your best qualities. Unfortunately, your foolish innocence leads you to trust the wrong people. Don't worry about me. I picked the place. You'll appreciate my choice. It's in an abandoned building less than two blocks from where they found my poor dead body. Ironic isn't it? I'll start my new life where I ended my old one."

I wasn't sure that was irony, but it didn't seem like the time to offer a tutorial on literary terms. "Okay, but if it wasn't you, who was in that car?"

"Just a guy I knew. Someone I used to work with." He waved his hand dismissively, and I wondered if it was the "friend" he introduced me to.

"Isn't it crazy, Claire? You and I have been working for the same person. Remember when you described yourself as a fixer? At the time I thought it was one of the more insipid things you'd said since you clearly didn't grasp what a fixer must be capable of. Later, I found it amusing. There you were complaining about having to deal with low-rent characters like our judge while you were sleeping with me. Hilarious, wouldn't you say?"

In another setting, I might have seen the humor, however dark, but being referred to as "insipid" pissed me off. I didn't trust myself to answer and feigned indifference with a shrug. My lack of interest had no effect on his enthusiasm.

"The more I learned about your job—covering up for the judge, painting him as a good man, hiding his racism—the more I realized you actually were something of a fixer. I even saw a little of myself in you. Of course, I'm more up front about my profession."

The safe response would be to nod and appease him until Mark showed up. But I'd had enough. It might have been the smug smile on his face when he suggested we were alike that caused me to forget a psycho with a gun held me captive. Or was it the flicker of doubt I felt at the thought he could be onto something in his assessment of my character? I didn't consider myself on the psycho level, but I had to question what kind of person would keep working for a man like Harrison.

"How dare you suggest you and I have anything in common," I hissed. "We're nothing alike. Yes, I have a shitty job that turned out to be entirely different from what I expected. Staying in it has been a bad move for my career and my soul. But it's nothing compared to my horrible decision to be with you. I mistook cold-blooded indifference for stoicism and strength. I couldn't accept I loved someone—no, some *thing*—more reptilian than human. Someone batshit crazy."

The expression that crossed his face made me miss the smug smile. He narrowed his eyes and set his mouth in a straight, lipless line.

"There's no need to be crude. But you always were a bit rough." He lunged across the desk and slammed both hands down hard. I jumped but refused to back away.

"Frankly, your entire family is a bunch of crass rednecks. And that blathering old fool Jams is the worst. What kind of name is that for a grandmother? I suppose it fits her primitive nature. All that with her countrified bits of down-home wisdom. I can't tell you how many times—"

Rather than complete his tirade, he emitted a howl of pain, startling both of us. Him because the business end of my Hathor letter opener pinned his right hand to the desk; me because thrusting the goddess of destruction into that hand had been such an automatic reaction to his criticism of Jams I didn't realize I'd done it until he began screaming.

His cry of pain devolved into a stream of extremely crass language as he tried to free himself. Although Hathor was tougher than she looked, it wouldn't take him long to break loose. I reached into the canvas bag and grabbed a canister, popped the top, and sprayed his eyes with Oh So Beautiful.

"You bitch," he shrieked. "I'm going to—"

Before I could hit him with another round of hairspray, I saw Emily holding an object over his head. When she slammed it against the back of his head, I recognized it as the fancy copper trashcan I considered too nice to use. The sound of metal against bone was sickeningly satisfying. She must have experienced the same pleasure because she continued the banging until he slumped forward, still attached to the dagger. Even then, she kept smashing him with the can until I ran from behind the desk, grabbed her arm, and dragged her from the room.

We dashed down the hall and into the reception area, where we found Mark outside the glass doors, holding a fire extinguisher over his head in preparation for some smashing of his own.

35

"Are you sure I stabbed him with the letter opener? Because I remember the hairspray but not the stabbing part."

Although the question had been asked and answered at least three or four times, I was unable to grasp the concept.

"Hell yes, you did, and it was awesome," Emily said from the backseat of Mark's car.

"I don't understand why I can't remember." I leaned my head against the passenger side and thought of Rob, bloody and unconscious, as the EMTs carried him out on a stretcher. Images came to me in no real order. Mark and Detective Atkins huddled together while uniformed men scurried around, sitting on the floor with Emily outside the reception area. Someone wrapping me in a blanket to stop my shivering.

"Shock makes it hard to remember things," he said.

I turned toward him, wondering for a second who he was and how I'd ended up in the car with him. My teeth chattered as I fought against the bitter fluid rising in my throat.

"I think I'm going to be sick."

"Emily, there should be a grocery sack back there. Throw it over the seat."

She tossed the bag to me, and I sat there trying to decide whether to breathe into or use it for barfing. Luckily, the nausea passed as quickly as it came, but I still shook so hard she handed me her dark navy sweatshirt, a good color because it camouflaged the streaks of Rob's blood.

"That must be why my memory of the stabbing is gone. Because I'm in shock,"

"Most likely, but don't worry. It's a common reaction."

"What about my car?"

"One of our guys is dropping it off at your grandmother's. You shouldn't be driving in your state of mind."

With my limited recollection of the evening, I wondered what he meant but gave up and watched a flashy red Porsche fly past, looking close enough to take off our side-view mirror. I despised traveling on Highway 400. People in Mercedes and BMWs zoomed by so fast they rattled the windows of those of us who preferred exceeding the speed limit by a mere ten or fifteen miles. They whipped in and out of traffic, oblivious to the chaos of slammed brakes and near-collisions left in their wake.

We passed the famous King and Queen. Part of a massive office and hotel complex, the royal structures towered above the surrounding buildings. The taller of the two has a rectangular crown. His consort's is an enormous yet dainty dome. Management changes the colors weekly in recognition of one of the many charitable organizations in the area and the nation. Tonight, they glowed red. Like the blood gushing from Rob's wounded hand and head.

"I called ahead, so your grandmother will be waiting with hot tea and blankets. You'll be fine."

"If that means I recall the attack, I'll pass. I hope I never remember plunging a letter opener into another human being, even one as awful as Rob."

"That's funny," Emily said. "I hope I never forget the way it sounded when I smashed the trash can on his head."

• • •

As soon as we turned onto my grandmother's street, we saw all the lights were on at her house. Franks' car remained in the driveway, and for a moment I imagined myself as the guest of honor at a surprise party celebrating my victory over evil. Very unlikely, considering the way Jams sounded when I provided her with an abbreviated account of the evening.

"Sometimes I wonder if you've got the sense God gave a goose. Going off like that. You could have gotten yourself and Emily killed. How would you feel then?"

I was wise enough not to point out that dead people generally feel nothing. I just let her continue to rant for a good five minutes before telling her she was right. I was sorry, and we would be home shortly.

If the memory of my grandmother's righteous anger hadn't already convinced me I wasn't returning to a party but from the scene of a crime, the SUV parked on the other side of Frank's vehicle banished all thoughts of festivity.

"Oh, shit," I said. "That's Mom's car."

"Is that a bad thing?" Mark asked.

I didn't bother to explain her presence most likely indicated Jams called her during the time I was missing or after I'd been found, and either way, I was screwed. There would be countless questions with answers they wouldn't like at all, along with recriminations for putting myself in danger and worrying them half to death. Then they would fight over where I should spend the night since I obviously shouldn't be alone.

If I was lucky, they would wear themselves out quickly and allow me to slink away in disgrace. Once home, I might still have enough energy to take a hot bath and try to forget my hellacious day.

I didn't want to think about what unlucky looked like.

Mark parked alongside the curb outside Jams' house, but I stayed put. "Can we just sit here for a few minutes?"

"Sure. I've got nowhere I need to be."

He probably had reports to file and people to call, which made his offer to stay even nicer.

"Why am I having such a hard time recalling what happened in the office? I must be a special kind of idiot."

"Hey, you had the presence of mind to get Evans to tell you where the judge was hiding and to give the location to me. Not many people facing down a gunman would be as composed. If you ever decide to change careers, I might have a spot for you on my team."

I hadn't realized until that moment but getting out of the PR business sounded good. I could revive my writing career, tell Mary's story, and donate the proceeds of my sales to her daughter's college fund.

"You should have seen her," Emily spoke up. "One minute she was sitting there all calm and everything. The next second, she snatched up that dagger thing and stabbed the asshole's hand. Then I started whacking him with the trashcan."

We sat quietly for a moment before she added, "I'm sorry, Claire. But I've got to pee bad—really bad."

"Can you hang on just another minute or two?"

"Not without ruining the leather seat." Her desperate tone reminded me of my own when traveling with a dad who hated making pit stops.

"You go on in. I still have a few questions for Mark."

"Okay, but please don't be long because I'm not coming out of the bathroom until you get there. Your mom freaks me out a little."

"She freaks me out a lot, but I promise it will just be a few minutes." I watched as Emily hopped from the car and ran to the door.

"Were you serious when you said you had some questions, or are you stalling for time? Either way doesn't matter to me. I can hang out as long as you want."

The streetlight cast a faint glow over him, making it impossible to read his expression. "I meant it. First, did I tell you how much I appreciate your coming to rescue us?"

"You've thanked me several times, but if anybody needed rescuing, my money would be on Thornwall."

The naked look of pain on Rob's twisted face—to me he would always be Rob—came to me, and I shuddered. "That brings me to my second question. What are his chances of surviving?"

"You don't have to worry about him. If that trashcan had been heavier, she might have cracked his skull. But the worst he'll have is a concussion."

"I'm not worried about him. I just didn't want to think about Emily having to live with having taken somebody's life, even somebody like him."

"It would be understandable if you had concern for the guy, what with the two of you being engaged and all."

"Except it wasn't a real engagement. He was only acting a part. Eventually, I would have recognized that and refused to settle for the relationship. I didn't want him dead. Honestly, I don't give a damn what happens to him."

Plus, his death would have been a little anti-climactic since it would have been the third announcement Rob Evans had met his demise. I kept that tidbit to myself.

"I guess it's time for me to face the music."

"I can walk in with you," he offered.

"Thanks, but no. If you go in, Jams is going to insist you have something to eat, and Mom will ask you a bazillion questions about what you do and where you went to school. You'll be stuck there forever, and it will only postpone their cross-examination of me."

I saw no need to mention that with Rob out of the picture, my mother would have a hidden agenda behind her interrogation. She would launch a campaign to find a suitable replacement for the criminal I planned to marry before my final egg died. Poor Mark wouldn't know what hit him.

"Okay, but Atkins wants to ask you and Emily some questions. Why don't I pick you guys up, say 10:30? Here or at your house?"

I'd forgotten about the attractive detective. I enjoyed the way he referred to the woman by her last name, as if they were buddies in a cop show.

I considered telling him I would drive to the meeting, but a wave of fatigue crashed over me, making me question if I would have the energy.

"Thanks. I'll text you when I figure out where we'll be." I dragged myself out of the car and up the path to the house.

•

"I don't know how I expected to react." Mom dabbed at her eyes as we sat on the king-size bed Walter and Jams shared for years. Emily retired to her room an hour ago. Frank and my grandmother were drinking bourbon-laced de-caf in the kitchen. Dad had fallen asleep on the couch in the den, leaving me alone with my teary-eyed mother.

The anger Jams released over the phone dissolved before we came through the door. Even Mom had no appetite for a full-scale assault. Whether from relief we got out alive or Frank's unexpected arrival, they looked close to collapsing. My mother's eyes were lined with streaks of red, and Jams kept dabbing at her nose with a handkerchief. Their smiles were halfhearted and fleeting. I imagined the combination of fear for our safety and the reunion of father and daughter had taken a toll on them.

"I thought things would be different," Mom said. "That there would be this immediate connection between the two of us. I mean, all this time I was so sure I would be able to pick him out of a crowd without even seeing his picture. But when we arrived, I was shocked to see a stranger sitting on the sofa with his arm around my mother."

She blew her nose and hiccupped. "And to think that stranger is my father. How about you? What kind of reaction did you have?"

"Pretty weird, I guess, mostly because I almost blasted the poor guy with roach and ant spray." No reason to tell her about the instant familiarity of my image reflected in Frank's glasses or the startling recognition of my smile on someone else's face. It didn't seem fair to have this unsought advantage over my mother when I hadn't been the one who longed to meet him for years.

"I suppose I built everything out of proportion." She sniffled into a tissue, then said, "And you know what's the saddest part of meeting him?"

She surprised me by waiting for a response because she usually supplied her own answers.

"What?"

"When I saw him, all I could think about was how much I missed Walter." Her sniffles turned to sobs. I held her close until they subsided.

"Enough of that," she said, sounding like my real mom again. "I'm just glad you and Emily are okay."

I waited for a lecture on how foolish I'd been taking off on my own to face down a homicidal ex-lover, but it didn't come.

"Your dad and I should go home. I've put that poor man through hell the last few weeks. And don't you worry, honey. My friend Barb from Bunco has a nephew your age. He's in real estate. Or could be retail? Doesn't matter because whether it's him or someone else, you'll find somebody better than that horrible Rob in short order."

She had that right. It would be no trouble at all improving on my choice of fiancé since the last one was a murderer who tried to add me to his list of victims. But the timing was off for sarcasm, and I chose to be thankful she hadn't brought up impending fertility issues, then walked with her to the den, where she woke my sleeping father. He stumbled along with her to the front door. They left without saying goodbye to Jams and Frank.

All the adrenaline from earlier in the evening had dissolved, leaving me with a fatigue so heavy I had to drag myself to the kitchen to announce I would be spending the night.

"It looks like you ladies don't need my protection. The way Claire handled herself tonight, I'm not sure you ever did. So, I'll head out." Frank took his cup to the sink, rinsed it, and set it on the counter.

I half expected Jams to invite him to stay, but she didn't. As he passed, he hesitated. "Would you mind if I gave you a hug?"

I've never been a fan of random hugging, even with family members. And I absolutely do not enjoy getting up close with people I've just met. Unlike my mother, however, I felt a connection to my new—or should it be old—grandpa. The hug was a little stiff, but we could work on that.

36

Before going to bed, I texted Mark where to pick us up and a group message to Anna, Lisa, and Sarge to assure them I was okay but wouldn't be in for a few days.

He arrived a little after nine. We were quiet on the way to Atkins' office. Emily had lost her revenge high, and I was still too rattled to do more than read the replies from my friends after sending them an abbreviated version of the last night's events.

Anna's responses included a stream of Spanish curse words because I hadn't called her but said she loved me anyway. Sarge commended me for a job well done. Lisa sent a barrage of happy faces and hearts.

Before we reached the station, images of the previous evening tore through my mind. The smell of my own fear-sweat as I looked into the eyes of the man I once planned to marry. The contrast of the flow of crimson against Rob's ashen face. But I couldn't arrange those events in any order, not chronologically nor by shock value nor least to most significant. I doubted I would be of use in clarifying the situation for Mark or Atkins.

Turned out my collections of the previous night weren't needed. Rob took Emily's phone when he kidnapped her, but he hadn't seen the girl tuck her mother's in her back pocket. During our meeting, she handed it, complete with a recording of the ordeal, over to the detective. Remembering her reluctance to share information with the authorities, I was surprised at how easily she relinquished it until she whispered that she'd saved the video in the Cloud for future listening enjoyment.

On the way home, we stopped at Wally's Waffle House for breakfast. Hungrier than I'd expected to be, I was on my third pancake when Mark's cell rang. He glanced at the number and excused himself to take the call.

"So, he's hot, right?" Emily asked with a mouthful of French toast.

"I hadn't noticed." I dragged my last piece of bacon through the sticky syrup on my plate.

"Uh hu, I noticed you not noticing." She grinned and washed down her food with a slug of orange juice.

My face grew warm. "Seriously, I am not interested in the man. He's nice and all. But after Rob, I don't trust my judgment."

"Your judgment is fine because you're a good person. Mom taught me it's better to believe in people and be wrong than to always expect the worst." Her grin disappeared, and she ran her fork through uneaten scrambled eggs.

Mark returned before I attempted to ease her heavy grief.

"That was Atkins. Thornwall's doctor called to say the patient has a serious concussion but has regained consciousness." He stirred cream into his coffee, keeping his eyes fixed on the cup.

"So that's good news, isn't it?" I asked. Emily snorted.

"Yes and no," he began. "It seems our suspect has developed a case of amnesia. The doctor thinks he's faking but says there's no way to be certain. They're transferring him to a mental facility for observation."

"Does that mean he can say he doesn't remember killing my mother and walk?" Emily demanded.

"Absolutely not. Harrison is spilling his guts about everything, trying to get a better deal than Delmar. Those two have been taking turns throwing each other under the bus, but there's enough evidence to lock up both of them. Thornwall can't keep up the pretense forever. He's bound to slip up, and when he does—bam!" He slapped his hand on the table, startling us both, then signaled for the check.

Fortified by breakfast, I wasn't overwhelmed when we returned to Jams' to find both Mom and Frank were there and a third car I didn't recognize.

"Looks like a party," he said as parked a half block from the house. "I'd offer to walk you in but—"

Emily interrupted. "You should come in. I'm sure Jams and Claire's mom want to thank you."

"Well, uh, I hate to intrude."

"She's right. My mother will never forgive me if I don't introduce you. And Frank should be happy to have you around for moral support."

"It would be awful if I disappointed my old friend." He smiled.

Before we got out of the car, my grandmother opened the front door and an older lady scurried down the walkway. The moment I caught sight of her poufy, reddish-orange hair, I recognized her as a member of my grandmother's bridge club. I couldn't recall her name, but her elaborate up-do suggested she was the retired beautician who kept trying to get Jams to liven up her brown bob.

"Duck," I said, much louder than I intended. "If she spots us, we won't make it inside until after dark."

Sunlight glinted off her helmet-head as she veered nearer to the car. I slid down in the seat, but she was moving surprisingly fast for a senior citizen and didn't glance our way.

"That was close," I said when she was gone.

"I've never seen anybody with hair like that," Emily remarked. "It's kind of amazing and scary at the same time."

I was too relieved at having dodged a barrage of conversational bullets to wonder what she was doing at Jams' on a non-bridge day.

While I fumbled with my seatbelt, she bounded out of the car and up the steps.

Mark put his hand on my arm. "I need to say something before we go inside."

He nodded toward the girl as she entered the house. "You should feel good about that."

"About what? You mean Emily?"

"Just look at her. She's a different person. Yes, she has a hard road ahead of her, but you and your grandmother have shown her things don't have to be so bleak. And you helped her get justice for her mother. Even though you were damn reckless doing it."

"I hope you're right. Without family to support her, it scares me that she might not make it. I'm not familiar with situations like this, but maybe the court will let her stay with Jams or at least be in contact with her."

"I have a feeling you won't have to worry about that. But that wasn't what I wanted to talk about. After the time we spent at the workshop, it almost killed me to have to keep lying to you. It makes sense you'd have trouble trusting me. But please understand this. I've always been honest when it comes to being with you. All that stuff about growing up in my family and how it affected me? I never said that to anyone before. Whenever I'm with you, I can't stop myself from blabbing on about my life and feelings and all that crap. And when we're not together, all I want is to hang out with you. I told myself it was because of the case, but that's done. And the idea I might not see you again is driving me crazy. You don't have to say anything now. Just promise you'll consider giving us a chance."

•   •   •

Bursts of laughter echoed down the hallway, and Dolly Parton sang in the background.

"Guess I was right about the party." Mark acted as if the previous conversation had never taken place, which made it easy for me to pretend it hadn't.

"Jolene," Emily squealed from the den.

As I followed the sound of her voice, I wondered when she became such a Dolly fan.

"Well, here they are." Jams rose from the sofa, arms full of what looked like a curly-haired fox although I doubted a creature with fur that color existed in nature.

"Can I hold her, please?" Emily bounded across the room. My grandmother transferred the squirming bundle to her. I noted she was not a fox but some strange breed of canine. The pup covered the girl's now radiant face with kisses.

"Meet Jolene," Jams said, wrapping her arms around girl and dog.

"Isn't she the cutest thing you've ever seen?"

"She's cute all right, but what is she?" I came in for a closer look, and the little creature stopped licking long enough to direct a wary gaze my way. When I held out my hand, she sniffed it, then returned to lavishing love on Emily.

"We suspect there's some poodle in her. Maybe a Yorkie-poo or a Malti-poo. Definitely some kind of poo," my grandmother answered.

"I've never seen anything, pure or mixed, quite that color."

"She's in disguise." Emily burst into giggles.

"You two sit." Jams motioned to Frank, who stood and scooted the rocker closer to the recliner. After a quick game of musical chairs, everyone except my grandmother had a seat. She perched on the arm beside her lost love, leaving the sofa for me and Mark.

Once we settled, she cleared her throat. "I guess you could say me and Emily are dognappers. You remember that poor pup the neighbors kept outside all the time and how I threatened to report them to animal control but was afraid they wouldn't be able to find a home for her, what with her being so dirty and matted up? Well, they started moving their stuff out, and I figured they up and left the sweet baby. So, we went over and snatched her. Then they came back."

She recounted how the neighbors hung around a few days, canvassing the neighborhood for information about their missing pet. They cleaned the dog up and took her to the vet. He said other than being malnourished and covered in fleas, she was in good shape. By then, the now-previous owners had disappeared, but Jams feared they could pop by again. So rather than have her shaved, which might not fool everyone, she requested a modified cut and enlisted the help of her bridge-lady beautician to use animal-friendly dye to change the off-white fur to a warm apricot. Something went horribly wrong, though, and the result was a critter with hair the same startling shade as her stylist.

"You can see why I keep that woman away from my gorgeous locks." She scratched Jolene's ear. "Don't you worry, sweetheart. When that nasty color wears off, you'll be pretty as a peach, and that scary lady will never come near you ever again."

"I hate to condone pet theft," Mom said. "But I don't blame Momma one bit."

Jams smiled, leaned across Frank, and patted my mother on the back.

Emily put the dog on the floor, where she immediately ran to Mark and flipped over. He bent down to rub her belly.

"You are a temptress, aren't you?" She moaned and he scooped her up. The ecstatic mutt had cast her spell on him.

After a few minutes, Jams said, "I bet she could use a walk. Janis, why don't you get everybody something to drink while Claire and I take little bit outside?"

I recognized the ploy: my grandmother wanted to isolate me for further questioning about what happened with Rob or what was happening with Mark. Jolene jumped off the sofa to allow Jams to attach her leash. Resigned to her upcoming inquiry, I followed them out the kitchen door to the backyard.

"I guess we'll have to put up a fence for her." She said as we walked toward her garden.

"And by *we*, do you mean you and Frank?"

"Well, honey, I'm not sure. Would that be awful?"

I enjoyed being the one asking the difficult questions but didn't want to upset her. "Just teasing you. I hope you guys become a *we* if that's what you want."

"It is. There's already been too much wasted time. Not that we're rushing to get married. Nope. We'll be living in sin, driving your mother plumb crazy." She stopped to let the dog squat. "My relationship is part of what I wanted to talk to you about. But first, I've got some good news, more like great news. I heard from Regina."

"You mean Detective Atkins?"

"She asked me to call her Regina. Anyway, she told me she pulled some strings, and if I was okay with it, I could be Emily's foster parent or grandparent or whatever. I hollered, hell, yes, I wanted that girl to stay."

"Oh, my God. That is the best news I've heard in a very long time." I grabbed her and got us both tangled in the leash. The little dog sat patiently as we untangled.

"I haven't asked her yet, but I think she'll be good with it."

I had no doubt she would be more than happy to stay.

"Back to me and Frank. Like I've said before, I can't regret the way I took off without asking what was going on because that would mean I wouldn't have had all those years with Walter. But I learned something from it. I let myself get taken in by doubt, by not trusting my heart. I'm not going to make that mistake again. Whether we stay together or not won't be because we didn't have faith in each other and what might be possible between us."

Jolene bit the head off a clover, sneezed, and pirouetted several times before resuming her walk.

"Honey, I don't want to see the same thing that happened to me happen to you. Just because you trusted the wrong person doesn't mean you won't find the right one. I'm not trying to throw you into the man's arms, but it's obvious Mark cares about you. And I think you care about him, too. You need to chill out instead of missing out."

Our party got livelier as the Bloody Marys flowed. Dad brought pizza and beer and grinned when my slightly tipsy mother greeted him with a kiss directly on the lips, the most PDA she'd shown in ages.

During the festivities, Jams took Emily aside to tell her about Atkins's offer. After dinner, they shared the news. It was official. She and Jolene had a new home.

Every time I looked at Mark, my grandmother's words about not missing out echoed in my head. For as long as I could remember, I wanted to be more like her: fearless, spontaneous, irreverent. It turned out I'd been more like her than I thought, but the wrong version. I was the girl she became after losing Frank—afraid to step out of line, to take chances or go with her heart. Lucky for her, Grandpa Walter was a fine man who practically worshipped her, and she grew to love him. She learned to trust herself and not give a damn about other people's opinions. And now, she was getting a second chance with the one who first taught her about love.

I might not be so lucky.

A little after eleven, Mark announced he hated to leave but had an early day ahead of him. When I volunteered to walk him to his car, I glanced at my grandmother and smiled. She winked her approval.

"What you said before, you know, about not worrying about us not getting to stay in touch with Emily. You knew Regina had worked things out with foster care. That was pretty sneaky." I punched his arm.

He leaned his back against the car. "Guilty as charged. But I didn't lie about it. Shouldn't I get some credit for that?"

I stepped closer. "I'm not sure how much credit you deserve." I stood on my tiptoes and kissed him softly on the lips. He cupped my chin in his hands, keeping his mouth pressed against mine. I melted into him, thrilled by the warmth as it flowed through me. When we separated, I gasped.

"I better get back to the party. They'll be wondering what's going on out here."

He sighed. "About that extra credit, I'll take anything you want to give. And I promise never to lie to you again."

"Never is a long time." His smile faded. I thought of how I felt after discovering my entire relationship with Rob had been an illusion and almost walked away. Then I pictured Jams and Frank locked in each other's arms in that Woodstock van.

"It wouldn't hurt to discuss the possibilities. How about dinner tomorrow night at my place?"

He launched himself upright. "That would be great. I'll bring wine. What do you like? White, red, pink?"

"Surprise me. Just make whatever you choose pairs well with Janis Joplin."

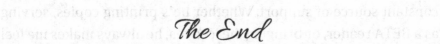

The End

Acknowledgments

As always, I couldn't do it without the help of my writing community. Wild Women Who Write (Gaby Anderson, Kim Conrey, Kat Fieler, and Lizbeth Jones) is a source of comfort, encouragement, and fantastic feedback. As a member of the Atlanta Writers Club, I meet talented writers who are generous with their time and advice. Sisters in Crime Atlanta has given me additional incentive to be the best writer I can be.

My book club friends remind me that to be better, I need to keep reading. Jan, Peggy, Jolly, Sharon, Ann, and Pat challenge me to dig deeper into contemporary novels and let me drink wine while I do it.

Black Rose Writing provides an extended family of writers, as well as incredible resources.

I couldn't do any of this without my family. My husband is a constant source of support. Whether he's printing copies, serving as a BETA reader, or bringing me iced tea, he always makes me feel special. My daughters, Laura and Kate, are my biggest fans. I love the look of excitement on their faces when I talk about my work. My sons-in-law, Brent and Brian, never fail to show up for me. And my grandchildren—Carson, Holland, Quinn, Heidi, and Grayson— give my life a greater purpose.

Special thanks for my headshot go to a talented photographer, compassionate counselor, and great friend, Madonna Mezzanotte.

About the Author

Katherine Nichols is the author of *The Sometime Sister* and *The Unreliables*. She is a vice president of the Atlanta Writers Club and on the board of Sisters in Crime Atlanta. She lives in Lilburn, Georgia with her husband, two rescue dogs, and two rescue cats. When she isn't writing, she enjoys walking, reading, traveling, and spending time with her children and grandchildren.

Note from the Author

Word-of-mouth is crucial for any author to succeed. If you enjoyed *Trust Issues*, please leave a review online—anywhere you are able. Even if it's just a sentence or two. It would make all the difference and would be very much appreciated.

Thanks!
Katherine Nichols

We hope you enjoyed reading this title from:

BLACK ROSE
writing™

www.blackrosewriting.com

Subscribe to our mailing list – *The Rosevine* – and receive **FREE** books, daily deals, and stay current with news about upcoming releases and our hottest authors.
Scan the QR code below to sign up.

Already a subscriber? Please accept a sincere thank you for being a fan of Black Rose Writing authors.

View other Black Rose Writing titles at www.blackrosewriting.com/books and use promo code **PRINT** to receive a **20% discount** when purchasing.

9 781685 130862